ManLove is a single author collection of some of my short stories pulled together from other out-of-print anthologies. There are no new stories in this collection, just time-worn, in some cases award-winning, shorts. The most recent title is *Jackson & Nick* from the *Storming Love: Wild Fire Series* in 2015.

These stories range from military men to computer nerd, tackling DADT to private fantasies, a kidnapping and an attempt to survive a natural disaster. It also includes two short stories that are part of the worlds in my existing series, the *Rough Series* and *Mexican Heat Series*. *Rough Ride* is a brief holiday piece and *South of the Border* is scene that was originally part of the first draft of the novel *Mexican Heat* was deleted before publication.

Featuring a roll call of some of the best writers of gay erotica and mysteries today!

Derek Adams	Kyle Adams	Vicktor Alexander
Simone Anderson	Victor J. Banis	Laura Baumbach
Ally Blue	J.P. Bowie	Barry Brennessel
James Buchanan	TA Chase	Charlie Cochrane
Karenna Colcroft	Ethan Day	Diana DeRicci
Taylor V. Donovan	S.J. Frost	Kimberly Gardner
Kaje Harper	Stephani Hecht	Alex Ironrod
Jambrea Jo Jones	DC Juris	AC Katt
Kiernan Kelly	K-lee Klein	Geoffrey Knight
J.L. Langley	Vincent Lardo	Cameron Lawton
Anna Lee	Elizabeth Lister	William Maltese
Timothy McGivney	Kendall McKenna	AKM Miles
Robert Moore	Jet Mykles	Jackie Nacht
N.J. Nielsen	Cherie Noel	Gregory L. Norris
Erica Pike	Neil S. Plakcy	Rob Rosen
George Seaton	Riley Shane	Richard Stevenson
Christopher Stone	Liz Strange	Lex Valentine
Haley Walsh	Lynley Wayne	Missy Welsh
Ryal Woods	Stevie Woods	Sara York
Lance Zarimba	Mark Zubro	

Check out titles, both available and forthcoming, at
www.mlrpress.com

MANLOVE

*A Collection of Contemporary
M/M Erotic Love Stories*

LAURA BAUMBACH

mlrpress
www.mlrpress.com

Published by
MLR Press, LLC
3052 Gaines Waterport Rd.
Albion, NY 14411

Visit ManLoveRomance Press, LLC on the Internet:
www.mlrpress.com

Cover Art by Winterheart Designs

Print format: ISBN# 978-1-944770-19-8

Second Editions Issued 2016

TABLE OF CONTENTS

BURN CARD

The locker room of the crime lab smelled like an odd combination of flower-scented body sprays and manly deodorant. Coed, so there were separate showers. It was essentially a room full of rows of metal clothes lockers divided by wooden benches.

Mid-morning, only a dozen or so officers and criminalists working for the Las Vegas crime lab were in sight, most having just finished an off-hours shift or overtime. This was a place to wind down from a long shift or rev up for a new one.

Only three hours into his usual dayshift, Cody Baxter was neither finishing nor preparing for a new day. But he was changing his clothes. He pulled a fresh black T-shirt out of an open locker and tossed it onto the bench behind him. It was identical to the shirt he was wearing except that the one he had on was torn, dirty, and splattered with what looked like dull, dark stains of a faintly deep red substance.

His locker was directly across from the main entrance to the room. He contemplated going and shutting the door, but he decided it took too much energy. Let the gawkers look.

Using his open locker door as a partial shield, Cody dropped to the bench, his jeans-clad legs slightly parted, balancing his small, wiry frame in a ready stance. A guy couldn't work with body fluids, debris, and dead bodies and not get dirty occasionally. While his compact, toned body was nothing to be ashamed of, he preferred to draw as little attention as possible when he occasionally needed to change his shirt. He was a private kind of guy, liking it best when people ignored him and let him do his job. The less attention, the better.

Lord knows he'd had enough attention this morning to last him for a long while. Even now, a copy of the offending paper lay on the end of the bench, the pages folded back to reveal the smiling candid snapshot of him and media darling Gil Turko.

The T-shirt just cleared his head, forcing spikes of dark hair to stick up at all angles. A recently abused muscle spasmed. Breath caught in mid inhalation, Cody waited for the twinges to pass, the lean muscles of his abdomen clenched while his arms were left encased in the soft cotton of the shirt, his movements briefly frozen.

He flinched, worked his shoulder to loosen it up. "Ah! Damn it." He let out a long, tired breath. "Whoa. That hurt." Folding the soiled shirt, he laid it in the bottom of his locker. He jerked only a little when an unexpected hand lightly touched his bruised arm.

"Hey, you need to see a medic before we go back out? You're moving slow, bud."

Working the shoulder more vigorously, he ignored a fresh stab of pain. Cody shook his head and grunted an unconvincing, "Nah."

"You sure? You took down two big guys, Cody. One of them had at least six inches and a hundred pounds on you." Eric Wren propped a foot on the bench beside Cody and leaned his arm on his knee, a casual stance that had the added benefit of blocking Cody from the view of the busy traffic in the hallway.

Tall, dark chocolate brown, with a wrestler's build, Eric was barrel-chested, with a voice as deep as his skin was dark. "Everyone here knows you're a feisty little bad ass. No one tangles with you if they can help it but," he poked a finger into an array of newly blossoming bruises on Cody's collar bone, "that has to hurt."

"It's not so bad, really." He gave Eric a wry grin. "It was more painful to listen to all the teasing about my picture in the paper this morning." He carefully slipped the clean shirt over his head and pulled it into place, unconsciously smoothing out the wrinkles as he tucked it into his waistband. "I can handle this better. It's business, not personal."

"Yeah, well, you pick a rich celebrity for a boyfriend, you're going to get a little of the limelight shining on you. You and Gil have been together for what, three years now?" Eric didn't wait for Cody to nod in agreement, but Cody did anyway. "I think you'd be used to it by now."

"I am used to it." Cody grabbed the paper from the bench and stared at the grainy photo of his lover. Gil Turko was a handsome man, his towering body a mountain of trim bands of toned muscle evident even under the tux he wore. His face was Latino dark, all sharp planes and broad bones with piercing brown/black eyes and jet-black hair he wore slightly longer than Cody's neatly trimmed cut.

"It's just" — Cody tossed the paper into his locker and firmly shut the door firmly — "it was my birthday. It was a great, intimate night. I didn't want to share any part of it with work. Not even the morning after." He gave Eric a ruefully, embarrassed glance. "You know what I mean?"

"Yeah, I do. But you were at the biggest fundraiser of the year for Children's Hospital and Gil is one of the major forces in raising money for it. Besides that, he's got a great mug. All those years of football, wrestling and skulking around the world as a special services operative never marred his pretty profile." Eric straightened and threw an arm around Cody's shoulders. His smile was completely without any hint of remorse when Cody grimaced and tried unsuccessfully to shrug him off. "Face it, dude, the camera loves him and so do the media."

"Yeah, well, not as much as I love him." Cody narrowed his eyes and smiled back at his friend. "I have some other, better bruises to prove it. Wanna see them?" He made a move to undo his jeans.

Eric instantly released Cody's shoulder, hands waving protectively in front of him. "TMI, Cody, TMI! I trust you."

Laughing, they both stopped short as a new man filled the doorway, files in one hand and a preoccupied look on his tanned, lined face. Grant Hewlett, section supervisor and their boss, peered up at them over his half frame glasses, clear, steady eyes sharply evaluating both men.

"Word has it you had physical contact with a couple of hecklers at the latest homicide scene, Cody. Are you all right?"

"I'll be fine."

"Good." Staring at Cody, Grant nodded, pursed his lips, seeming to think hard about something Cody couldn't see. Grant straightened marginally and nodded again. "Rodriguez called off for nights. Flu. You're next up on the float list. Go home. Rest up and be back for the graveyard shift. You can take the next day off to make up for it."

"I can finish out my day shift now, then come back for graveyard." Cody darted a look at Eric, hoping the man would keep silent about the extent of Cody's bruises. He was fine. He could do his job. "It's no big deal."

"It is to me. We're skeleton enough on nights without staffing it with tired people. Go home. Take a nap."

"Yes, sir." He tried to keep disappointment out of his voice but he caught Grant's eyes narrow, and he flushed, feeling like he did when his dad had caught him in a lie. "I'll leave as soon as I finish the report on what happened."

"You do that, Cody." Grant gave Eric a hard look then moved back out into the hall and began to walk away adding, "You see to it that he does, Eric. Leave, I mean."

"Yes, sir."

Both men waited until Grant was out of hearing range then sighed loudly. Cody walked back to his locker and began stowing his gear. "Well, damn. Happy birthday to me."

"Luck of the draw. I'd trade with you, but I don't think Grant was in the mood to be messed with about this."

"Nah, it's okay. I'll go soak in the hot tub for a while and ease away a few of these sore muscles."

"Hey, you didn't tell me. What's a guy get for his twenty-eighth birthday from his rich and famous boyfriend?"

"Among other things, a new watch. It's got everything but a full keypad on it, I swear." Cody raised his wrist and admired the gleaming gold watch. It sported a heavy mesh band that hugged his smaller than average wrist perfectly. "It's even got an emitter in it."

"You're kidding?"

"No, I'm not."

"He actually put a tracker on you?"

"You know how much he obsesses about safety, my safety."

"Yeah, but a tracker? Gil lojacked you?"

"It's not on. I have to activate it." He flashed his watch at Eric again, fingering a third stem in the side of the watch. "This button here." He flashed it on, showed Eric how a red glow highlighted the watch dial. It buzzed and vibrated for a half a second, then he shut it off.

Eric raised his eyebrows, suspicion written all over his face. Cody frowned back. "He isn't spying on me, you jerk. I turn it on if I need it."

"Simmer down. I didn't think he was. I'm just stunned." Eric laughed and leaned against the lockers. "You let the man lojack you! Holy shit! You must be in love."

"You're an ass." Cody shut his locker and walked toward the hallway.

Eric hurried to match Cody's determined stride. Once he reached Cody's side he murmured in a sing-song whisper, "And your ass is lojacked!" Eric had to dance out of the way to avoid a hard jab to his ribs.

"A huge, irritating jackass."

On the up side of things, he was going home in the middle of the day with nothing to do. Maybe Gil would be available for a little afternoon delight. Cody's day just got brighter.

§ § § §

The offices of Body Armor, Inc., bodyguards to the rich and famous in the Las Vegas area and around the world, were smaller than most people might imagine. But what they lacked in size was more than made up in elegance and style. Two rooms in the east wing of Gilson Turko's mansion were devoted exclusively to his business needs.

Off the main foyer was an outer office where Trudy Davis, Gil's personal assistant, managed the phones and the day-to-day business matters, nine-to-five, Monday through Friday. A dedicated workaholic, Trudy took any off-hours or emergency calls from home. Trudy was married to one of Gil's most requested bodyguards, and she claimed it helped her deal with her husband's dangerous job better when she was able to keep a handle on what was happening around the clock. It gave her the illusion of control in the often dangerous job in which her husband worked.

Gil understood and empathized with her need to stay connected with the love of her life any way she could, so the arrangement suited them both just fine. Besides, she was efficient, intelligent, pleasant, and pretty. Plus, she could be as tough as any of his guys if she needed to be.

"Morning!" Trudy entered Gil's office, a thin file in hand. "This is everything we have on Walter Bead, that Tryst Casino accountant whose file you asked for, Gil." She took a moment to peek into his ignored coffee cup on the edge of his desk.

"Morning, Tru." Gil smiled then shook his head to let her know he didn't want a warm up. He shifted more comfortably in his seat. The black swivel chair was oversized, but the desk it sat behind was even more massive, all black glass and chrome steel, thick, solid and substantial, like the man sitting at it. The surrounding panes of window glass gleamed, reflecting Gil's sharp features and imposing six foot six, two hundred sixty pounds of hard-muscled Scandinavian build.

"Ex-accountant, you mean, Trudy. The guy's going to have a hell of time getting a job after this. Nobody likes a snitch." Bruce Bukowski grunted, his thick, blunt fingers alternately rubbing then tapping a metal key ring. He shifted it from hand to hand, the empty ring clicking against its pink lacquered face. The medallion's painted surface, a decades old Playboy Bunny head, was covered in fine cracks. Gil couldn't remember a time when Bruce didn't have it on him.

Gil had known Bruce since grade school. They were as close

as brothers, separated only during the years Gil was in the special services. Bruce was rough around the edges but savvy, an ex-wrestler, and brutal when he needed to be. He was Gil's right hand, one of three people Gil trusted implicitly.

"You sure about the coffee?"

"No thanks. I'm good, Tru." Gil reached for the cup and sipped at the still hot liquid just to reassure her. It was rich and full-bodied, one of the best roasts available, but a few morning sips were all he wanted. Too much caffeine wasn't good for a healthy body, something of which he couldn't convince Cody.

Gil had to make sure the kitchen pantry was stocked with can after can of Colombian ground to keep Cody happy. The little guzzling shit didn't even like it fresh ground. Only cheap coffee from the supermarket sated his lover's daily caffeine needs. Gil didn't understand how Cody kept so fit and trim with all the coffee and junk food he snarfed down. God knew the guy didn't have an ounce of fat on his lean, smooth, wiry body. Gil had checked the situation just last night.

A smile he couldn't stop tugged at Gil's face.

Cody was all smooth lines, tight muscles with a firm little ass. A great ass, really. Great ass, great mind, and a great soul. His Cody had it all. And right about now he wished he could be sharing that great ass all over again. Last night had been a hell of a good time.

Shifting uncomfortably in his chair, Gil accepted the folder from Trudy and leaned forward. He held the file at waist level to disguise a growing bulge in his lap.

Trudy smirked and added, "Detective White even dropped off a copy of the court transcript since the case is closed." She tried to raise the edge of the file covering Gil's lap.

"Jared's the best." Gil moved the folder from her reach, covering his lap more completely with it. "Isn't that your phone ringing? Shouldn't you be at your desk?" The only sound in the room or outer office was the muffled ticking of a grandfather clock in the foyer.

"Slave driver! Huh! I need to go polish my nails anyway. I chipped one." She wiggled her shocking pink fingertips in front of Gil's face. One was missing a moon shaped chunk at the tip.

He batted her hands away when she made another grab at the file. "You're making me uncomfortable in my workplace, Tru. I'm feeling defenseless here." He flexed his broad shoulders and made his biceps bulge, turning the sexual harassment implications into a meaningless tease.

"Like you'd care! Ha! A girl can't have any fun at work anymore." With a last taunting wiggle of her eyebrows she turned and walked out, tossing a farewell over her shoulder. "Later, Bruce." The double doors to Gil's office closed firmly behind her.

Swiveling absentmindedly, Gil silently looked over the papers in the file, willing his mind to get back to the subject at hand and off Cody's ass. Without a teasing audience, he leaned back and relaxed in the comfort of his personal sanctum.

"I can't believe Bead didn't run the minute the trial was over. With the temper Enrico Sabo has it's surprising the guy is still alive, let alone still in town." Bruce jiggled the key ring hard and fast. "You can't turn in a casino for bad books without expecting a few marks on your ass afterward."

"And that's why Mr. Bead wants us to protect his currently unmarked ass until he liquidates all of his assets and catches his flight out of town in three days. You're going to like the suite at the Tangiers we booked him into."

"Tangiers is good. I can do room service and cable for a few days." The key ring clicked loudly then fell silent. Gil watched Bruce rub the rabbit's lined metal ears, his gaze automatically tracking a glint of shiny pink as it tumbled to the floor.

"You might want to take it easy with Bunny, brother. She's showing her age." He gestured to the key ring.

"What?" Bruce stared at the ring, fingertips caressing the fine cracks in the paint and lacquer. "Christ, you're right, she starting to strip again. Can't have that. I need to put another coat of sealant on her. Been awhile." Fumbling a slim leather card wallet out of his pants pocket, Bruce carefully slipped the key chain into it. He squeezed it tightly in his palm before sliding it into this pocket.

Gil smiled at him and nodded.

Bruce shrugged, quietly defensive. "Gotta be careful. You know it's all I got left of mom and pops. The only thing that scumbag left me."

"I know, Bruce. I remember."

"Pops had been robbed a half dozen times. It's not like he didn't know to just hand the creep the money and stand back. The bastard didn't need to kill them."

They shared a look that told Gil they were thinking the same thing, as they so often had in their years together. This was an old wound. Gil knew Bruce had wanted to protect his parents during the liquor store robbery, but he had been ten years old at the time of the shooting. They both were. All they had been able to do was watch and hide. Now they devoted their lives to protecting other people from bad things. The past shapes the future, and this tragedy had definitely shaped theirs.

Gil hit on the first thing he could think of to break the solemn moment. "Have you tried out that new micro surveillance camera I gave you?" The past might shape the future but it wasn't going to overshadow the present. "Does it interface with your phone the way the salesman said it would?"

Bruce patted his pocket. He pulled a gray Blackberry from his jacket and gestured with it. "I played with it a little bit, trying to learning the commands, but I need some time actually working with it and the camera. I'll work it in over the next couple of days. Can't be any harder than my Blackberry."

"Great, let me know how it does. I'm thinking of getting several of them if they work out."

Bruce nodded. "Sure thing. You want a written report on it?"

A buzzing drew their attention. Gil glanced at the display on his cell before he smiled and flipped it open, one hand gesturing to Bruce that he was interrupting their conversation. He nodded wordless agreement for the written report.

"Hey. What's up, lover?" Gil nearly purred into the phone, aware he sounded like a smitten teenager and not caring. If there was one thing in life he was sure of it was his relationship with Cody and he didn't care who knew they were in love. "You're coming home? Now?...Sure you're okay?...We can play doctor, I'll check you for bruises...See you in ten."

Hanging up, Gil closed Bead's file and stood. He was halfway around his desk when Bruce chided, "That's it? Cody's coming home for lunch and business is done for the day?"

"Nothing's more important than love, Bruce. Find yourself a nice woman, you'll understand."

"Says you." Bruce rolled his eyes and followed Gil out of the office with a resigned, thoughtful, "Everything in your world stops for Cody. You'd think I'd remember that by now."

§ § § §

Grueling work had its rewards. Gil had earned his six-pack abs on the college football field and the pro wrestling circuit and then in a stint in special services. He kept his physical bulk and strength by a fortunate mix of good genes from a Viking-descended father he'd never met, nature's generosity, and as many hours of physical labor as he could steal from a work day. He liked nothing better than to be out in the sun, working in the dirt and sand, volunteering his time and energy on things like the latest project to build a playground for a new preschool across town. Unless, of course, he could be where he was right now, getting the workout he liked best — making love to Cody.

"You have the whole day off now?" Gil pulled his shirt off and tossed in onto one of the chairs opposite the foot of their four-poster king bed.

"No, just the afternoon." Cody turned down the comforter and rolled the sheets back, neat and tidy. Gil had to smile at the meticulous way Cody did things, as if he was in a crime lab, detailing vital evidence. Talk about a man with obsessive compulsive disorder! His Cody was so OCD.

When he was done, Cody slipped off his shoes and socks, tucking them under a chair out of the way. His shirt came next, draped neatly on the back of the same chair. "I told you, I have to go back in for the swing shift seven to seven. Why?"

"The way you've been wasting time I thought you had all day off." Gil kicked off his shoes and sent his socks spinning off to a corner of the room. "We've been in the bedroom three whole minutes and you're still dressed." He deftly unsnapped his waistband, yanked the zipper down and slipped out of his trousers and boxers all in one smooth move. They pooled on the floor and he left them there and began to stalk his prey. "That would make one of us."

"Not everyone can strip at the speed of light, macho man."

Gil grabbed Cody from behind, arms wrapping around his lover's slender waist. He ran his hands gently over the superficial scratches and deepening bruises. "You okay? Want to take a rain check for now?"

"I gave a lot worse than I got, Gil. It's only a few bumps and scrapes." He tugged Gil's arms more tightly around him. "There are no rain checks being issued today, lover."

"As long as you're sure. I promise to be gentle." Gil pulled Cody close and began kissing and licking his way up Cody's exposed neck into his dark hairline.

"Like hell you will." Cody laughed and squirmed, warm and playful in Gil's embrace, his voice teasing and sultry. "Maybe I'd like you to undress me. Ever think of that?"

Gil hummed his eager agreement against Cody's scalp, his hands swiftly sliding south to work Cody's jeans open. "Absolutely not a problem, gorgeous." Once inside, he found plenty to keep him occupied.

"Holy shit, Gil!"

He loved it when Cody's voice got that breathless tone to it.

He slid one hand around to the back of the jeans and worked them over the plump swell of Cody's firm ass, admiring the way the smooth globes fit perfectly in his grip. He couldn't resist sliding a finger down the warm crack between them. His other hand found a better handle to grasp in front.

"Damn. How many hands do you have?" Cody grunted, his body lifted for a moment as his jeans dropped from his legs and were yanked from under his feet. Gil tossed them over his shoulder. A loud thud and the sound of dresser items falling over mixed with a rainfall of loose change pelting the carpeting.

"Be careful. You'll break the mirror." Cody's tone had gone from breathless to broken and needy, despite his attempts to admonish. He was writhing and bucking in Gil's arms, his slim hips working with the slow pumping of Gil's hand on his cock, his ass pressing back to get more of the finger rubbing over his opening. "And you're picking up all that change and putting it back in my pockets before I go to work."

With a sudden twist of his arms, Gil turned Cody around to face him. He kissed Cody hard and quick then grabbed him by the rib cage and underarms and lifted. His voice came out husky and raw to his own ears. "Stop talking."

Tossing Cody through the air was as easy as tossing Cody's jeans, but this time Gil aimed for the center of their bed and managed a direct hit. He took great pleasure in watching Cody and all of Cody's body parts bounce on the mattress. Finally, his lover lay sprawled on the sheets, naked and laughing, eyes bright with a combination of desire and love that Gil could never get enough of. He leaped into the air, landing beside Cody — at least once Cody and the bed stopped moving.

"Hey, watch it; you'll bruise my birthday bear!" Rolling slightly to one side and then back, Cody pulled a twelve-inch stuffed bear out from under a pillow.

"Bruise him my ass. He's a Grizzly." Gil plucked the smiling bear out of Cody's grasp and jammed him back under the pillows. "He can take being mashed for a good cause."

"You're grinding him into the mattress." Cody crawled partially on top of Gil, his body pressed hard against Gil's side and chest. His cock was firm and wet where it rubbed over the muscle of Gil's abdomen. The playful gleam in his lover's eye had turned sultry, needy. The dark side in Cody was breaking free from Cody's normal quiet reserve, just the way Gil liked it. His Cody was a little spitfire once his East Coast primness fell away.

Gil shifted and threw on an arm over Cody. He rolled, pinning Cody to the mattress, their cocks suddenly aligned, duel shafts of satin-encased steel. "I'd rather grind you into the mattress."

"Put up or shut up." Cody groaned and bucked, increasing the pressure on their cocks.

Gil could feel the tip of Cody's cock nudge the sensitive underside of his cock's head, sending a rush of excitement up his spine. "I can do that."

He captured Cody's lips with his own, running his tongue over the full lower lip until Cody's mouth parted for him. He explored, starting out as a slow lazy stroking over teeth and palate but soon turned to a fevered need to claim and possess.

Cody answered his demands in kind, harsh grunting and labored panting filling the bedroom. Their bodies fell into a rhythm learned over the last three years of living together and loving each other.

Sliding his open mouth down Cody's skin, Gil worked his way to one dusky nipple. The nub was already swollen. He nipped it, rolling the sensitive flesh between his teeth while lapping at the captured tip with his tongue.

"Christ, Gil!" Cody squirmed under him, one hand coming up to press his face hard into Cody's chest.

Gil obliged, sucking the whole teat into his mouth, working the entire rosy disc until it was puckered and hard. Cody moaned between each shallow pant. Gil did the same thing to the other nipple, one hand pinching and teasing the first, still wet nub. He knew he'd teased enough when Cody arched and pulled his legs free from under Gil, knees bent to force their bodies closer. Cody's cock left a trail of creamy white on Gil's abdomen and chest as he slid down Cody's torso. His lips, tongue and, occasionally, his teeth left behind their mark as he inched his way lower.

Cody moaned and raised his hips, pressing his groin into Gil's face, wordlessly asking for more. Gil licked a long, slow path down the dip between leg and torso, then did it again just to hear the little panting it wrung out of his lover. It was one of the sweetest sounds in life, Cody's needy moans and tense, tiny breaths he was reduced to during sex. The sounds were music to Gil's ears.

He loved everything about Cody — his above average smarts, his dry sense of humor, his lean masculinity, and his slender beauty. Even Cody's innate need to help people was in sync with Gil's desire to protect and care for others. They made a perfect match inside the bedroom and out. But at this moment, he was focusing on the here and now of Cody's physical attributes.

Running his hands over the smooth, firm flesh of Cody's lean hips and tight thighs, Gil dragged his thumbs down along the groin creases on both sides following the wet trails left behind by his exploring. Cody opened his legs wider for him, urging him lower. Gil obliged, mouthing the tight, hairless sac before sucking it into his mouth, first one small sphere and then the other.

"Christ, Gil! More. Something more!" Cody's hands were in his hair, tugging one minute then massaging his head the next, urgent and needy, control slipping, on edge. Just the way Gil liked him. He pulled back, letting the wrinkled sac slip from his lips in slow, wet cascade of flesh and moans. Saliva dribbled from it. Gil caught the droplets on two fingers, sliding both down to Cody's opening. He rubbed and teased the tight ring until Cody bore down on his fingertips, trying to capture and pull them inside. Gil eased them in an inch or two, twisting and curving them, touching everywhere he could.

As Cody began to hump against his open palm spread over quivering ass cheeks, Gil leaned in to lick his way up the slender, dusky cock that bobbed beside his chin. Cody shook and grunted, ass twisting this way and that, trying the impossible: to get his cock into Gil's mouth and impale himself on Gil's fingers at the same time with the same frenzied stroke.

Gil spread a hand across Cody's lower abdomen to slow the frantic move. "Slow it down, Cody, slow it down. Enjoy the ride. I'm going to take you straight to Sugartown, baby."

His hand crawled up Cody's sweaty chest to pinch and roll the swollen nubs, each bud still hot and hard. He worked his other fingers deeper into Cody's ass in short leisurely thrusts until they couldn't go any further. He brushed over the tiny gland he found there every few strokes, his own erect, eager cock jerking and swelling with each grunt, moan and panted breath that escaped Cody's parted, silently begging lips.

The tugging in his hair bordered on painful. Gil knew Cody was near his boiling point. His opened his lips wide and sucked the tip of Cody's cock into his mouth, just enough to capture the head and hold it there. He swirled his tongue over the smooth, slick surface, flicking the tip of his tongue into the creamy slit to taste the salty, bittersweetness that was all Cody.

He loved the feel of his lover's cock as it slid down his throat, the firm softness, the spongy, pulsing give of the satiny flesh, the ridges and dips that teased his tongue and massaged the roof of his mouth, all coupled with the crisp, musky scent of Cody's body. He even liked the way the soft curly hairs of Cody's groin tickled his nose and scratched his cheek.

He increased his sucking rhythm to match the thrusts of his fingers, swallowing deep when he was knuckles deep in Cody's channel and sucking hard on the out stroke. Cody's hands suddenly left his hair and slapped the sheets, knuckles going white as he fisted the covers, arms tense, hips bucking. Cody's legs trembled to stay bent, a fine sheen of sweat on his flushed chest.

Gil looked up at his lover's face to see half-closed eyelids over a smoldering stare, wet lips — the lower one a deep pink pinned between even, white teeth, a complexion smooth and tanned, the gaze staring back at Gil lusty and caring, passionate, desperate, but only for Gil. He could see that in Cody's expression. Only he could do this to Cody. Cody, a debauched angel fallen to earth who had landed in his bed. And Gil planned on making sure the angel never thought about flying away. His heart, his pride, and his cock swelled. He could feel the buzz of a creeping climax gnawing in the pit of his abdomen, simmering, swirling, sending startling jolts of electricity up his cock and down into his balls.

The cock in his mouth jerked and Cody's head snapped up and back down, bouncing against the mattress. He cried out, his body stiff as his cock pulsed, bathing Gil's throat and tongue with strands of bittersweet cum. Gil swallowed the first few spurts, savoring the taste and texture, then swiftly released the shaft to move closer, kneeling up to straddle one of Cody's legs.

He aligned their cocks, holding them tight in one hand as he pumped, the still spewing cum from Cody's cock lubricating each rapid, hard jerk and yank. He kept his other hand's fingers still buried deep in Cody's hole, twisting his hand so a knuckle raked over the hidden nub in an irregular tapping motion that made Cody hiss, arch and then bear down eagerly each time it happened.

Gil's own orgasm boiled up, pulling heat from every fiber of his body, making his limbs heavy with the burning spread of icy pleasure. It wove its way through his veins to erupt from his cock, mixing with his lover's spent fluids. Slowly the buzz began to fade.

Mindful of being nearly a hundred pounds heavier than his mate, Gil dropped onto Cody's chest, bracketing Cody's shoulders and face with his powerful forearms. He wiped his hands on the crumpled sheets then laced his fingers through the dark sweaty curls of Cody's hair to yank his lover's flushed startled face into the right position to capture Cody's mouth. The kiss was deep and blistering, containing the heat and fierce love swelling in Gil.

He felt almost choked by the sensation of need, wanting to be inside of his lover and have Cody inside of him at the same time. It was as if he were a starving man coming across his first meal in months. He knew other men might collapse under the heavy weight of his need for Cody, but for Gil that weight was what made him stand tall. Cody was his inner strength, a match for his straight moral compass and a companion for his soul.

No one rocked him like Cody did. It should be a sin how good the man made him feel. The lips under his own had turned soft and compliant, gentling the embrace. Gil took his cue and eased back, returning to peck tiny kisses around Cody's face, touching eyelids and temples, the hollow of Cody's throat and the sensitive inside of his lower lip as a last caress.

Gil rolled off to one side and pulled himself up to a sitting position against the headboard, recharged and energized. Cody lay limp and drained for several deep breaths, then crawled up to snuggle beside his lover.

"Eric notice your birthday present?" Gil pulled Cody back to rest against his chest. Cody tucked his head under Gil's jaw, resting over the big man's heart.

"He liked it." Cody raised his wrist, admiring the new timepiece for what Gil guessed as the hundredth time since Gil had given the watch to him. "Even if he thought the tracking device was just hilarious."

"Hilarious?" Gil tilted his head to one side so he could read Cody's expression. "What'd he say?"

Cody mimicked Eric's low bass and wisecracking tone. "'You let Gil lojack your ass.'"

"Ha! Really? He said that?" Gil tugged Cody closer. He slid a hand low to grab a handful of Cody's naked ass. "Lojacked?" He snorted to keep from bursting out laughing. "I never thought about it like that." Gil made a pleased face and grinned. "I like it." He squeezed and Cody jumped.

Cody punched Gil's offending forearm but didn't move away. "And I'm telling you the same thing I told him — you're an ass. Both of you!"

"Oh, come on, Cody. You know it's for your protection." He wrapped his arms around Cody's shoulders and hugged him tightly. "I've made a few enemies over the years. It's not wrong to protect the people you love, Cody."

"I know." He patted Gil's arm hugging his neck. "Eric knows it too. He was just yanking my chain." He turned slightly to look up at Gil. "And yours too, when he sees you again. Be ready." He settled back into the embrace. "Secretly I think he thinks it's the coolest birthday present ever."

"Did you read him the inscription?"

"Nah, that's for just you and me." Cody slipped the watch off his wrist and angled it so he could read the fine text engraved on the back. "'Cody, my strength, my sanity, my heart, Gil.' It says it all, Gil, for both of us." He immediately slipped the watch back on.

"Not too sentimental for you tough CSI guys?"

"Nah, not when it comes wrapped around the neck of a grizzly bear! Rugged he-man packaging offsets all possible girly tendencies." Cody wrestled the bear out from under the pillows behind them and set the stuffed animal on his chest. His fingers automatically combed through the layers of downy soft fur on the plump body. "He'll go great with the Kodiak and panda from the first two birthdays!"

"I picked him to remind you of me — fierce and wild, king of all he surveys."

Using the bear as a club, Cody playfully smacked Gil on the head and shifted his weight off Gil and more fully onto the mattress. "How 'bout you go survey your domain downstairs and let me grab a couple of hours of sleep before I have to be up all night. You wore me out."

"Glad to hear it." Gil started to rise up off the bed, but Cody rolled over, presenting him with a magnificent view of his naked ass. Unable to resist, he leaned down and bit the swell of one exposed cheek. Cody yelped, pelting him with a pillow for his evil deed. Gil laughed, slapped the abused skin, adding a pink tinge to the faint wet teeth marks. "Usually you're the energized rabbit afterward."

"Usually, I haven't just taken down two dudes twice my size and then had great sex. I gotta recharge. Toss me the covers, okay?"

A microsuede comforter billowed in the air to settle over Cody's lean, compact body, taking it from Gil's appreciative view. "Night, super science geek."

"Leave, grizzly man." Cody didn't even open his eyes.

Gil watched as his lover tucked the bear to his chest and snuggled a tanned cheek into the soft, brown fur. He left with a smile that matched Cody's.

§ § § §

The tiny, dime-sized surveillance camera reminded Bruce of a piece for tiddlywinks. He'd played the game on the back step of his parents' liquor store during the summer he broke his collarbone. Gil had spent that entire summer with him, content to play board games and study baseball card stats while their other friends raced off to hit home runs and pound each other into the ground with touch football.

It was bittersweet, like all of his childhood memories. If things had turned out differently he'd be a thriving businessman beside Gil, owner of his family's chain of liquor stores, an independent man. Not that he didn't make a damn good living working for Gil. Gil was good to him, like family, and it was a good life, but it wasn't the same as working for himself.

Bruce peeled the backing off the camera disc and pressed it to the center of the top frame of the entertainment cabinet facing the foot of the king-sized bed. Whether the doors were open or closed it was high enough and far enough away from the rest of the room; he would have an unobstructed view of the main area around the bed. He tapped the bottom edge of the camera disc, and it tilted slightly down, giving the pinhole for the microphone a better position.

"That should just about do it." Bruce glanced around the luxury suite, taking in the mess of discarded clothes, half-open luggage and crumpled takeout cartons with which Walter Bead had already violated the beautiful room. "Prime location...good sound and visual range...crappy subject matter." He sighed and took his key ring out of his jacket pocket, fingers already working over the worn pink surface. "I'd give my eye teeth for you to be a size double-D showgirl, Walter, but a guy's gotta take whatever the cards deal him."

The sound of the shower from the adjoining bathroom ended. Bruce moved smoothly out of the bedroom despite the bulk that he carried on his squat frame. He pulled the bedroom door silently closed behind him.

Once out in the main living area, he put his back to the far wall so he could watch the bedroom door and the front door to the hotel suite at the same time. Comfortable, he pulled his Blackberry out of his pants pocket, slipping his empty key ring over one finger to make it easier to handle the small device in his large hands. He couldn't remember if the rotating asterisk meant it was just receiving or recording.

Inputting a series of keypad strokes and then a few more, he tried several commands before the camera icon that indicated it was active showed on the small screen. The viewing pad gave him a clear view of Bead, in all his wet , skinny-legged, naked glory struggling into a pair of Bermudas and a polo shirt. The guy was pure geek from thinning hair with the balding spot on the top of his head to the worn flip-flops into which he scuffed his bony bare feet. The guy had even found a polo shirt with a breast pocket to stuff his array of pens into.

Bruce thanked God he hadn't been born a nervous, whiny pencil neck. Bead was all over the room, rifling through his open luggage, tossing aside clothes then grabbing them back up to shove into a bureau drawer then taking them back out again to drop into the suitcase. Ever few minutes Bead would look at his watch, twitching fingers tapping the crystal as if he was checking to see if the hands were stuck.

Bruce watched as Bead silently shoved the open suitcase on the bed to one side, jamming it into a gym bag lying on the foot of the bed. The second bag slipped and hung partially off the end of the mattress, the open suitcase spilling part of it rumpled contents over the coverlet. Bead didn't seem to notice or care.

He threw himself down on the bed and grabbed the phone to dial a number from memory. It only took three seconds of Bead's jabbering and gesturing his way through an animated conversation before Bruce realized the mic wasn't on.

"Christ! Trial runs always bite my ass." Bruce stabbed at the keypad, highlighting icon after icon until a thin, nasal voice assaulted his hearing. "Never thought that annoying sound would be music to my ears. Almost as good as the payout bells at the slots."

Bead rubbed his bald spot and nodded vigorously. "Yes, yes that's right. The transfer has to be in the Cayman account as soon after deposit as possible. How soon can that be done?...Are you sure?...No holdups?...Okay."

He hung up without a goodbye and hurriedly made another phone call. For this one he had to take the number out of the open phone book on the side table. He bounced on the bed in an effort to drag the thick book onto to his lap, the motion jiggling the gym bag hanging over the foot of the bed. It was enough to shift the contents, the added weight on the zipper causing the teeth to pull open.

Bruce studied the screen, tapping buttons and arrows until the picture was brighter. Frustratingly, the display changed but only to flash the current time of three twenty-one p.m. at him. He hit a few more combinations. The sound of Bead changing his airline departure time came crisp and clear in the earplug he'd attached to the Blackberry to see if it improved the sound quality. It had. Enough to know Walter Bead was skipping town. The weasel was shorting Bruce days of bodyguard pay by heading out early. Which was pretty cheap of him considering the number of ten thousand dollar bricks falling one by one out of the now open gym bag onto the lush carpeting of the hotel floor.

§ § § §

The streetlights were dim and dirty. Every other one was burned out. The darkness painted the entire block in pasty shades of gray. Just after nine p.m. and life in the less successful side of town was awakening, its inhabitants creeping out of their respective holes.

The only bright spot on the street came from the flashing lights of the police cruiser blocking the road from any possible, but so far nonexistent, traffic. Shadows from the surrounding buildings reached out from every angle. The garish neon signs in the few closed, barred, and gated pawn shop windows only made the area look desperate and abandoned instead of colorful and lively. Of course, the dead body in the middle of the alley drained a lot of the cheeriness out of the scene.

Cody backed the official CSI SUV into the mouth of the alley, stopping where the uniformed officer instructed him to so he didn't breach the outer perimeter of the crime scene. He jumped out of the driver's seat and grabbed his processing kit from the back seat, glancing at his partner for the night, Emily Warady.

"Ready for some fun, Em? I can take the vic if you'd rather not." It was Emily's partner who had called off with the flu, but Emily wasn't looking too perky herself.

"I'm good. Why ask? I don't have a problem with bodies." There was no defensiveness in her tone, but she gave Cody a frown. He noticed a sheen of sweat on her forehead that the mild temperatures didn't account for.

"Well, honestly, you look a little green around the gills. You getting the flu, too?" Cody tried not to pay attention to shop gossip, but rumor had it Emily and her partner shared more than just the same shift.

"I'm fine, Baxter. Don't think you have to baby me." She pushed open the SUV's door and jumped out, wasting no time taking her gear from the back of the truck. Cody silent joined her and they moved off together toward the primary scene.

Good at her job, smart and efficient, Emily was a dedicated field agent but cool and distant enough that most men seemed too intimated to approach her on a personal level. She was a tall blonde with wide blue eyes, and a lean, athletic body. She routinely turned the head of quite a few males. Tonight she looked a lot less stunning than usual. Gray was not her color.

"Okay." Cody nodded at the blood spatter as they approached body. "I'll work the scene and you take the body."

The closer they got, the slower Emily walked until she paused ten feet away from the dead man. The smell of urine and stool floated on the air toward them, the result of loosening bowel and bladder control after death.

Emily gagged, one gloved hand pulling Cody to a stop beside her. "Okay, I was wrong. You take the body." She gagged again and covered her mouth with her forearm, taking quick, shallow breaths through the fabric of her jacket. "I'll take the perimeter and surrounding area."

"Deal." He smiled to let her know it wasn't a problem, but kept his manner brisk to reassure her he didn't think less of her for a momentary weakness. "I'll check in with the detective on the scene." He tilted his chin at a tall, dark-haired man in a suit talking with a patrol officer and taking down notes. Everyone seemed to be keeping a distance from the dead guy. "Looks like White's on this one."

"Okay." Emily nodded and stepped back a few paces. "Thanks." She cleared her throat and turned a shade paler, but looked Cody in the eye to firmly add, "I owe you one, Baxter."

"It's a team effort, right?" Cody shrugged off the debt and moved toward White. "I got your back."

"Right." Emily got a better grip on her kit, pulled her flashlight out of her CSI vest and started exploring the dark alley pavement in a wide circle spiraling in toward the body.

Cody shifted his kit to his left hand and held out his right as he approached the patrol car and the men surrounding it. "Hey, Jared. Isn't it kind of late for you to be out?" His hand was caught in a stranglehold for a millisecond before it was released. Jared White's heavy hand patted his shoulder in welcome.

"I got the call just as I was leaving." Jared nodded his thanks at the officer and tucked his notepad away in his jacket pocket. His hand still on Cody's shoulder, he guided Cody toward the deceased as he talked. "Amy's going to be hopping mad. Third night this week I've missed dinner."

"Better take her out this weekend, Jared. You'll be bunking over at our house again if you're not careful." He glanced around, noting the position of the surrounding cars and officers.

Emily was off to his right, slowly working her way in with a tight circle. He hadn't noticed any flashes from her camera and there were no markers on the ground. She was coming up empty so far.

"There are worse places than ending up at the Turko–Baxter mansion when you get kicked out into the street." Jared stuck a piece of gum into his mouth and chewed slow and deliberate, waiting patiently as Cody worked his way around the body.

"Who kicked this guy into the street? Any witnesses?" Cody hefted the large evidence camera that hung around his neck. The camera snapped crisply with each picture he took of the dead man and the area around the body.

"No. But that's not exactly a surprise in this neighborhood. The patrol officers found him on their rounds. Usually they just roust a few drunks or homeless out of the doorways down here."

"Just my luck to have the graveyard shift on the night the animals come out to play." The man was lying face down on the wet pavement, his clothing and hair still damp from a brief evening rain. He was dress in shorts and a polo shirt, a pair of flimsy sandals askew but, amazingly, still on his feet.

"Look at his feet. His flip-flops are still on." Cody crouched beside the body. He was careful to keep out of the surface puddles, not knowing yet if they were blood or rain. "It looks as if he dropped to ground without a struggle. Like he didn't have any warning he was about to die."

Cody looked up at Jared. The detective was leaning over his back, close to him, a position of trust between friends. "Like he knew his killer, trusted him." He looked back down at the victim's deformed head. "That's kind of sad, huh?"

Jared grunted a noncommittal answer and straightened up.

"Coroner released the scene; it's all yours." His tone was all business, telling Cody he was refusing to take the discussion further at the moment. Cody knew Jared cared about the homicides he investigated, but the detective didn't let the human factors distract him from the job of catching the killers. He honored the dead in his own way — by solving the crime.

"I'm heading out. The patrol officers that found him will stay with you and Emily so if you have any questions, ask them. I don't have anything to go on yet, no witnesses, no weapon found, no security cameras in the area, no abandoned cars, nothing. I'm hoping you get some kind of hit on his fingerprints. He doesn't have any ID on him. No wallet or money in his pockets that the uniforms could find without disturbing things. No watch or jewelry either."

"A mugging?" Cody knew his expression conveyed his disbelief as much as his voice did.

"Maybe. But I got a preliminary cause of death as gunshot wound to the head. Single shot, close range, execution style."

"So maybe not a mugging."

"You tell me, you're the super science geek."

"You spend too much time listening to Gil."

"Hard habit to break after ten years."

"Well, he's wrong. I'm a gifted science geek."

Jared huffed and turned to walk away. "Well, gifted, I'm heading back to the station to make my report. If you get anything, leave me a voice message. I'll check my mail later when Amy isn't looking."

Cody skirted a pool of brown, odorous fluid seeping out from the man's pants and slowly turned him over to snap photos of his face. All the time he worked, he continued talking to Jared. "That's a slippery slope, my man, slippery slope. Next you'll be telling her we're just 'friends'." He laughed and looked away from the camera's eyepiece long enough to give Jared a huge, mocking grin.

"Laugh all you want, funny man. I'm going home to a beautiful wife," Jared clapped Cody's shoulder hard, "while you get to spend the night with our vic."

Without another word, Jared strode off. He waved at Emily before getting into his car. Cody watched him pull out, then waved at the waiting coroner's attendants to come bag the body.

Emily was getting nearer, but she wasn't looking like the break from the action had helped any. Her eyes looked sunken and her lips had started to crack.

Cody helped the two attendants lift the body onto the gurney then stood back until they were out of the way. As soon as they left he crouched to check the area where the body had been. The alley was littered with discarded paper, tossed fast food containers, and rotting garbage. The pavement under the body had more of the same.

As he peeled away a flattened sandwich wrapper, a dark rectangle caught Cody's eye. He picked up a small leather pouch like the kind people keep credit cards in. Instead of plastic cards, a sliver of pink stuck up past the edges, glossy, and hard like metal.

He looked up to see Emily approaching, her face in the shadows as she hurried forward. "Looks like I found a wallet."

"Baxter. Cody. I don't feel good. I mean really not good." She stumbled, regained her footing, and continued to Cody's side.

Cody dropped the wallet on the ground and rose, grabbing Emily by the arms just as she swayed and her knees buckled. He caught her and held her upright. Both uniformed officers came at a dead run, and Cody passed her off to them. He used his flashlight to check her pupils and study her face. Sweat beaded on her brow and upper lip, her color ashen.

"You look like crap, Em."

"I'm ...just...probably haven't had enough to drink today." Pushing away the helping hands, Emily straightened up. She ran the back of her hand over her mouth then pushed strands of hair from her ponytail off her face.

"You're so dehydrated you can't stand? Why?" Cody frowned.

Emily's tone turned defensive and hard. "I just got a little lightheaded, okay? It's been creeping up on me all day. I thought it would go away once I got busy working. My partner had already called off; I couldn't call in too. Listen, guys, I'll be —"

Emily spun around and lurched several feet away to vomit by the rear wheel of the patrol car. She had to lean over the fender to stay standing up. When she was done, she wiped her mouth on a tissue from her pocket and turned around to smile weakly at the three men watching her.

"Sorry."

"I think you should go home, Em."

"I can't leave you alone —" Another round of sudden vomiting interrupted her. This time one of the officers had to support her so she didn't end up kneeling in her own stomach fluids.

Trading concerned glances with the officers, Cody said, "We're all done here, Em. I can pack up the evidence bags and take everything back to base myself. There wasn't much to begin with. Why don't you let these guys take you home? I'll let the supervisor know what's happened to you."

She hung her head, taking deep breaths instead of answering him.

"I'll take that as a yes." Cody glanced from one uniform to the other. "You okay with that, guys? I'm good here. I just have to bag the rest of debris that was under the body. Less than five minutes and I'll be out of here. Okay?"

The older of the two officers cast a look around the deserted street and alleyway then finally nodded when Emily made a gagging noise that she eventually managed to bite back. The officer supporting Emily helped her slide into the back of the cruiser. He handed her a paper barf bag and gently shut the car door. Both men rolled their eyes at Cody. He smiled but didn't add to the mockery.

Before the cruiser pulled away, Cody gathered up the few bits of evidence he had already bagged and dropped them into the locker in the back of the SUV. Then he strode back to the spot where the body had been. Crouched over the flattened litter and debris, he reclaimed the wallet he had dropped when Emily had almost toppled over onto him. Taking a closer look at it, he noticed that a chip of the pink was now missing, the glint of metal catching the light were there hadn't been any visible before.

"Crap! First Emily tries to throw up on the evidence and now I break it. This is not a good night."

A garbage can rattled fifty feet down the alley and the streetlight two posts away suddenly burned out. Darting a look at the new shadows surrounding him, Cody slipped the case into a bag. "Okay. I think my five minutes are nearly up."

He touched the gun on his hip and scanned the empty street again as he walked back to the open tailgate of the SUV. The truck was sitting in a new shadow made by the burned out streetlight and the building between it, but the SUV was a symbol of safety and security, tough and familiar.

Even if he was talking to just himself, he liked the alleyway better when his voice was bouncing off the walls. "I'll pop this into the locker, get the rest of the litter bagged and be out of here like a flash." He wasted a glanced at the shadows behind him then went to work with an odd sense of urgency prickling at his skin. He leaned into the back of the truck to drag the locker closer.

As he pulled back, both hands dragging the heavy metal case, a large shadow came off the darkest side of the SUV, swift and unexpected. It engulfed him, all strong arms and vapor-soaked cloth. It swallowed him whole, making the alley go instantly black and silent.

§ § § §

"I know it's after midnight, but I thought you'd want to know, Gil. Can you believe that weaselly jerk fired me? Bastard."

Gil closed the front door behind Bruce. He led the way into

his study, wordlessly offering the man a drink from the bar. Bruce nodded and Gil automatically poured a neat whiskey and handed off to his friend. "It happens. Don't worry about it. Bead's a big boy." Gil raised his hands in the air in a 'whatever' gesture of frustration. "His decision."

"Yeah, well." Bruce pounded back half his whiskey in one gulp. "I saw the lights on here so I stopped. Sorry."

"I couldn't sleep anyway." Gil eyed Bruce as the man finished his drink in another single swallow.

"Something wrong?"

He took the glass, contemplating whether or not to refill it. Bruce wasn't usually much of a drinker. Having Bead cut him loose must have really pissed him off. He poured a short one and handed it back.

"Not really. Cody's working the night shift." He poured himself a few swallows of brandy and sipped, enjoying the burn and smoky flavor. "I was up."

"Yeah? Nights? Why tonight?" Bruce averted his gaze, leaving it riveted to the floor.

"Sick call. His turn to cover the hole." Gil studied Bruce's dejected slump, frowning.

"Too bad. I know you feel better when he's home. You know — safe." Bruce fished his key ring out of his pocket. The new recording micro device tumbled out with it. In the effort to catch it, Bruce dropped both the key ring and the box.

Gil picked them up before Bruce could react. "Hey, you've got a chip missing from the ear, Bruce. Better get it lacquered back up, buddy. This thing is showing its age." Gil handed Bruce the key ring, but kept the recorder.

"Cody can handle himself. He'll be okay." Gil fiddled with the controls, bored and not really interested but looking for something to keep himself busy. Damn, he'd forgotten how much he hated sleeping without Cody. "It just plays hell with his sleep cycle. Both of ours."

"I hear ya. You're used to him being around to keep you busy." Bruce tossed the key ring into the air, his fingers worrying a spot over and over again. "I was counting on those two extra days with Bead to keep me busy before that Middle Eastern sheikh got into town." He sniffed and tossed down another swallow of his drink. "Goddamn geek."

"He probably just got scared." Gil sat down in leather club chair, eventually setting the recorder on the table beside him. "I'd run a lot faster than he did if I'd just screwed over Enrico Sabo. At least it gave you a chance to play with the new camera."

Bruce remained standing, pacing the room, restless.

"Yeah." Bruce's gaze darted immediately to the table where the recorder lay. "I gotta practice with the keypad more. I don't have all the commands and icons figured out yet. I'll work on it." Bruce held out his hand for the device, but Gil waved him away.

"I'll check it out. It'll keep me busy until I fall asleep. Maybe even read the manual."

"You sure?" Bruce looked longingly at the small black box. "I can play around with it some more."

"You're more bored than I am!" Gil laughed. "Thanks. If all else fails, I'll ask Cody to scope it out. He's great with these compact things. Then he can show us both how it works." Gil took another sip of his brandy then set it aside. If he was actually going to work on the recorder he needed a clear head. He picked the box up.

Bruce grunted a noncommittal sound. "Yeah, well, little hands probably work better with it."

Any response Gil was going to give was forgotten when the doorbell rang.

"Is everyone awake tonight?" Gil was out of his chair and striding through the foyer before the door chime stopped echoing in the hall. He glanced at the grandfather clock and frowned at the hour. Was there this much activity every night? Had he and Cody just sleep through it?

He could see Jared White's drawn face through the sectional panes of glass in the door. Yanking open the door, he chided, "Jared, what's up? Amy throw you out again?"

"It's not Amy, Gil." He crossed the threshold, followed by three other officers, two patrol uniforms and Sid Kraft, a detective Jared occasionally partnered with. "It's Cody."

§ § § §

It was the muffled silence that bothered Cody the most. The blindfold was tied tightly around his head, hard against his eyes, dipping low to a walnut-sized knot at the base of his skull. He'd once thought that blindfold play might be exciting with Gil in the bedroom, but he'd never look at it that way again. This was too disorienting. Frightening.

The material was stiff and rough on his cheek, like leather. It covered his ears and muted the sounds of the room, making his own breathing echo harshly in his head. It was distracting, annoying, and a little scary. Most normal people didn't keep leather blindfolds lying around in case they needed them. Sadist and murderers, now that was another story. They were known to have entire toy chests full of 'special items' for their victims.

Victim. It was hard to think of himself as that. Before this, it had been just a word that described some unfortunate person from whose body he was gathering evidence or photographing from every unnatural angle possible. Victims were the dead, the discarded, the helpless.

A shudder of terror ran down his spine and his body shook from the strength of it. He needed to calm down and get a grip. He wasn't dead, and Gil would never let him be discarded. But man, he sure felt helpless.

Lying partially on his chest and right side, Cody found his face was pushed into a musty-smelling mattress. His knees were bent, his legs held oddly close and parallel. His wrists were tied together at an awkward angle, palms together so he couldn't touch the binds with his fingers no matter how much he worked them. From the sharp bite that cut into his skin each time he twisted his hands he knew they were fastened with nylon wire ties, unbreakable and unyielding.

He could feel the soft nap of a flannel sheet or a thin blanket. His ankles and feet were bare. They were bound with the same nylon bands, each of his ankle bones pressed tight into the flesh of the other leg, one slightly raised into the curve of his other heel making it impossible to put both feet on the ground if he stood.

Whoever had him had experience at restraining people. Lots of it. Whoever had kidnapped him.

He was a kidnap victim.

Suddenly the muffled breathing echoing in his head got louder and more labored, the sound overwhelming, deafening in the confined space. He thrashed against the bed and linens, trying to work the blindfold off, desperate to shove it away even if only a fraction of an inch. Up or down, it didn't matter as long as it moved off his ears and stopped the raspy, frantic sound in his head.

He tried to scream out his frustration, but his tongue was trapped in the dry cavern of his mouth, his lips held immobile. By the way his skin pulled and pinched across his jaw and cheekbones, he judged at least three pieces of wide duct tape had been used. What felt like a balled up hanky trapped his tongue, jammed between it and the roof of his mouth.

The smell of the adhesive on the tape drifted into his nostrils. It reeked of chemicals and oil, probably from sitting in a toolbox or the trunk of a car. Cody's head spun and his stomach churned, a combination of the lingering effects of the drug that had been used to knock him out, his own rising fear and thrashing movements, and the heavy odors in the poorly ventilated room he was in.

A sudden fear of drowning in his own vomit if he threw up while gagged instantly halted his frenzied movements. He lay still on the bed, chest heaving, skin clammy with sweat. He could feel hot pools of moisture line the edge of his covered eyelids. Tears trickled into the corners of his eyes and stayed there, unable to flow down his cheek, trapped in his eyelashes, scalding his skin. He had a sudden vision of his co-workers finding his body with his eyes sealed shut, crusted closed with the salt of his own tears. The sob that dragged out of him was weak and choked.

A few sobering deep breaths and the tears slowed along with his breathing. After several anxious minutes, his head cleared enough that he remembered what he should have thought of when he first woke up. Cody turned and yanked, rolled onto his stomach and then onto his back, but no matter what position he managed, he couldn't get his fingers twisted around enough to tell whether his birthday watch was still on his wrist or not. The nylon cords bit into his skin, never giving that tiny quarter inch he needed.

If his socks, shoes and jacket were gone, he'd bet a twenty his belt, cell phone and watch were gone as well. He wasn't even going to think about the odds of the police actually finding him. Alive. He knew the reality of his situation all too well. But then the odds didn't take into account that the police weren't the only ones searching for him. The odds didn't take into account Gil Turko.

Just thinking about Gil made his chest ache, part of it loneliness and terror, part of it hope. He didn't know hope could actually hurt. Cody was amazed by what he thought about when he was scared shitless.

§ § § §

"Cody? What's going on, Jared?" Confused, Gil stepped back to let the men enter, moving to stand with Jared.

"We can't find him." Jared paused, and Gil could see him searching for his next words. They seemed to stun both of them once Jared said them out loud. "We think he's been kidnapped."

Bruce hung in the background at the study's door, close enough to hear what was going on. He shrugged when Gil looked at him, his gaze wandering away to scan the other officers in the foyer.

"Kidnapped? Cody?" Gil slipped the recording device into his pants and pulled out his cell phone. He hit the speed dial, listened, waited. He snapped it shut after the recorded message repeated itself three times. "His phone's off. He never turns his phone off." He inhaled deeply and focused all his energy to deal with the immediate problem, forcing imagines of a dead or dying Cody from his mind. "When? Where?"

"Around ten. He and Emily Warady were called to a murder scene over on Lancaster at eight twelve p.m. Looked like a professional hit. Not much for them to do besides bag a few leaves, take some pictures and let the coroner bag the body. It was a laundered scene."

"Pros." Jared nodded his agreement. Gil shook his head. "So what went wrong? There's always backup out there when the criminalists work the field."

"There was. But his partner showed up sick. She got so bad Cody asked the remaining uniforms on scene to take her home while he packed up and brought the evidence in. He had five minutes of work left to do. They agreed."

"If that's all he had to do why didn't they wait for him to finish up?"

"Apparently Warardy almost passed out at the scene. Looks like the same flu as her partner called off with. Anyway, the patrol car swung back around to the scene after dropping her off at home. They found Cody's official vehicle still parked in the alley with the doors wide open. All the collected evidence was missing and so was Cody."

"He didn't make it back on his own some other way?"

"I checked. He never went back to the lab."

"How? Jared, you can't just pick Cody up and walk off with him. He may be small, but he'd kick the average guy's ass no time flat."

"Guess he didn't meet up a with an average guy then, Gil."

"A pro? Think the hitter came back for something?"

"It's looking like it. Can't say for sure yet. But since you haven't been contacted with a ransom demand, it just might be all about the murder."

"Who's the vic?"

"You're not going to like it."

"Jared."

"Walter Bead." Jared turned his frown on Bruce. "I thought you were doing protective services with him, Bruce."

Bruce worried the key ring some more then slipped it away to his pocket. He cleared his throat. "The geek fired me earlier this evening. I was here telling Gil about it."

"When did you last see him?" Jared pulled out his notebook and began jotting.

"About five o'clock. He made some phone calls, changed his flight out of town, told me he didn't need my services anymore. So I left." He shrugged again. "I hit a bar or two for a drink and came here."

"Maybe Enrico Sabo decided letting a snitch loose was bad for his reputation after all." Jared looked to Gil for an opinion.

"Taking the homicide evidence points to someone wanting to remove evidence of the killer, but why kidnap Cody, too? Just knock him out and take the bags." Gil paced a circle, tightly contained and coiled for sudden action.

"And if they wanted Cody, why take the evidence?" Jared shook his head. "It doesn't make sense."

"There's one guy that might know. Let's go find Enrico Sabo and ask." Gil was out the door before Jared could protest.

§ § § §

"You know you're always welcome in my casino, Mr. Turko." Enrico Sabo flashed his pearly whites at Gil then toned down the smile for Jared. "It goes without saying for you, Detective White. I would prefer it wasn't in your official capacity, but we can't always have what we want, now can we gentlemen."

Both large men stood in front of Sabo's gleaming desk where the casino owner had opted to remain sitting when they entered the room. Gil decided it probably made the man feel safer. If Gil had the tiniest hint that Sabo has anything to do with Cody's disappearance a concrete wall wasn't going to protect him.

Gil gestured at the luxurious trappings that decorated Sabo's office. "I'd say you're pretty used to getting what you want, Mr. Sabo."

Sabo smiled in wordless agreement. "And what do you want, Mr. Turko? My casino isn't one of your usual drinking holes."

"Walter Bead was found dead tonight. Just a few hours after firing one of my men."

Sabo actually looked surprised. "And you think I had something to do with it? Or is your ego bruised? Your firm was protecting him, wasn't it?"

"My ego has nothing to do with this." Dangerous vibes started emanating from Gil. Jared moved closer to his friend.

"Of course, not. What was I thinking." Sabo frowned and looked questioningly at Jared. "Detective White, are you here officially about Bead's death or just as Mr. Turko's drinking buddy?"

"Officially. But not so much about Bead. The crime scene investigator working Bead's murder has disappeared."

"Disappeared?" Sabo looked from Jared to Gil and back again. "I don't get it."

"Disappeared as in taken," Gil leaned on the desk, both fists planted in the middle of the glass surface, his face hovering close to Sabo's, "along with all the crime scene evidence collected on the murder."

"So? What's it to you?" Sabo still didn't get the connection.

"The investigator was Cody Baxter." Gil said through clenched teeth.

The light went on for Sabo. He blinked several times before asking, "Your...friend?"

"My partner."

"That's unfortunate," Sabo licked his lips, "but what's that have to do with me?"

"It was a professional hit, Sabo." Jared studied Sabo's closed expression. "The only guy in town I know of who had a reason to take Bead out would be the guy he just cost a whole ton of money. You."

"No chance." Sabo looked relieved. "Court costs and fines didn't even come close to what this casino makes in a single day. I walked away from that fine with a hand slap and a lot of free publicity." He laughed. "In Vegas, it actually helps to have a gangster rap for the tourists. They think they're hanging with the dangerous crowd for the week they're out of the cornfields of Iowa. The geek did me a favor."

"And you didn't want to make an example of him when it was all over? Sooth your ego? There were rumors he might have covered up more than he reported." Gil left the implication hanging in the air.

Sabo just smiled and leaned back in chair, at ease for the first time since Gil and Jared had entered the room. "I settled all accounts with Bead like a gentleman. He left my employment an extremely happy accountant." Sabo winked at Gil. "I didn't kill him or arrange for him to be killed. No reason to. It was all taken care of."

Gil studied Sabo face for a full minute before straightening up, then quick as a flash he reached across the desk. His fist mangled Sabo's silk shirt and tie as he dragged the man out of his chair to stand so that their noses almost touched. Jared was there, a useless restraining hold on Gil's arm. Gil didn't bother to shake him off. It was more threatening to Sabo to have both of them in close even if Jared was trying to force Gil back.

"If something happens to Cody and I find out you had anything, anything to with it, the coroner's office won't be able to tell what species you were before you died, understand me?"

Jared whispered low and urgent, "Gil, let him go."

Gil didn't waste a glance at him.

Sabo had to swallow twice before he could answer, and then his voice was tense and reedy. "I didn't have anything to do with Bead's murder or whatever happened to your guy. I swear."

Gil stared at Sabo then shoved him back into his chair. "I'll take that as a blood oath, Sabo."

Jared grabbed Gil's arm and tugged him toward the exit.

Sabo straightened his clothing, rattled but regaining his composure rapidly. "I learned a long time ago that it's easier to clean green from the books than red from the carpet. I hope you find your guy. For everyone's sake."

He hated to admit it, but Gil believed him. He let Jared shove him out into the hall, and then silently followed the detective through the maze of flashing lights and buzzing slot machines to the unmarked car parked in the drop off zone of the casino.

Once in the passenger seat Gil punched the dashboard until it cracked. The sound stopped his pounding fist, but it opened a new wound inside of him. Pent up frustration flowed like hot lava. It was replaced by a feeling of helplessness so profound he almost wept.

"You believe him, Gil?"

"Yeah, I do." Cody was slipping away from them.

"Me, too." Jared eased the sedan out into traffic and headed back to Gil's house.

"We're out of leads."

"If it wasn't about Bead, you'll get a ransom call. I left the uniforms installing a wiretap at your house. Maybe we can track the kidnapper."

"Track him! That's it." Gil slapped the cracked dash with his open palm, trying not to add to the damage. "Why didn't I remember that?"

"What is it?" Jared shot him a worried glance, keeping one eye on traffic and one on his passenger.

"Cody's got a tracking device on him. He has to activate it, but if he's alive, he should be able to turn it on. Even if he's tied up."

"A tracker?" Jared was confused and it showed. "But they didn't take his car."

"It's not on his car."

"Not on ...." Gil saw the disbelief in Jared's eyes. "He has a tracking device on his body?"

"In his watch." He refused to feel guilty for looking out for Cody in his own overbearing, but loving, way. "Birthday present." It was best to keep his admission short and to the point. It cut down on the questions.

Jared was silent for a moment then he said, voice filled with amazement, "You lojacked your lover?" Gil gave a guilty shrug but didn't elaborate. "That is so wrong on so many levels, Gil."

"So I'm told." He checked his Blackberry to make sure the receiving unit was on and waiting for a signal. He hoped Cody was in a position to activate it. He didn't realize until that moment that hope could feel an awful lot like dread. "But if it helps us find him, I don't give a shit."

§ § § §

Cody's blindfold was still securely in place, but his other senses had started compensating for his lack of sight. He could hear the distant hum of what he decided were central air fans, and if he concentrated really hard, he picked out a dull constant hum as if electricity charged the air.

His skin felt cool. Dry air and the absence of outside noise suggested that he was in a basement. That meant a fairly expensive house in a secluded neighborhood, probably one with a wine cellar with a sampling room. He could smell the fruity odor and alcohol. Bruce had a small wine room that had smelled like this. Cody hadn't visited often but he remembered the smell well. He just hadn't realized he remembered it until now.

If a wine cellar and basement equaled an expensive house,

this was about more than getting a load of cash from Gil. But if it were about covering up the murder he had been working, why not just take the evidence and leave Cody behind or kill him right then and there? Why kidnap him? It didn't make sense.

The one piece of evidence he did find at the scene had been the metal object in the leather case, and he hadn't taken the time to examine it before being grabbed. He tried to conjure a mental vision of it, but the cramps in his legs and arms and the ever-expanding fullness of his bladder kept interfering. Now he wished he hadn't had that third cup of coffee on the way to the scene.

Facedown on the bed, he shifted his weight to turn onto his side. His shoulders ached from having his arms bound behind his back. His wrists felt raw and sticky from his attempts to twist them around. He finally managed to drag his arms over the thicker waistband of his jeans enough times to ascertain that his watch wasn't on his wrist. No hard edges dug into his hips, so he guessed his cell phone was missing too.

A soft jingling sound like loose change in a pocket along with a faint scuffing tread told Cody someone had entered the room. Something about the jingling noise made him listen harder, but no brilliant revelations sprung to mind about the source of the sound.

His thoughts were derailed when a heavy hand touched his cheek. He jumped and pulled back, but a large hand grabbed his jaw and held him still. The tape was peeled off his face fast enough to make him flinch. A grunt escaped him at the sharp pain of having facial hairs none too gently pulled out by the roots. The wad of cloth dried to the roof of his mouth was slowly pulled out, freeing his tongue.

He couldn't stop himself from gasping, dragging in a deep breath of air through his mouth, and savoring the ability to inhale with his mouth and exhale through his nose. The heavy smell of adhesive disappeared. A thin line of sticky tightness remained on his face. His lips felt raw and cracked. Cody suspected more than a little of his skin was on the discarded tape. Even so, he was thrilled that the tape was gone. It didn't improve his predicament, but he felt less like a helpless mummy.

The same large hands grabbed under his arms and pulled up so he sat with his back and arms in the pillows. His head hit a wall or a headboard. His legs were still awkwardly bound together, making his calves cramp. His ankles burned from the constant strain against the nylon ties as his body tried to regain its natural alignment.

The soft shuffling sounds of footsteps moved away and came back to the bedside. Cody rolled his head against the pillows and wall, trying for the hundredth time to loosen the blindfold just a bit.

Knowing danger was standing less than a foot away and being unable to stare it in the eye were unnerving. But getting an eyeful of the man who kidnapped you, thus making you a liability, was even more unnerving. Cody stopped moving, but he couldn't remain completely submissive.

"What do you want with me?"

In answer, an object was pressed to his lips and up against his teeth. It took him a second before he recognized the smooth circular shape as a straw. Despite his full bladder signaling an urgent need to empty, he knew he was dehydrated. Spitting out that one sentence had been almost painful with his dry, raw lips and tight throat. Whether it was drugged or not didn't matter. He dipped his head to get a better hold of the straw and drank down the cool water until his stomach threatened to rebel.

"Thanks." He eased back against the pillows again, trying to think of a way to get a response from the man. He knew it was a man by the feel of his hands and the strength he had used to bodily move Cody on the bed. The guy hadn't even grunted with the effort of moving a hundred and fifty pounds of dead weight because it hadn't been an effort for him. This guy, someone's hired muscle maybe, was big. The only other person who had ever moved him so easily was Gil.

Jesus, what Cody wouldn't give to have Gil's hands on him

instead of this guy's.

"My shoulders hurt. Could you..." The footsteps shuffled away, heading out the door. Cody knew it had been a long shot, but he needed to try to find an opening to escape, fruitless as it probably was. "Wait! Please, wait a minute. I need to relieve myself." The shuffling stopped receding, but they didn't grow closer either. "I really need to piss. Please? I promise not to do anything stupid. I just need to go, okay?"

If his feet were unbound to walk to a bathroom, he might be able to kick the guy and make a run for it, blindfolded or not. He was perfectly capable of disabling an assailant, no matter how big, with a few well-placed kicks, but it worked so much better if he could see them. Considering it might be his only avenue for escape, he was willing to try, blindfold or not.

The waistband of his jeans was suddenly yanked on. Cody thought for a triumphant moment that he was being pulled forward so the tie around his ankles could be cut. The surge of excitement died an abrupt death when the tension on his abdomen loosened, accompanied by the sound of a zipper being opened.

"Hey! What the hell!" A heavy hand pressed on his abdomen, forcing Cody to be still or lose control of his bladder. He really didn't want Gil or anyone else to find him lying in his own urine. Bound and blindfolded was bad enough.

With no room to roll away, he was forced to endure the fumbling of hot fingers on his cock as they freed it from his boxers. The digits felt oddly smooth and the familiar sound of latex rubbing on latex told him the man had gloves on.

Visions of the grisly handy work of the long list of perverts, gaybashers, and murderous deviants he saw in his day-to-day job clicked through his mind at lightning speed. He saw color photos of all the horrors his crime scene camera had recorded at each newly discovered dead body.

His breath caught in his throat and his limbs went cold and numb. Just when he thought he'd black out from lack of air, he felt his limp cock tucked into something cold and hard. He knew some guys got hard when they were scared but the idea of some faceless pervert touching him did nothing for his arousal, voluntary or involuntary. His stomach roiled. He panted just to keep from vomiting.

The sides of the object rubbed along his inner thighs and pressed up to loosely contain his cock. An impatient thud snapped against the object and he realized it was plastic. Not a sex toy or a torture device, but a container to urinate in — a bottle or even a hospital urinal.

It was difficult, but he managed to relax enough to go. God knew he didn't want to do this again if he could help it. When the last drip trickled off his cock, the bottle was removed and he was tucked back in and zipped up. No lingering touches, no exploring gropes, no open zippers to expose him for hungry gazes he couldn't protect himself from.

He hadn't realized he was holding his breath until the footsteps disappeared and he was alone again. Suddenly he could hold back the tears any longer. They were hot and brief, pooling against the blindfold again, seeping into his lashes and under and over his closed eyelids. He knew the leather was probably absorbing the tears so two wet spots would darken the hide on the outside. That thought alone helped him blink them back.

His arms hurt, his head and stomach hurt, he wasn't sure if he was going to live. The one thing he wanted more than anything else was Gil. Cody never admitted it to anyone else, but he understood part of his attraction for Gil was the sense of solid protection and security the man gave him. He was honest with himself if no one else.

Fuck being a stoic he-man, he wanted to be rescued. He'd even be happy if Jared's overly cautious attitude or Bruce and his constantly clacking key ring showed up to find his sorry ass. As long as Gil was with them.

Suddenly the wallet from the crime scene popped into his head along with the jiggling sound of change. Cody visualized the pink painted edge of the object in the wallet, and his heart skipped a beat. He suddenly knew what that pink metal was.

This wasn't about him or money or a murder. It was all about Gil.

He rolled off the bed and hit the floor with a muffled thud. Squirming around to a kneeling position he found the edge of the mattress and the board holding it in place. Grinding his forehead into the firm surface, he began raking his face across it. The blindfold caught every now and then, allowing a tiny breeze of cool air to touch a spot that had been covered by warm leather. He didn't care if he scraped his entire face off. He had to get out of here and warn Gil.

§ § § §

The grandfather clock in the foyer struck three a.m. The chimes echoed off the walls, forlorn and empty. Gil usually considered it a rich, reassuring sound, but tonight it was plain lonely. It reflected his solitary state of mind pretty well.

Tru had been at the house waiting for them when Gil and Jared returned, alerted Bruce. She was busy making coffee and sandwiches for the officers who had stayed with the phone tap. A few drinks under his belt, Bruce had excused himself to grab a quick nap in a guestroom.

Back in his study, Gil reclaimed his abandoned brandy glass. He splashed a small amount into the snifter and sat staring at the wired house phone.

The receiving software for Cody's tracker was tied to his Blackberry, not the house line. He leaned back and fished in his pants pocket. The recording device he was saving for Cody to decipher brushed his palm. He pulled both out, laying them both on the table. One was a lifeline to Cody while the other had been a witness to a dead man's last hours.

Having paced a rut into the carpeting in front of the wide window at the west end of the study, Jared snapped shut his cell phone and joined Gil on the sleek leather sofa.

"The coroner removed the bullet from Bead, and now

ballistics is trying to match it to something in the system, but no luck so far." He jerked his chin in the direction of the coffee table and the electronics array that Gil was busy exploring. "What's that?"

"New surveillance hidden mini-cam. Bruce was trying it out on Bead." Picking up the recorder, Gil turned it over in his hands, checking the power source and function keys.

"Think he got something on it that could help?"

"I doubt it. He said he couldn't get the record program to function. The keyboard isn't a QWERTY configuration and some of function symbols looked like Russian." He thumbed through a few more symbols then shook his head. "Bruce is usually good with this kind of stuff, but unrecognizable icons and symbols make any new program a bitch to learn in the beginning."

He played with it, trying to retrieve any recordings on it, but it refused to respond. Just as his limited patience was about to snap, the house phone rang, a jarring, ominous, trilling. Everyone in the room shifted into high gear. Gil waited for the signal from the officer with the wiretap before picking up the receiver.

Tru came at a run, breathless and pale, to stand in the doorway. Her knuckles were white where she held onto the doorframe. Gil stopped her in her tracks with one calmly lifted palm to ensure silence.

"Turko."

"I have him." The voice deep, rough, filtered through an electronic synthesizer, but very much a masculine grunt to the tone. It seemed to fill the room, magnified by the wiretap's speakerphone.

"Prove it." Gil could barely shove the words out between his teeth, his jaw clamped tight to hold back his rage and hurt.

"Cody, my strength, my sanity, my heart, Gil." On this monster's lips, it sounded more like an epitaph than the declaration of love it was. "That's what the back of this watch has inscribed on it. I'm guessing there aren't two like it in the world."

There was a muffled gasp from the doorway. Tru slipped into the room and sat down heavily in the nearest chair she could find.

Gil couldn't convince his lungs to work. Any response his brain could formulate was lost in the haze of pain that boiled up from his chest and stuck fast in his throat.

"If you've hurt him—" He could barely see through the red haze that settled over everything, the room narrowing to focus completely on the voice in his ear, the people and furniture around him disappearing altogether.

"He's alive and he'll stay that way as long as you agree to do what you're told."

"I want to talk to him. Hear his voice."

"Too damn bad."

"I won't agree to anything without knowing he's alive."

"Then I might as well hang up."

"Wait!" The line was silent but it hadn't been disconnected. "What do you want?"

"Nothing."

"What?" If this was all just a game, Gil was going to dismember this guy with his bare hands when they caught him.

"I want you to do nothing. A few days from now your firm will be protecting a visiting Eastern oil sheikh, Atullah ibn Mojad. You will instruct your men not to interfere with any unusual events that take place on the second day of his visit. All they have to do is nothing. Stand back and do nothing. It's a simple thing; even a bodyguard can do it."

"That would be accessory to murder."

"The sheikh's murder or your guy's murder. Which one do you want to be responsible for?"

"If Cody doesn't make it back to me, I promise you, I'll hunt you down. Your own mother won't be able to ID your body when I'm done."

"As if she could. Save your breath for sweet-talking your

boyfriend. When he wakes up, I'll let you talk to him. Wait by the phone. I'll only call once. You miss it, you miss your only shot at it." The line went dead.

Gil turned to the wiretap monitor but the officer shook his head and said, "The signal was cloaked by several connections. We didn't make them all before he hung up."

"Gil, you're not going to do what he asked." Jared took the digital recording chip out of the machine and bagged it for the lab. An officer replaced it with a new one.

"Of course not. I was trying to buy more time. We get anything usable on the tape?"

"I'll take it to headquarters, see if Eric or one of the lab guys can find anything useful in the background noise. I'll check out this sheikh while I'm there."

Trudy finally found her voice. "I ran a full background check on the sheikh when we got the job. There was nothing in it that made me think he was in danger any more than the average zillionaire in Vegas is. I'll go get it and you can look it over again." Finding something useful to do seemed to re-energize her. She breezed out of the room under full sail.

Jared nodded. "I'll check anyway. I'll run by ballistics while I'm there, too." He clapped Gil on the shoulder. "You going to be okay?"

"I won't be okay again until Cody's home, Jared. The inscription on the watch was the truth."

§ § § §

Cody's face felt like it was on fire. Scratched raw down his right cheek, it was bruised and bleeding where he'd rubbed it repeatedly over the thick, corded edge of the mattress and sharper wooden frame in the hope that the mask would snag.

His whole body was shaking with the effort to stay on his knees on the cold concrete floor, legs secured in an awkward and now painful angle. His back was hunched over while he tried to keep his balance and work the blindfold loose at the same time.

His clothes clung to him, damp areas dotting his shirt. Tiny rivers of sweat ran down his face. He wiped them off in the bed covers, scraping his face over again and again with each new attempt.

What seemed like hours later, the blindfold began to curl up on his cheek, the leather moistened by blood, sweat, and a few frustrated drops of moisture Cody refused to call tears. Several more minutes of rubbing and dragging his skull down the bed post, and the leather slid up, aided by the sweaty strands of his own hair. Once he had it over the ridge of his brow bone, it crept off his forehead, popped off his skull to hang down between his shoulder blades, a tuft of hair caught in the secure knot at the back of his neck.

Cody didn't waste time trying to get rid of it. It didn't matter. Gil was all that mattered. Letting Gil know he had an enemy in his home camp was all Cody could think about. Gil was in danger. Maybe more so than Cody was. Cody understood the hand that had been dealt to them. Gil didn't have a clue.

The lighting was low, a single lamp on a small bedside stand three feet away. Cody blinked and brushed his face on the covers to clear dried crusts from his eyelids and lashes. He desperately wanted to sit back and relax, to catch his breath and wallow in the success of the moment, but there was no way of knowing when his captor would be back. And he needed out of here.

Once his sight adjusted to the lighting, Cody fell back on his training, scanning the scene, looking for indications of activity from the perpetrator and laying out the room in his head.

The room was small, eight by eight, the stand, lamp and bed the only furniture in the place. The floor was bare concrete. Still kneeling by the bed, Cody ran his gaze around what he could see of the perimeter. His boots were beside the stand. A dark coil lay beside them, a glint of metal in its midst telling Cody he'd found his belt, as well. He eagerly ran his gaze over the small square tabletop but it only held an empty glass and straw. His cell phone and watch were still missing.

Disappointment coursed through him like an electric shock. They had to be there. Then as his vision adjusted to the lightning, a small dark knob on the front of the stand caught his attention. A drawer. Trying not to cry out as the nylon wire ties cut deeply into his ankles during each painfully slow inch of the trip, Cody covered the three feet between him and the table on his knees. He thought of easing down to the floor and rolling over to the stand, but he wasn't sure if he would be able to get back up to his knees once he was down.

His boots sat in front of the table, blocking him from getting close enough to grab the drawer knob with his hands when he put his back to the stand. With an impatient nudge of his shoulder he sent one boot skidding aside. It thumped a foot to his left and fell over. He swayed, the effort knocking him off balance, and he jarred the stand, knocking over the lamp. It landed, heavy and hard, the sound abnormally loud in the quiet, nearly empty concrete box of a room.

Cody froze. When no one came pounding back into the room, Cody heaved a shaky sigh of relief, sparing an evil glare for the fallen boot. A glare that quickly changed into a closed lip hum of triumph. There on the floor, having slipped out of the overturned boot lay his watch. His bright and shiny new birthday watch with the overprotective, embarrassing, absolutely wonderful tracking device. He was so going to give Gil a night to remember for this gift — if he got out of this situation alive.

Turning his back to the fallen boot, Cody scrabbled for his watch, fingers numb, swollen and nearly useless. Once the smooth surface of the crystal touched his fingertips, he closed his eyes and envisioned the dial, walking his finger around the edge, counting the buttons and feeling for the right trigger to activate the sending unit. A light buzzing tingled his fingers for a second then stopped. The silent signal that he'd properly engaged the tracking feature.

§ § § §

"Yeah." Gil started speaking before he even had the phone to his ear.

"Gil?"

He recognized the deep, streetwise twang of Cody's work partner immediately. "Eric. What have you got?"

"Nothing, sorry, Gil."

"Nothing? What kind of nothing?"

"Nothing as in 'not a clue'. Jared doesn't think the sheik angle pans out. The guy is mad wealthy but nothing that warrants a hit shows up in his profile. He's a playboy, not a power broker. Jared thinks it's a bluff."

"Something else to confuse us."

"Yeah. Looks like it." Eric sighed. A dull thud echoed in the background. Gil knew from the sound that a metal locker was now sporting a new fist-sized dent. "One other thing. The investigators working Cody's kidnapping tell me the entire crime scene where he was taken is clean. Cody and Emily processed the original scene and whoever took Cody cleaned up after himself."

"All of it?"

"Except for one thing."

"What?"

"They found a tiny chip of pink paint in the debris in the spot where Bead's body had been lying."

"Cody missed it? I find that hard to believe."

"Yeah, I know. Mr. OCD never misses anything."

"Then maybe he didn't. Maybe our kidnapper left it behind after Cody bagged the scene."

"If he did, it'll be the only thing he left beside the bullet in Bead's head."

"All the evidence Cody collected at the scene is missing, too?"

"Every bag, envelope, and glove. Even the evidence lockers are gone."

"Maybe this has nothing to do with the sheik. Maybe our guy was really trying to hide evidence of kidnapping Cody. Or evidence of the first murder?"

"Don't know. He could have taken the lockers just to make us think it was about the murder or he could have taken Cody to throw us off the murder. I just don't know, Gil. It could be either."

"Or both."

"I guess."

"Did trace run the paint chip?"

"Yeah, the whole department is on overtime working on this. Trace said it's twenty-year old lacquered paint they used to use on metal toys and trinkets. You know like those windup monkeys or letter openers you buy on vacations as souvenirs. My girlfriend uses a stupid pink flamingo for her house keys she got when we went to Florida last year. Junk like that."

Something sparked a memory, but Gil couldn't pin it down just yet.

"Thanks, Eric. If you find out something more—"

"You'll be one of the first to know, Gil. Promise."

"Thanks."

Gil picked up Bruce's forgotten camera relay phone and idly punched buttons activating and deactivating functions, replaying conversations in his head. Slumping back in the chair, Gil ran over all the information Eric had given him, none of it making any more sense than it had when the two of them had been discussing it.

He tried hard not to let the memory of his and Cody's afternoon of lovemaking enter his mind. He couldn't afford to be distracted now. Besides, he'd need those memories to hold him over for the rest of his life if he didn't solve this soon. Kidnap victims that weren't found in the first 12 hours of being taken were rarely found at all, at least not alive. The clock was ticking.

Hitting the camera cell's keypad to bring up the current time, Gil accidentally called up the replay function for the hidden camera footage. Bruce had used it in Bead's room earlier in the evening but wasn't sure if he had recorded Bead's phone conversations. If he had, maybe it would give them some idea of who Bead had been talking with. Who he had gone off to meet before dying.

The image of Bead filled the small screen as the audio, low but crisp, replayed the man's calls. When the money began to fall from the bed, Gil just stared at it, surprised at first. Surprise that quickly turned to disbelief as the pieces of the puzzle started to form a conclusion he couldn't believe. Didn't want to believe. At least not at first.

Then a kernel of real fear blossomed on his gut, slowing his reactions. He hands felt clumsy as he used the speed dial on his own phone, his lips numb and his tongue thick.

"Jared? We have to find Cody."

"We're trying, Gil. You know everything possible is being done. The entire department is working on his case."

"No, I mean we have to find him now. Things have changed." He shut off the camera footage and slid the device into his pocket.

"What's happened?"

"Cody knows his kidnapper. No victim survives who knows his kidnapper, Jared. You know that. I know that."

He snapped the phone closed and was slipping it into this pants pocket when a low, insistent beep almost made him drop the phone. It took him all of two seconds to realize Cody's tracker had been activated.

Out the door at a dead run, he only paused long enough to make sure he had his gun and an extra full clip on him.

§ § § §

The cellar door creaked open and Cody froze, barely daring to breathe. He kept his head buried in the blanket, hoping the missing blindfold wouldn't be noticed in the dim, eerie shadows made by the fallen but still lit lamp.

Cody had managed to crawl and squirm his way back onto the

bed, wrists and ankles still tightly tied, but the lamp lay on its side in mute testament to his earlier activity. His watch rested in his back pocket buried as deep as he could shove it. Its heavy weight and warmth-leeching metal were reassuring, like having a piece of Gil with him, solid and sure.

He pressed his numb hands over the bulging pocket, willing Gil to track the signal faster and rescue him before he had to turn over and see the face of the man he knew was standing there. A face he didn't want to be on the man who had done this cruel thing to Gil.

The silence grew until Cody almost couldn't stand it then heavy familiar footsteps approached the bed. He heard a deep, regretful sigh then he was seized, his entire torso engulfed by huge meaty hands. He was gently but firmly flipped over, arms pinned behind his back, to face his kidnapper.

Cody blinked and looked away but then his gaze rose to meet the troubled face studying him.

"Hey, Cody." The big man sighed and sat down on the edge of the bed. He patted Cody's arm for a moment then guiltily pulled his hand back.

"Hey, Bruce."

"Sorry about all this, kid."

"Untie me and call Gil, Bruce. We'll work it out."

"Not this time, Cody. Not this time."

"You know Gil will forgive you."

"Nah, this will be the end of things between him and me."

"Bruce—"

"You're my burn card, tucked back into the deck for safekeeping. When I get to where I'm going, I'll call Gil and let him know where to find you. I swear."

"Why? Just tell me so I can help Gil understand later, when he realizes the guy who he thought of as his brother all his life betrayed him."

"Money. I killed Bead for the cash Sabo paid him off with. Bead found a lot more than he told, and Sabo paid to keep him quiet. Two million in cash. It's good working for Gil, always has been, but this is my chance to get the life my folks intended for me. If they'd lived, I'd be my own man now, own a chain of stores, be a big businessman just like Gil."

"We can work things out, Bruce. You haven't hurt me."

"You said it already, Cody, this is betrayal of the worse kind. There's no going back from this."

"Why didn't you just go, leave while you had the chance?"

"At first I was making sure no one connected me to Bead's murder. Give myself time to get out of town. This was a kind of a spur of the moment decision. I needed time to pull it together. Then I saw you, alone with the evidence against me, and … maybe I thought I could take something from Gil, too. For a little while, anyway."

"You'd wanted me?"

"I've always wanted everything Gil had."

A crash and thud from upstairs made both of them jump. A new surge of hope, thrilling and even more painful than before, gripped Cody, squeezing the air from his lungs and sending ice cubes to rattle around in his stomach.

"Now that —" Bruce gave a thoughtful glance at the ceiling, then at the open cellar door. "That would be the front door being kicked in." He heaved a sigh, eyes closed for a moment. Then he looked at Cody. "Cavalry's here." Bruce grew calm and relaxed, resigned. "Or maybe just your white knight."

He shook his head and smiled. Cody was sure there was pride in his voice. "Damn, Gil really is the best." He stared at Cody, then reached out and mussed his already disheveled hair. "He must actually love you as much as he says he does." His eyes glistened in the dim light. "Tell him I'm sorry. But it was my shot at a life that was supposed to have been mine."

"He's called my bluff. Time to fold." Bruce pulled his gun, his expression sad and tired. "Guess the only thing left to do is give the burn card back." Shoving the gun firmly under his jaw, Bruce looked Cody in the eye, his gaze watery, his eyes rimmed in red, his intentions clear.

"Christ, Bruce! NO!"

"Tell him I'm sorry."

The shot reverberated in the small room. Cody wished he could cover his ears to block out the deafening sound, his gaze glued to Bruce's face as it suddenly became misshapen. Blood and brain tissue splattered over the wall behind Bruce while streams of red jetted out to pelt Cody's clothes and face. He turned his head into the pillow but it was already too late to avoid the main splatter.

The noise from Bruce's gun had been deafening. But the silence that followed was frightening.

Who was upstairs? Police or Sabo's men come to collect their money back? Was Gil up there? He wanted to call out to let someone know he was there, but the thought of Sabo's men finding him bound and helpless stopped him cold. They might not have been sent to kill him, but they wouldn't leave a potential witness behind either. If they were here, he didn't want to see them.

Cody could hear footsteps pound on the stairs. The door creaked, slowly drifting open. Heart pounding in his ears as if he had the blindfold back on, Cody turned to watch the door, torn between looking strong and impatient or playing dead. It all depended on who was on the other side of the door. It pushed open the last foot with a forceful shove.

Framed in the doorway stood the white knight Bruce had predicted. But this one was tall, dark and Latino. Cody's heart skipped a beat. He felt a rush of icy cold flush through his body and out his toes. For a fleeting second he thought he might pass out from the relief. Then exhilaration made him choke up. Tears burned at the back of his eyes and his voice deserted him. All he could do was nod at Gil's questioning stare before the big man was at his side, murmuring nonsense words of comfort as he cut Cody's wrists and ankles free.

"Found you." Gil almost managed to make it sound as if Cody had gotten lost in the shopping mall. His voice was soft and tender and oh so broken as if Gil couldn't get the syllables out all at once the way they were meant to be said.

The tears broke free, but Cody didn't need to worry about any condemning stares from other officers if they looked into the room, not with his face buried hard against Gil's chest and his entire body shielded from the doorway by Jared's broad back.

Thank God this night was over. It had been a one graveyard shift that had lived up to its name.

§ § § §

A sound that could only be described as a purr vibrated through Cody's body. It escaped from him into the bedroom, the soft low satisfied sound mixing with the swishing of oiled skin rubbing leisurely over oiled skin.

"Better, Cody?" Siting astride his lover's ass, Gil's open palms ran the length of Cody's back and then back up again, fingers kneading the cramps and kinks out of the sore, strained muscles.

"Oh, yeah. Much." Cody ached in places he didn't think should feel the effects of the last twenty-four hours but did. The doctor in the emergency room has cleaned and dressed the wounds made by the ties, even having to suture one vicious laceration on his left ankle. The raw circles around his wrists and ankles still stung as if they had been cut into his flesh by fire, not mere plastic. White gauze dressings encircled all four of his extremities. Gil seemed to have trouble keeping his hands off the dressings, a frown marring his face every time he touched them.

The biggest lingering discomfort was Cody's strained shoulder muscles. His private masseur was handling that problem, much to Cody's delight. He purred again and nodded.

"You've got amazing hands, Gil. If you ever give up being a bodyguard you can make a living doing this." He sighed and rolled his head. Gil took the hint and immediately moved one hand to massage the slender curve of Cody's neck.

Gil laughed softly and blew a stream of air over Cody's warm skin, making Cody shiver. "Maybe I should just offer it as a package deal along with personal protection services. 'Bodyguarding and More.'" Gil rolled off to one side, propping himself up on a mountain of pillows.

"And then, maybe you shouldn't." Cody crawled up and into Gil's arms, his head resting comfortably on Gil's chest for only a moment before he rolled over. Spooning against his lover's side, Cody pressed back so he was plastered to Gil. Cody wasn't as at ease with displaying his emotions as Gil was. He could talk about them, but he was more comfortable if he wasn't facing Gil when he did it. One hand fished under the pillows and emerged with the stuffed bear he'd received for his birthday.

"Who's being the possessive one now?"

"I am." Cody choked up a little. "I know what it feels like to almost lose you...almost lose us." He glanced quickly over his shoulder at Gil, for once uncaring about the unshed tears in his eyes. "I don't want to do that again. All I could think of was that you were in danger. If Bruce was desperate and crazy enough to kidnap me, he would be unstable enough do something to you." He had to pause a moment to keep his voice from shaking. "I couldn't imagine you gone...dead."

"Cody." Gil wrapped his arms around Cody and pulled him in close. "I'm not going anywhere, babe."

Cody forced himself not to turn away. "You want to talk about Bruce?"

"Not yet. No. One day. Right now I just want to concentrate on being here with you, forever."

Feeling exposed and suddenly very young, Cody tucked the bear under his chin and closed his eyes, as if he was going to sleep. "You can't promise that."

"No, I can't." Gil kissed Cody's temple and slid his hand down the front of Cody's pajama pants, his fingers lightly stroking over the soft skin just above Cody's cock.

Cody could feel the smile on his lover's face when Gil playfully added, "But what other guy do you know who has his boyfriend lojacked just so he can find his cute little ass when he wants him? All in the name of love, babe."

Without turning his head, Cody raised the bear and whacked Gil with the stuffed animal. "You have reduced our relationship to a country and western song."

"'Lojacked for Love.'" Gil roared with laughter. "I like it."

"And I say again, you're an ass. I love you, but you're definitely an ass."

DESIGNATED
TARGET

"Don't worry about the stuffing, Mike. I've got it covered. I don't have any place else to be tonight. You just keep the food coming. I'll dish it up."

Steam rose from the eight-foot serving stand, the warm, moist vapor a welcome change from the frigid fall air outside. Carson slipped the large metal basin of stuffing into the open rack and quickly covered it. The heavy rectangular lid clanked against the steel base adding one more cheery, riotous sound to the noisy room.

Thursday nights he donated time to the food bank. Tonight was one of the coldest of the year and a holiday to boot. The basement was packed, mostly with people just looking for a warm place to spend a few hours out of the cold. The free meal didn't hurt either.

Hands covered in a pair of thin silicone gloves like all the other volunteers working the food line, Carson used the absorbent sleeve of his Henley to wipe away the newly formed sheen of steam-generated droplets from his toasty cheeks. He closed his eyes, buried his nose in the crook of his elbow and drew his arm down his face. Unexpectedly, the two-day-old bruise on his left cheek soared to life. He winced and pulled his arm away fast. A small, annoyed breath escaped him. *Christ, I need a shower.*

He wished he could wash away the memories as easily as the sweat he was working up. The painful area around his eye throbbed, making his eyes water.

Steve, you wanker, you certainly left your mark on me, man. Literally. Goddamn control freak. Two dates and you were trying to run my life more than Jim did when I was fifteen. Big brother Jim would beat the crap out of you if he was around, you'd better believe it, asshole. He'd use every Army Ranger skill he had to make you suffer in ways you couldn't even imagine and he'd get away with it too…

If he hadn't died two months ago in some mysterious, classified mission. Fucking 'need to know' rules wouldn't even let me know where or how or why. Jim loved the Army but sometime the U.S. government sucks big time!

Wincing, Carson sighed and scratched his nose with his wrist, waiting for the tears to evaporate so he could face the people around him. He had friends here but he wasn't going to explain the bruise or the watering eyes. Or talk about the pain in his chest whenever he thought about his brother's untimely death.

The people here weren't that close to him. No one was, not since grade school. He'd been out of high school for six years, losing contact with everyone from home when he moved across the state to join the research and development division of Advantage's software house. Communications *was* his thing. But with computers not people.

Which is why you're alone in a room full of complete strangers for the holiday instead of spending it with someone.

Regret mellowed to resignation that mixed with a touch of lingering anger with himself. *Whiner. Suck it up, Crosby! Spending the holiday here alone is better than spending it in the emergency department again. Sure, you've got great health insurance, but let's not put it to the test. And yeah, it would be better if Jim was here, but he's not and he's never going to be again. Get used to it.*

Raising his head, Carson opened his eyes to look out over the crowd. The church basement was laid out with long tables placed end to end the length of the large, drafty room. Lines of folding chairs that had seen better days were arranged down both sides of the tables and more were stacked in the corners of the room. Holiday decorations dotted the tables and the walls, all of them looking like they came from the Sunday school and day care patrons' busy little fingers and eclectic imaginations. They were colorful and bright if not always recognizable, but still pleasing to Carson's watering eyes.

Pleasing. Just like the man standing less than six feet away, towering over the service table, talking to Mad Lacey, the old eccentric who haunted the four city blocks surrounding the church they were in. Mike, the food bank's overworked coordinator, said she had a home of her own and never seemed to need anything. She was such a constant figure at the food line, Carson tended to forget she wasn't one of the many homeless that came to the basement. He watched a rare smile light up Mad Lacey's face, the old woman seemingly as captivated by the towering man as Carson.

Carson hadn't even heard the stranger walk up to the serving area. Which took a fair amount of stealth and skill, considering the guy had on heavy boots and was no lightweight. Carson had excellent hearing, even in a noisy room.

He had to wear earplugs when he was writing software—to block out the rest of the world. Something he maybe did a little too often outside work. Right now he could hear the deep timbre of the man's smooth voice—low, strong, and confident.

Broad and brooding, tall and dark. The guy's six foot plus frame had several inches on Carson's five foot nine, and the man outweighed him by at least seventy pounds. All of it in hard muscle. The man's tan T-shirt stretched across his linebacker shoulders and thick upper arms, straining around a thick neck, smooth as a second skin over hills and valleys of sloping, taut skin.

"Lord, have mercy." It popped out before he could stop it, but what the hell. He *was* in church. This guy was definitely attractive.

Being a detail junkie had its drawbacks, but now the talent served Carson well. He couldn't stop himself from taking in every possible bit of information he could pull in visually about the man. The guy was all testosterone and steroids, alpha male, macho to the max and hard as stone. And probably so straight he had trouble bending to sit down. Some days it wasn't easy being gay when all you were attracted to was big, bad, macho men, most with an eye for ladies only. The last thing Carson needed was another shiner to match the one Steve-the-Asshole had gifted him with last night.

The tan fabric clung to the man's sides and sculpted abdomen, showing muscle that told of hours of physically intense, daily workouts. The deep tan and calloused hands said the guy did his workouts somewhere besides a gym. The short, spiky dark hair, ironed fatigues and polished, high-top black boots shouted military loud and clear. Carson could see a worn spot on his belt where Carson's imagination supplied weapons to hang off the webbing.

Carson closed his eyes. Everything about the man screamed control and order. *Walk away, now.* But he couldn't. He needed one more look before he crossed the guy off his list of things to wish for this holiday season.

The thighs under the pant legs looked like sides of beef, powerful and long. The man's boot size had to be over thirteen. Carson's gaze jumped to the calloused hands again. They were proportional to the rest of him.

An old wife's tale sprang to mind. Before he could stop himself, Carson's eyes dropped to the man's crotch, instantly wondering what lay tucked away behind the rough, bulky folds of thick fabric and fasteners. His imagination supplied a vivid reason for the respectable fabric bulge, making his own close-fitting jeans suddenly less comfortable.

He blinked when he felt heat rise in his cheeks, embarrassed by his body's immediate reaction. *You're supposed to be here helping out, not mentally feeling up the patrons.* But he really didn't think this guy needed a soup kitchen to grab a hearty meal. *Not with that body.*

Christ, how hard up are you, Crosby? It hasn't been that long since you got laid. Okay, maybe it has, but how many teeth do you want to lose for copping a look?

His frustrated libido grabbed his common sense and stuffed it into a bag. Darting a guilty glance to get one last longing look at the rugged man's tanned and weathered features, Carson physically flinched. His unguarded and needy gaze was hit full force with a dark, unwavering stare.

Sometime during Carson's inspection of bronzed muscle and long bone, Mad Lacey had wandered away leaving Military Man alone. Alone and staring straight at Carson, his dark eyes, almost black, glaring out under squinted lids.

The man's gaze followed the path Carson's had traveled, dropping down to his own groin. The stranger's stare moved from his crotch to Carson's, slowly, pointedly crawling up Carson until their gazes met again. The expression on the man's face was controlled, measuring, without a hint of what he was thinking.

He might have been thinking how attractive Carson was. Or he might have been thinking of a dozen different ways to kill him without being caught. He was definitely military and Carson knew from his brother that any well-trained soldier could kill if he wanted to eliminate someone.

Carson didn't doubt the guy could do the job. There was a distinct element of danger to that inky, silent stare. Then the squinting eyes relaxed a tiny margin and the man's unsmiling lips parted slightly, a mere twitch that smudged the edges off the man's hard look. The sudden change whispered of physical attraction.

Carson felt a chill sweep down his back, a shudder of anticipation, while the flush of embarrassment still heated his neck and face.

It was times like these he hated his fair, unusually pale complexion, starkly framed by even paler blond hair. Added to his slight but athletic build, quiet personality and geeky job, he was often invisible to hunky guys like this one. Once in a while someone noticed his eyes. Since this guy was trying to bore a hole through Carson's head with his eye-to-eye laser beam gaze, Carson guessed this one had noticed them.

Every memory Carson had of a comment about the way he looked hinged on his eyes, the swirls of white streaked through the vibrant green gave them the appearance of green turquoise. His parents had described them as bright, intelligent and stunning. His classmates in school had called them alien, bizarre and freakish.

At twenty-six he'd finally come to accept them as natural, mother nature's own unique stamp. Women seemed to find them exotic. Most men wouldn't maintain eye contact for long, as if being attracted to his eyes made them sappy schoolgirls.

But this guy was no giggling pre-teen and he didn't seem to

have any problem staring into Carson's eyes. As a matter of fact, for once Carson was the one getting uncomfortable from the prolonged moment.

The heat in his face receded but the stirring in his jeans snugged the fabric tighter. He shifted his weight, moving just enough so he could angle his hips behind the cover of the steamer. Eye contact remained unbroken. Carson felt his breath turn ragged and his heartbeat quickened, thudding against his ribs.

Now who was acting like a pre-teen?

The clock kept ticking and the guy kept staring.

Carson wanted to step back and run, hide out in the kitchen, find a nice mindless job like peeling potatoes for the next three hours where the only thing he had to think about was the ache in his bruised face and the burning of his scratched cornea. Steve 'I-don't-take-rejection-well' Fuckwad just had to be wearing a ring when he lashed out. The staring contest was making his eyes dry but he refused to be the first one to turn away. For some reason he didn't want to look submissive to this guy. One dominant jerk brushing up against his life at a time was enough.

A thick, mucous tear trickled down Carson's cheek from his injured eye. He needed to put more ointment in it. The hours went so fast between applications he had trouble keeping track of them. Eye red and weeping, Carson knew he looked like he had been crying. One more reason to dislike the abusive want-to-be boyfriend. *Bastard.*

Carson carefully brushed the streak of wetness off his discolored cheek. Too much pressure would make his whole face throb. Then again, maybe the tearing had a higher purpose. Maybe GI Joe would think he was just a blond twink, a sniveling weakling, and walk away, giving Carson a chance to take a deep breath.

Pain won the battle with his ego. He closed his eyes and counted to five, then blinked rapidly to clear away the gathered moisture, determined to look at something other than dark eyes and mountains of perfect muscle when he opened his eyes. He'd give the guy plenty of time to break away. He counted to five again just to be sure.

Or not.

'GI Joe' had moved but it wasn't away. Now he was so close, just a thin serving table width away, that Carson could see the gray flecks in his eyes and the light shadow of stubble on his square, rugged face. Movement caught Carson's attention and his gaze dropped to dusky pink lips; lips that were taut, moist, inviting and, oh yeah, moving. Moving like in saying words.

"What?" Carson blinked again.

"Your eye. You seen a doctor?"

"A doctor?" The concern in the guy's voice sounded genuine but Carson shied away.

He liked looking at the guy but the last thing he needed was another control freak trying to pin him to a wall and fuck him standing up instead of saying goodnight and leaving like Carson had desperately wanted Steve to do. He might be small but he could knee a guy with the best of them. Having an Army Ranger for a big brother had its benefits. Jim had made sure Carson knew how to protect himself if he needed to.

"Yeah. It's okay."

"Doesn't look okay." That laser stare grew impossibly more intense. The soldier rested both meaty, tanned hands on his fatigue-covered hips, his broad shoulders losing a degree or maybe even two of rigidity. "Cornea scratched?"

Relaxing minutely, Carson nodded. "A ring." Studying the man's less threatening stance and sympathetic expression, he added, "How'd you know?"

"Been sucker punched a time or two." The man walked to the end of the table. Now the guy was only two feet away. "Doesn't have to be fist metal to do damage. Gloves will do it too with enough force behind the hit." The hard glare returned and washed over Carson again. "You don't look like the type to go looking for trouble."

It was harder to hide Carson's physical reaction to the man with him this close. Hoping to keep attention focused away from his obviously interested crotch, Carson kept talking. "I don't, but I don't run from it when it happens either."

When that bit of bravado was met with silence, Carson grabbed at a few conversational straws. He was not going to talk about dating disasters with this stranger. "Why don't I think you mean class rings when you say fist metal?"

"Because I don't."

The quiet statement hung in the air, letting Carson's imagination fill in the blanks. He shrugged off a cold touch on his spine. Yep, this guy was all power, control and steely force. *Walk away! Walk away!* Absolutely not Carson's type.

"You get in a bar fight?" He was nothing if not persistent.

"No."

Fed up with the questioning, suppressed anger pushed aside any attraction Carson felt. *Might as well let the jerk think he was a wuss.* At least the questions would stop and the guy would go away. "I don't drink."

Sticking a serving spoon into the stuffing, Carson turned and moved away from the table toward a small alcove beside the kitchen doors. He leaned his back into the cool plaster wall and closed his eyes, letting some of the tension drain away.

When he opened them, a wall of tan over a very well-defined chest blocked his view of the room. One look up and those dark, curious eyes pinned him in place again.

Christ!

If he Googled 'tenacious' Carson bet this guy's picture would turn up with the definition. He'd check when he got home. Home. It sounded like a good idea right about now. His headache was back full-force.

"Why?"

"Why what?"

A whiff of aftershave mixed with the food odors—dark, sharp and spicy. The vision of this macho guy rubbing a mixture of gun oil and cinnamon on like cologne popped into Carson's head. Then the gun oil dripped onto other body parts and Carson had to blink to clear away the mental picture before his jeans strangled his dick.

"Why don't I drink?" His cock ached and his sac turned heavy, the weight frustratingly thrilling. He hated to admit it but being this close to the guy was like being handed a big bag of warm, buttery popcorn and then being told you could look and smell, but not have any.

"Why did the guy hit you?" A large finger pointed at his face. Carson instinctively flinched then reddened at his own reaction. Frowning, the guy froze in place. Slowly he lowered his hand to tap Carson's unbruised cheek in a brief, tender caress. He dropped his hand, adding, "You can answer about the drinking later." His low voice sounded huskier to Carson for some reason.

He fought the overwhelming urge to spill his guts. It wasn't like he could tell his friends about his latest dating mistake. And he wouldn't have to. By the time the first of the year rolled around and he was due back to work, most of the outward evidence of the assault would be gone. That's one of the reasons why he was here helping out in the soup kitchen instead of attending one of the many holiday parties planned by his buddies from work. At least the whole mess had distracted him from thinking about Jim being dead and his having to spend his first holiday truly alone since their parents had been killed.

But this stranger demanded to know what he couldn't tell anyone else. And damn it, Carson wanted to tell him. Whoever the hell he was.

"Who are you?"

"Nobody." The man shrugged and then smiled, a smile that touched his dark eyes. "Someone who doesn't like seeing beautiful things crushed. The world can be ugly enough without some A-hole marring some of its best scenery."

He paused, studied Carson's face intently then flatly stated, "You've got great eyes. Not just the color, that's a looker, sure. But the swirls of white make them almost hypnotic. You could be damn dangerous to be around."

Was this guy actually trying to come on to him?

"And you're crazy." The last person he expected poetic charm from was this muscle-bound mountain of spit and polish. It was unexpectedly sweet but… "Crazy with a capital 'C'."

Pain flared in his face. Carson gently pressed his fingertips over his bruised eyelid, the burn increasing with each passing minute. Fumbling in his pants pocket he worked the tube of eye ointment out into his palm, the warm metal of the tube oddly reassuring. Relief was on its way. As soon as he got rid of Mr. Romance.

"Crazy? I guess you could call me that. But most call me China."

"China? Like in dainty porcelain?" Surprise made Carson arch his eyebrows. Pain shot through his face. "Sonofa—!"

A tear ran down from the corner of his eye and he carefully palmed it away. He couldn't wait any longer. The emergency room doctor had cautioned him to keep the scratch from becoming too dry. He didn't need an infection in his eye.

He opened the tube of ointment, but needed a mirror to do it right. Maybe the dirty glass in the kitchen door would work. Before he could take a step away the tube was plucked from his hand.

"Give me that."

A rough finger under his chin gently tilted Carson's face up. He tried to keep his gaze focused on anything except the rugged face looming six inches away. The smell of spice and physical heat made him inhale sharply. He lost the battle to refrain from making eye contact.

China stared back at him, dark eyes watching, powerful body still as death until Carson realized the man was waiting for some indication that he could continue. The guy was big enough to flatten Carson like a bug, take whatever he wanted, and he was silently asking for permission to touch him.

This was unexpected. Nice and unexpected.

Looking at the pitted, grease-spotted ceiling tiles, Carson nodded, steadying himself with a hand on the wall behind him. His legs felt shaky. "Crazy, like I said." He was startled to hear the slight waver in his voice. Maybe China wouldn't notice but Carson somehow doubted much escaped this guy.

"They both start with 'c' but China works better. All my friends already know it."

The lower edge of Carson's irritated eye was pulled gently downward. He tried not to blink, anticipating a spurt of ointment flooding his eye. Instead, a thin ribbon flowed onto his lower lid, easing into his eye as the skin was slowly released back into place.

It felt so good. Like the heat of the warm palm pressed to his jaw and throat holding him steady, encouraging him not to jerk away. A blunt fingertip massaged the red-purple skin in light, soothing strokes.

Carson automatically closed both his eyes, letting the medication melt with his body heat. Back against the cool wall, his chest nearly touched a wall of sweltering human heat. Carson's cock moved on its own, trying to close the small gap between them. He tried to move away, but there was nowhere to go. Thank God the alcove blocked them from the direct view of the dining room.

Take a step back, big guy, before I embarrass myself.

Coffee-laced breath fluttered his eyelashes. Low words brushed his cheeks. 'China. Like in the third largest country in the world, not counting disputed territories. Can you say that for me?"

The sarcasm wasn't hard to detect, even with his eyes closed. "Like a bull in a china shop?" Carson blinked through the blurry goop and focused on China's face.

The wry smile there startled him. GI Joe had one killer smile when he tried. Especially when that sparkle of mischief glinted in his eyes. Carson felt his insides melt. *This guy is in serious danger of losing his straight card!*

"You know the Chinese invented the compass and gunpowder?"

"Important needs for an action figure like you, I bet."

The teasing was fun but the tight squint was back around the dark eyes. The sparkle was still there but the squint kind of canceled it out for Carson. Carson nodded at the tattoo on China's muscular forearm proclaiming its owner a member of the U.S. Army. "I mean…you being military. World travel, guns, bombs."

"They *are* important. How can a guy find treasures like you and set off fireworks to celebrate without them?"

Okaaay, GI Joe never owned a straight card. Ever.

The hand dropped from Carson's face but its heated imprint lingered. A funny, twisted, tingling sensation uncoiled beneath Carson's sternum. It surprised him, made him duck his head like a schoolgirl. It even pulled a smile to his lips. "Christ, you *are* crazy."

"Never said I wasn't." But the squint vanished. "Sometimes crazy can be a good thing."

Crazy for you, maybe? Yeah, right. In the space of three minutes. Dreaming doesn't make it so.

There was that certain…something about the way China looked at him now and then, like he was supposed to be able to read between the lines and hear the rest of the man's thoughts, the ones that were too private to say out loud. It was irritating and intriguing. It made Carson want to spend more time with him just so he could figure out the unspoken communication code the big man used. The guy was becoming a challenge to Carson's puzzle solving fetish.

Even so, Carson was unable to ignore the nagging voice in his head. The one that muttered about how long it had been since a guy had said nice things to him without wanting sex. He rubbed his chest, trying to lessen the tightness. "Carson."

"Carson?"

"My name." It had actually come out before he'd realized he was going to say it. The tightness uncoiled a little. He couldn't resist flashing the smile he knew had helped him win over everyone from coffee shop waitresses to college professors all his life. "You China, me Carson. You know, like the huge, powerful country versus the small, but prosperous and charming city."

The smile seemed to have the same effect on China, making the big man's quirky half-smile widen into a grin that showed even, white teeth and a dimple in one cheek.

"Carson. I always thought that was a nice name." China said it just the way Jim had, splitting it up between the 's' and the 'o' to make it sound like 'cars-un'. "Thought I was going to have to call you *Dangerous* all day."

No one had said his name like that since Jim's last phone call home months ago. The huge gaping hole that had just begun to heal after his brother's death split back open. His throat constricted and the pit of his stomach grew heavy, cold as if he'd swallowed a giant snowball whole. It didn't seem right to feel good, not today.

"I'm not going to be here all day. As a matter of fact I have to leave right now." Carson slipped around China, doing his best not to make physical contact with him. His dick had lost interest the moment he heard China say his name, but he wasn't taking any chances. His desires had to take second place to doing what was right. "Excuse me."

Without waiting for a reply, Carson was through the kitchen doors and out of reach. He caught Mike's attention as he wove around volunteers and boxes of food, gesturing at the back door to let it be known he was leaving.

Mike frowned but nodded, concern making his eyes narrow, but he did his usual one-shoulder shrug of acceptance. Carson grabbed his yellow ski jacket off the wall and shrugged into it, pulling a brown knit cap over his blond hair that failed to capture all the wayward, pale curls. He zippered the coat as he walked out the door, taking the back steps two at a time despite the slippery, rapidly accumulating ice and snow.

Shoving his hands deep into the pockets to search for his gloves, he realized they must have fallen out back in the kitchen. He'd grab them later. Mike would know who they belonged to and keep them safe.

Head down, Carson buried his nose in his jacket's high collar, thankful for the warm down and thick nylon to break the icy wind that had kicked up. Ice and snow crunched under his boots.

He was just past the recessed archway that led to the tiny church cemetery when he was suddenly jerked to a halt, his back hitting the stone wall deep inside the archway hard enough to knock the air from his lungs. Stars danced before his eyes but not enough that he didn't recognize the sneering face looking down at him from far too close a distance.

§ § §

"What are you doing here, Steve?" It was hard to talk with a fist jammed up against his chin. Steve's gloved hand gripped Carson's ski jacket, pulling it and Carson up until Steve's jaw practically scraped Carson's nose.

Winter wind licked at Carson's cheeks and dry lips. Icy fingers wormed under his scrunched-up jacket to numb his unprotected ribs and belly. Carson looked toward the doorway he'd just come out of but couldn't see past the archway. No one was going to notice them from inside the church unless they walked out here into the freezing cold, and the odds of that happening were slim. He'd have to deal with this alone. The rough surface of the brick behind him abraded his exposed lower back, the sharp points of mortar gouging his skin like needle points. Still, the sensation was more pleasant than either the sudden rising nausea in his gut or the twisted, dark look on Steve's face.

"Just passing by, Angel. Thought I'd say hello. Miss me?"

Steve studied Carson's swollen eye and colorful array of bruises. "Looks like I gave you plenty to remember me by."

It was tough but Carson managed to force the words past his clamped teeth. "You're an abusive creep, Steve." He forced both his arms between them and pushed hard. "Let go of me."

Startled at the sudden move, Steve changed his stance slightly to one side. It gave him more leverage on Carson's upper chest. He forced Carson higher up the wall, shoving his fist hard under Carson's chin.

Up another inch Carson wouldn't be able to stand on his own without help. He figured that was pretty much the asshole's plan. One of the first things he'd learned about the guy was that Steve liked control.

"Harsh words, Angel. I don't think you gave yourself enough time to get to know me properly." He leaned down and nudged Carson's hair, working the knit cap off in the process.

Carson felt the hat roll off his shoulder and disappear. He shivered at the sudden loss of protection, feeling exposed and vulnerable to both the wind and his attacker.

"You know what, Angel? Since it's the holiday season I decided to be generous. Give you a second chance. I'm a great guy. Ask anyone."

"Yeah, you're a real fun guy, Steve. The staff in the ED thought so, too. Now let me go."

"Did you tell them my name?"

"Touch me again and it'll be cops I talk to not nurses." Carson worked at keeping his tone level and firm. The asshole didn't get to know how scared he really was. Steve was big. Not as big as GI Joe had been but big enough to be a problem. "Get your hands off me."

"You ungrateful little shit!" Steve's restraining hand gripped Carson's face and turned it to the wall, grinding his cheek into the brick.

Day-old bruises scraped over centuries-old brick and stars

danced behind Carson's eyes. *Enough already, asshole!* He grabbed a hold of Steve's jacket with both fists and pulled his legs up, hanging from the other man's body only long enough to drive a knee into Steve's crotch. The ragged shout was as satisfying as it was explosive. If he got another round of bruises from it, it was worth it just to hear the surprise in the jerk's voice. *Should have expected it after last time, dumb fuck. Some guys never learn!*

Steve curled forward, his weight partially pinning Carson to the wall, but his grip lessened enough that Carson's feet were back firmly on solid ground. Before Carson could wiggle out from under him, Steve pulled back a fist and let it fly at Carson's face. All he could see was Steve's fist and the guy's malicious grin. Then a vise wrapped around Carson's upper arm. His feet left the ground for real this time, his body yanked sideways. Steve screamed like a little girl when his fist hit the brick wall.

Confusion clear on his agony-contorted face, Steve turned around and slumped against the bare wall. One hand clutching his groin, he cradled the other to his chest.

"You fucking little shit! You're going to regret that."

"I'm not little and I never have regrets about taking out scum."

Steve's feet were swept out from under him and he hit the ground hard. Seconds later he was on his back looking up. Carson stood beside a man that made Steve look like a Gold's Gym wannabe.

"Who are you?"

"Doesn't matter." China's voice was soft, barely heard above the panting, partially stifled moans and the wind. Even so, it struck Carson as one of the most threatening things he'd ever heard from another human being.

"What *does* matter is that you just made yourself a *designated target*. Come near this man again and you'll lose more than the temporary use of a hand."

Steve was an obnoxious jerk. But China…China-man was *deadly*. Carson could actually feel the fatal intent in his words.

"Got it, Ace?" The last was punctuated with a fairly gentle size-14 boot nudge to Steve's ribs.

"I hear you." Steve sat halfway up to drag himself a safe distance away. He stopped when his back hit the brick wall. "Didn't like the little bastard anyway. Just teaching him a lesson." Steve slowly pushed to his feet, swaying a little in the wind.

Carson watched as China took in the man's protective crouch, guarding his injured groin and hand. A genuinely pleased smile spread across his face, giving rebirth to that single dimple again. "Looks like he taught you a few things, too."

He gestured Steve toward the road. "Now get out of here."

Steve didn't even look back.

Carson decided that, when he was the cause of it, he could get used to that look of pride on the big guy's rugged mug. It was rare that a guy so much larger than he was respected Carson's ability to defend himself. Even so, he couldn't resist adding, "I told you I can take care of myself."

"And I believed you. You had it under control. For the most part." The smile widened then quirked with a touch of restrained amusement. "But everyone needs a helping hand now and then." He swept the dropped knit cap off the snow and pulled it over Carson's hair. "Even a tough as nails, little fighting cock with killer green eyes."

Okay, the only reason his teeth *weren't* in the snow was because China had ripped him from Steve's grip at the last second. Carson knew that. And appreciated it. And since Carson hadn't heard China approach on the crusty ice and snow, the guy must have been standing there watching. Watching but not intervening until Carson needed him.

"You following me?" His eye burned from the wind. At least his face was growing numb, saving him from the immediate joy of fresh raw scrapes over tender bruises.

"You dropped your gloves inside." He pulled Carson's brown leather gloves from his jacket pocket and handed them off. He stared into Carson's eyes long and hard. "Thought you might need them."

Attraction, concern and what Carson thought looked like the need for a friend shone down at him. "You mind walking in this?"

"I've been places that make this look like a sunny day at the beach." China zippered his jacket closed and pulled on a pair of worn gloves and a dark knit cap from his other pocket. "I can walk for a bit, yeah."

"I'm going to see my family. Say hi for the holiday." Carson began to walk but turned around to face China as he stepped out onto the sidewalk.

"Okay. I got some free time on my hands. Can you talk while you walk?"

"I've been known to, yes." Carson spun to face forward as China joined him, arms brushing as they strode through the gathering snowfall.

"Good. I like to listen to your voice."

Carson hesitated, unsure how to take that. "I already told you that you were crazy once, right?"

"Yeah, but you'll find out with me—once is never enough."

Carson wasn't ready to touch the double meaning in that one. The warm glint in China's glance said it all anyway. They weren't talking about crazy anymore.

And surprisingly, Carson liked it.

§ § § §

It was unnerving how comfortable he was walking beside China. He'd always been attracted to large, beefy hunks, but most of them had towering egos to match their towering bodies. Steve was a perfect example, even if a slightly more manic one than most guys were.

But China was all quiet confidence and restrained, if hulking, power. And he respected Carson enough to let him handle his own fight; at least to the point where he was about to get pounded into the pavement. Most other guys treated Carson like he was fragile or helpless. He was slight, but he could take on more than most guys gave him credit for. He didn't like to fight, but he knew how. Jim had been insistent about it.

Jim. The ache started up again in his chest. Jim dead. Thanksgiving here. Mauled by a jerk, not once but twice and the best companion he'd had in months was a complete stranger. Well, almost. He knew China was a soldier.

"What branch of the service were you in?" He glanced sideways and caught China's surprised expression. "Come on, man. You scream military. The way you walk, the way you hold yourself so straight."

"Army. Specialty unit. Active status."

Carson reached high to ruffle his gloved fingertips through the short fine dark hair barely seen around the edges of China's knit cap. "The hair, the boots, the confidence. I recognize the... attitude."

"Attitude? I'm giving you *attitude*, son?"

The line was delivered in a barking, mock-General-Patton bellow that made Carson chuckle. "Just a little."

It felt good to laugh, good to let go and enjoy the moment. It even soothed the flash of loss that came with it. "My brother is...was a sergeant. Army Rangers. Career soldier. I know what to look for. You remind me of him in some ways. He'd have probably liked you."

For once China was silent. Carson studied the man as best he could in the gray afternoon light. China's lips were drawn into a hard, tight line as if they were holding back words trying to escape. His dark eyes scanned the surroundings as if he was scouting a mission, looking for enemies behind trees and in alleyways. Could be, but Carson had the impression they were just trying not to look his way.

The fine lines at the corners of his eyes were more pronounced as he squinted into the growing shadows. His stride was easy, loose, but Carson felt the power his body housed when their arms and thighs brushed as they walked. China was solid muscle.

The man was handsome in a dark, brooding kind of way, rugged and brawny, but with a keen intelligence and sense of humor that appealed to Carson. Besides, the Army didn't take just anyone for a special unit, whichever one it was. China-man was top shelf.

"Do you like being in the Army?"

"Second tour. What do *you* think?"

"I know the Army doesn't let you off for holidays. Are you on leave? Do you have family around here?"

"Looking in on a family member for a friend. He can't be here himself so I promised I would." He shrugged his shoulder but Carson thought it looked more like he was trying to knock something heavy off his back instead of make light of the generous offer. "I'm on medical hold. I'll be going back on active duty in a couple of days."

"You get shot?"

"Something like that."

"Can't talk about it, can you? You haven't even mentioned what division you belong to. Must be dangerous work."

"Talk about it? No. Dangerous? Sometimes. But it's pretty simple. We have a job to do. We do it."

"You sound so much like my brother. He loved the Army. Everything about it."

"How do you feel about it?"

"*Hate* everything about it. The rules, the discipline, the orders." He tugged at the olive drab Army issue field jacket China wore. "The dress code."

He caught China's narrowed glance and smiled to take the offense out of the words. His grin widened when the man gave him a dimple-punctuated half-smile in return.

"Anti-establishment, huh?"

"No, just anti-'tell me what to do all the time'. I don't even like the regulations at my job and they are pretty lax compared to most big corporations."

A car horn blared, the noise muffled by the heavy snowfall. The wind carried it away like shreds of old newspaper.

"Yeah?" China gave him a questioning glance but didn't ask for more. His lips got that purse-string tightness again.

Carson decided to make it easy for him. Besides, he wanted China to know more about him. It was a two-way street, he hoped. "I'm a software programmer. Developer, really. I work for Advantage. They do a lot of government work there. I have a security clearance that impresses even me."

"Hot shot programmer? Nice skills. Useful for a lot of things."

"I have *flexibility*." Carson laughed, self-conscious about the way that sounded out loud.

"Good to know." There was that warm look again. The one with the double meaning behind it. It didn't hurt any that China had dropped his voice to a raspy bass. And that damn, sexy dimple was still in place.

Panic, a good panic for a change, twisted his gut and Carson rushed to change the subject. "When's your enlistment up?"

"A few months. I was going to go for indefinite status but after this—"

"Getting hurt?" Silence again. "Was it serious?"

"One of the worst times of my life. But I'm healing. Every soldier knows the risks. It's not the first time for me to take a hit." He sighed.

Carson tracked the rise and heavy fall of China's shoulders by stepping in closer. The sound of his breathing was ragged, his voice sad, almost like he was in pain.

"This time was…different. So much was lost."

He shook his head once and glanced at Carson, an unspoken question in his eyes, one Carson couldn't even begin to guess at.

"I've been thinking it's time for a change."

"Really? What would you do?" The sidewalk was framed by large old trees and the sounds of traffic disappeared as they turned a corner. An old iron fence marked the park-like area to their left. The houses were left behind on the main street, but China never questioned their direction or asked about their destination.

"Couple of things. Got a degree in business management. A little nest egg put away. I should put it to good use. Maybe do private security. Something with rules and order. I like order. Combine the two things I'm trained for."

"You can take the guy out of the military but you can't take the military out of the guy!" Carson chuckled and clapped his hands to chase away the growing numbness in his fingers. The temperature must have dropped ten degrees since they had left the church.

"I hate rules and routines, but I'd love to have my own software business. I want to expand my development skills past the walls they make me work with now. I use my free time to create security firewalls and then spend hours breaching them for the fun of it."

"That's what you call fun? You need to get out more."

"Hey, your idea of fun is getting shot at. Guess we're complete opposites."

"Not really. We're like the first great Chinese inventions."

"What?" China lost him there. Who knew what the Chinese invented if they weren't Chinese?

"Seriously. The Chinese had four great inventions. Gunpowder, the compass, paper, and printing. I think maybe the first two fit me just like the last two fit you. Action and power paired with knowledge and innovation. They fit together. Like us."

Okay. So maybe you knew about this stuff if your nickname was China. Or you needed an original pick up line. Sweet talk and muscle. Who would have guessed?

Carson liked it.

§ § § §

"We're there."

Carson strode through the open gates of the cemetery without looking back, his back ramrod straight and his head held high. China could read determination and pain in the too-rapid pace the younger man suddenly adopted.

The gates were ten-foot-high spiked wrought iron bolted into massive cement pillars topped with grotesque stone gargoyles. The falling snow blanketed the ground, turning the tallest headstones China could see into white shrouded ghosts in the fading light.

He stopped to assess the area closer, his years of training taking over, honed instincts telling him this was just another jungle filled with land mines, but this time of the emotional variety. He'd rather have bombs and bullets coming at him, but he'd come this far, he had to see it through. If not for his own sake, then for others.

Besides, Carson was growing on him something fierce. The young man was funny, smart and feisty as hell. Toss in those marbled green eyes, almost platinum blond hair and that firm little body and China couldn't resist flirting with him. He knew he shouldn't...but, hell, dangerous little treasures like Carson didn't cross a man's path every day.

"Christ Almighty!" China ran a hand over his eyes to wipe away the image of Carson laughing, hair in his eyes, smile on his lips and nothing hiding his pale smooth skin as he lay on crisp sheets beckoning for China to join him.

"China! Are you coming?"

China snapped around at the sound of Carson's voice. He located a shadowy figure a hundred yards away, one arm gesturing toward him, beckoning him like in his dream. He swore softly and muttered, "Not yet, but there's always hope."

Striding up the pathway, his boots crunching down through layers of thin ice and slushy snow, China waved back. "Hold up.

I'll lose you in the dark."

"I doubt that." But Carson stayed where he was, waiting patiently until China was at his side. "Guys like you don't *get* lost."

"Maybe I just think you could use a friend. A guy shouldn't be alone for this. Not today." The wind bit through his multiple layers of clothing. China suppressed a shiver, noticing that Carson's teeth had begun to chatter slightly.

"How do you know I'm alone?" Carson turned to his right to march down a row of low headstones. He walked with a sure step that told China he'd done this a hundred times before, barely glancing at the stones, secure in his destination. China kept pace at his side.

"Carson, come on. You're spending Thanksgiving at a church shelter feeding the homeless, avoiding a stalker ex, we're going to visit your family so you take me to a cemetery. I'm not a rocket scientist, but I can figure this out."

"Okay, maybe that was a dumb question. You're right anyway. Jim was my only relative and now he's gone, too."

He stopped in front of a small grouping of markers protected from the wind by a thick hedge. Three of the graves were long established—all three showing the same final resting date. Carson stood in front of a grave that still hadn't settled completely, its surface slightly rounded and the grass sparse under a thin layer of snow. China knew it belonged to Carson's brother but he avoided reading this headstone. There was time for that. Carson was his concern at the moment.

"These are my parents. They were killed by a drunk driver when I was fifteen. My sister Amy was in the car, too. She was seventeen." Now China understood the 'I don't drink' comment Carson had made earlier. A drunk wiping out most of his family must have made a big impact on a fifteen-year-old's ideas about life.

"Jim was twenty-two. He finished college and joined the Army so he could take care of me. He was always there for me, even when he was away. He'd make sure I had one of the other families to stay with when he was out on a mission. And he'd check on me every chance he got. I earned enough scholarships to pay my own way through college, but Jim helped me out if I needed something extra. Taught me to drive, helped me buy my first car. Taught me to defend myself and stand up for what's right. He was my big brother but he was my best friend, too."

"I'm sure he loved you very much."

"I know he did. He didn't even blink an eye when I told him I was gay. I thought he'd be disappointed but he just nodded and said, 'Okay. I guess I'd better teach you how to fight like a soldier now.' So he did. It didn't matter to him."

"He made a great leader with that attitude. Not everyone in the Army is that accepting. Some but not most." His voice was raspy, filled with an emotion he couldn't afford to let run loose. This wasn't the time for his own pain. Not now. "His men must have loved him."

"They did. Will and Brad were like brothers. And Vinny, he practically worshiped Jim."

"They were a four-man team?"

"No, five. A fire team. Jim was their sergeant. One guy left after a few months. I didn't know his name. Didn't know the replacement either. That was back a couple of months before Jim died. It all kind of runs together sometimes."

"Grief plays hell with your time sense. Regret, grief, pain, it all tears you up if you don't have someone or something to hold on to. The Army used to be my strength. But…things change."

And Lord, things had changed.

§ § § §

"The Army was Jim's life. He would have been a Ranger his whole career if he hadn't gotten killed. We're not even at war! Some stupid secret mission nobody cared about except some idiot general behind a desk! I don't even know how he died. They wouldn't tell me. I didn't even get all his personal effects, just a pack of official papers and his dog tags. I know Jim loved it, but

I hate anything to do with the Army."

China did that tight-lipped thing again, his eyes so narrowed Carson doubted he could see anything. Not that Carson could look at much of the guy's face when China hung his head like that.

"How'd you end up with that thug, Steve?"

The sudden shift in conversation rattled Carson for a moment. "Trust me, I was never with him. I knew by the end of the first date that he wasn't my type but he wouldn't take the hint."

"Wouldn't take a hint," China tilted Carson's face into the fading light from the pathway street lamp, "or take a 'no'?"

"He's not a fan of rejection. I'm not a fan of being forced." Carson turned his face out of the light, easing away from China's touch and his unhappy stare. "To do *anything* I don't want to, least of all that."

"He got 'rejected' then?"

"I might take a couple of lumps, but I can handle things pretty well. Most guys won't take things as far as Steve did. I'm small but I know what brings a man to his knees."

"I'll bet you do." The heated look was bad enough, but that raw, husky catch in China's voice almost undid Carson. It didn't help any when China added. "I knew I should have stuck to calling you 'Dangerous'."

"Walk me home. And that's not a question."

Now it was his turn to sound ragged with need.

§ § § §

The walk back was done mostly in silence. The wind and freezing temperatures stifled any lengthy conversation. But it had the benefit of making both men seek shelter in the other's personal space. Carson had to admit, 'The Great Wall of China' did a terrific job of blocking the wind.

Carson ducked his head and shoulders down, leaning a bit into China's side. It only took an instant before a comforting arm pulled him in closer, shielding him from the worst of the wind and faltering snow. It was only another block to his apartment and Carson irrationally found himself wishing it would take longer.

The big man radiated heat like a furnace. He smelled great close up, clean and crisp, like spearmint. The odor of tobacco clung to his jacket but Carson couldn't detect any on his breath, just cool spearmint and fluid warmth. If China had any vices they didn't appear to include smoking. God knew the man ate right. He couldn't keep that body without it. Clean living, killer looks and raw macho attitude in a caring, understanding guy who picked a career protecting the entire, freaking nation. And who wanted to keep protecting people once he was in the private sector. Now there was a man Carson should be dating.

Except the guy didn't live here, would be gone for months at a time risking his life, and be unemployed if he survived to his discharge date.

The downside of China-man was steep.

Carson glanced up at the strong, clean-shaven profile, taking in the long angles and square jaw, deep-set dark eyes, noticing for the first time that China's upper lip was thinner than his bottom lip, marred by a white scar that ran the length of one side. Instead of detracting from China's appearance it gave him a rakish, take-no-prisoners look that appealed to Carson's outside-the-box taste in life.

A modern apartment building towered between two clapboard houses to their right. Carson nudged China toward the freshly shoveled pathway that led to the apartment house, leading him through the entrance, lobby and into the elevator before he felt warm enough to waste energy on speech.

The elevator was a steady seventy degrees, toasty warm and welcoming. It trapped the scent of their bodies in the small space, mingling spearmint with a musky masculine smell Carson suspected was hormones wafting off the both of them. He hadn't felt this attracted to a man in ages. He briefly entertained the idea that he liked China so much because he reminded him a bit of his brother but he dismissed it almost as quickly. China made him feel attractive and flat out horny. That was not brotherly. No sir, Sergeant! They may have both been Army but that was where it ended.

A deeper, more intoxicating heat spread out from the pit of his stomach. It wandered down to his groin so that by the time the elevator doors opened his entire body buzzed with barely restrained interest. The silence had been companionable and comforting but Carson had to say something eventually. And it couldn't be the one word he had in mind—stay.

"Thought you might like a chance to warm up before you took off to wherever it is you need to be." He was startled to hear his own voice, the seductive tone to it, the unspoken questions implied.

China must have heard them, too. He didn't answer right away, just turned and stared down at Carson, dark gaze flickering from Carson's eyes to his mouth, down to his waist, and back to his mouth before linking back up with his own now self-conscious stare. Carson bet he looked like a deer caught in China's headlights waiting for the hit and run.

Opening the apartment door, Carson turned to usher China in, but found the big man still standing outside the threshold, his expression unreadable, his body language stiff, unyielding.

"I think maybe it's best if I go. I…You need some time." The only sign of lingering attraction China couldn't hide was the hungry look in his eyes.

But it was more than enough for Carson.

Grabbing China by the lapels, he yanked the man over the doorstep and down so their lips almost touched.

"What I need is *you*. Stay."

§ § § §

"Warmer?" China traced the curved of Carson's ribs with the line of his jaw. His five o'clock shadow rasped over the smooth flesh with a light scraping sound. Carson shivered and tried to move, but China held him to the mattress, his bare chest pressed to Carson's naked abdomen anchoring the slighter man down.

" Ah! Ummm."

Carson sucked in his chest to remove it as a target but China felt Carson's hips grind against his own belly, the hard cock trapped between them leaking slick pre-cum. He licked at the swollen, dusky nipple nearest him, liking the way Carson gasped and pushed into the touch.

"Ugh!"

"I do like an articulate man." China took the swollen nub between his lips and teeth, enjoying the heat radiating off the tiny bit of wrinkled flesh. Carson moaned and ran his hands down China's back, fingers unconsciously tracing the raised scars and slight dips where a dozen suture lines had yet to fade.

"No talking. I thought you were a man of action."

He sucked the nub deeper into his mouth, pulling it tight then teasing it with nibbled bites.

"Shit!"

Fists pounded on his shoulders, knuckles sharp, bony. Then the hands relaxed, as if Carson suddenly noticed the scars. China felt Carson hesitate then inch his hands back to the wounds, the touch gentle, a caress that both soothed and examined the healing flesh. He released the thoroughly tortured teat, licking it once to soothe it and to hear Carson make that funny little high-pitched gasping sound he found so arousing.

"These scars..." Carson pushed at his chest to get him to raise his head and look him in the eye.

Talking about his wounds was the last thing China wanted to do. Now or ever. At least with Carson. Definitely not while they were making love. Fleeting as it was, he wanted at least this much.

"Are ticklish." Grabbing both of Carson's wrists, he pinned them to the bed, shifting his weight so he was kneeling over Carson. He nudged Carson's thighs apart with a knee and settled between them.

Carson panted, a light sheen of sweat popping out on his upper lip as he tried to wiggle free. China inched slowly down until he could lick the beads of sweat off Carson's lip, moving the tip of his tongue in little teasing swipes. Carson held still, seemingly hypnotized, his gaze locked on China's, their stares unbroken as China moved to explore Carson's parted lips.

The kiss tasted of cranberries and coffee, warm, silky and so very inviting. He closed his eyes, deepening the embrace, need and desire bursting to the surface like a round of gunfire. Carson groaned into the kiss making it all the sweeter, his tongue battling with China's, each taking as much as they could.

At last Carson surrendered and allowed China to take control, his legs wrapped around China's waist, his cock stiff and slick against the hard flat planes of China's belly, his body exposed and submissive except for a continuous effort to free his hands.

China refused to relent. He had seen the pain and loss on Carson's face at the graveyard. He understood the basic human need to be held, cradled, cared for, even if it took the form of being physically restrained. It was a guise even the toughest of men could live with. No one could call you weak if you had no choice but to be held, caressed, cherished.

And if truth be told, China needed to be the one to give that to Carson for reasons that had nothing to do with his unexpectedly intense attraction to the younger man. He finally pulled away, panting. "I told you we could find a way to generate some heat."

"Use your mouth for better things than words, soldier."

The raw, bare need in the command inflamed him more than China thought possible. Carson was smaller, pinned down, restrained and still calling the shots.

"I should remind you that China, the country, is ruled by a powerful military figure." He pressed Carson's wrists into the mattress to remind him to leave them there then rapidly moved his hands to Carson's thighs, pulling Carson's slim hips into his lap. He slipped his powerful arms under Carson's knees and yanked the man so close Carson's straight, jutting cock touched his chest. He leaned down and raked his jawline's stubble up the shaft then stared into green marbled eyes that were wide with heated surprise. He smiled, heaved Carson's hips higher and leered, "And right now…so are you."

He felt the shudder that ran through Carson all the way to his own aching dick, but it was the strangled scream when he deep-throated Carson's slim, hard cock that made his balls tighten and his passion rage hot enough to forge steel.

"Shit! *China!*"

It had been a long time since he'd heard his name screamed like that. A long time since he'd allowed himself to indulge in the pleasure of a lover, a real lover, not a quick blowjob in a nameless bathroom where he wouldn't risk outing himself. Military and gay meant silence and loneliness. But not now, not here.

He bent forward and thrust his hips, grinding his cock against the swell of Carson's pale ass. His cock slid along the hot valley of flesh, lubricating the path with beads of slick cum. He found the tight puckered opening and worked his dick over it, teasing it with the lip of his cock head, loving the way Carson tried to capture his cock and shove it inside the dusky, tight hole.

Palms massaging the firm globes of Carson's ass, China used his tongue to caress the length of the dick in his mouth. It was slick with saliva, firm, and long enough to slide past his gag reflex but not so thick as to cause him to choke. It fit him like it was made for him, a treat to savor and taste at will.

He had to give Carson credit. The young man managed to keep his hands on the bed by grabbing onto the pillow, but when China slipped a spit-moistened fingertip past the tiny rosebud entrance to Carson's body, Carson couldn't stop from reaching up to press his hands into China's short, dark hair.

Letting the cock slide from his lips with a slurping, dirty, arousing pop, China leaned in to look Carson in the eye, expecting to see passionate lust but getting a bright, hesitant, pleading stare. The need for a more personal, more emotional connection shone in Carson's face.

Fuck, this man *was* more dangerous than any enemy China had faced in the field.

But the fact was this needed to mean more to both of them than just a one-time roll in the sheets. China knew he was a goner before the fingers of one hand laced with Carson's lean, twitching digits. He couldn't tear his gaze away from the wide, mesmerizing swirls of green and white, even if that meant losing more than he had a right to offer.

This minute, none of that mattered. He had to take what Carson so desperately wanted to give. Right and wrong be damned.

Just like he would be when it came time for explanations.

Nothing could stop him now short of a barrage of heavy artillery fire. He used his other hand to guide his pre-cum and spit-slicked dick to Carson's asshole. The moment the broad head eased past the spasming muscles, a consuming mandate to own Carson raged through him.

He eased in slowly, timing his short thrusts to the sound of Carson's ragged breathing and the growing return thrust of smooth, firm asscheeks down his cock. His fingers held tight to Carson's, as the other hand stroked over every inch of smooth, firm skin he could reach, raking nails over swollen teats, tracing rib cage and collar bones, tugging hair, and turning Carson's chin.

He thumbed over Carson's parted mouth, stealing moisture from satin slick lips and rubbing it over a willing tongue as that same tongue curled to suck and taste the offered appendage. He retreated to explore more skin, encouraged by soft grunts and sporadic thrashing of limbs as Carson tried to take more of China into himself, more cock, more taste, more touch, until it seemed they were almost one.

Carson suddenly stiffened and cried out, the sound of his voice lost in the muffled shout of China's own orgasm, prompted by the glorious spasms of Carson's tight ass around his buried shaft. Cum shot onto their chests, thin streams of pale white fluid, almost lost against the fairness of Carson's flesh. Each gush of his own ejaculation bathed Carson's insides, making his urgent thrusts deeper, almost to the point of being painfully exquisite.

Spent, China slowly pulled out, and collapsed forward landing on top of Carson, his weight carefully eased to one side to allow his still gasping lover a chance to breathe. The last delicious spasm shuddered down his spine.

China rolled onto his side and pulled Carson over to him, tossing an arm over Carson's chest and pressing a kiss onto his lips. It was chaste but tender, an unspoken declaration of affection from a man who preferred actions instead of words.

Carson responded in kind, his lips lingering over China's mouth then moving down to touch newly healed scars on China's chest and arms. Some were red, ragged masses of webbed flesh marking bullet holes and shrapnel wounds. Others were concise thin lines, dark pink and more faded made by surgeon's blades in an attempt to repair the other wounds.

China knew they weren't pretty but they were a fact of life and he'd stopped noticing them a few weeks after the bandages had come off. This was the first time anyone besides hospital staff had seen them. Carson had been curious about them earlier but other things more pressing, like their hard-ons, had distracted them both.

"These were serious injuries."

China had to concentrate to keep from squirming under Carson's light examination of one very long jagged scar. "Others got worse."

Silence consumed part of the air in the room. He cursed silently, remembering Carson's recent loss. Carson's questing touch stilled for several seconds, then continued. Air eased back into China's lungs as he searched for something to say and came up empty.

"It looks like they had to do a lot of surgery. You're sure you're okay to go back to active duty?"

"They went back in three times. Docs said I could ask for a medical discharge and they'd grant it, but—"

"But what?"

China couldn't ignore the disbelief in Carson's voice but he had to tell the truth. "I finish what I start. I'm Army. That says it all for me."

It was quiet for several moments before Carson sighed dramatically. "So we're back to that 'you're crazy' thing again, aren't we?"

§ § § §

Carson heard the shower running. The slap of water splashed against the shower door as China moved and rinsed in the gentle hiss of the spray. Even the air smelled of soap and steamy warmth. It was comforting; so different from waking up to a still and lifeless room every morning.

He yawned and stretched under the blankets, noticing the pleasant ache in his ass and a lingering burn on his skin where China's five o'clock shadow had left a reminder of their lovemaking. Carson luxuriated in the reminder, hating the fact it would be a long time before it happened again. If ever. He had no idea how long China planned to stick around before he was due back on base. Before he went back to a life that Carson couldn't be a part of.

At least not openly.

But maybe…when China was formally discharged…Maybe.

The bedroom was normally cool in the mornings but Carson could hear the furnace running. China must have turned up the thermostat to drive the chill off before he got in the shower. That was nice. The smell of coffee laced the air, making his stomach growl and his taste buds beg.

Giving in, he threw back the covers and rolled to his feet, grabbing his discarded jeans off the floor from under China's fatigues. The heavier pants clunked to one side, coins, a scrimshaw-handled penknife and a folded photograph tumbled out onto the carpet. Barefoot and bedraggled, Carson paused to scoop the items up, intending to return them to the pants. The coins and knife rattled back into the pocket of the fatigues but curiosity got the better of him.

What picture's so important you carry it in your front pocket, China-man? Or maybe—who is so important?

Insecurity reared. What if China had a lover? They hadn't talked about things; they had both allowed the attraction between them to rule the moment last night. Who else would a guy carry around with him besides someone special to them?

With a guilty glance at the closed bathroom door, Carson couldn't resist unfolding the photo. He had to look. He didn't want to admit it, but he might be falling in love. If China was involved with someone else, Carson was going to have to deal with it. He'd rather do that on his own terms, in his own way without making a fool of himself in front of the other man.

He smoothed open the somewhat worn, wallet-sized photo, holding his breath, hoping to see a picture of China's parents. What he did see choked him on his next breath, his eyes blinking rapidly to be sure he was seeing right.

It was a photo of him. The one Jim had taken of him on his last birthday. It was shot outside in the local park, sunshine making his pale hair look white as it was tossed by the light wind. He'd been smiling, delighted in the impromptu outing, excited by the day with his usually absent brother.

Even he admitted it was a good photo. Jim had carried it with him all the time, torturing Carson by showing it to waitresses and cashiers whenever he could, bragging about his brilliant little brother.

It hadn't been in the personal effects the Army had sent back. Carson assumed it had gotten destroyed when Jim was killed. His brother who had accepted him, raised him, and loved him. Who had been proud of him, proud enough to carry his picture with him all the time. But now…now that photo belonged to a stranger.

He dropped the photograph on the bed next to the crumpled trousers. The clothes of a stranger.

A stranger who had entered Carson's life under false pretenses. China was just as bad as Steve. He obviously had known Jim and how close he and his brother had been. But here he was, stalking Carson, using him, making him feel comfortable and secure while he was being lied to and deceived.

The sound of the shower stopping jarred him out of his stupor. He needed answers but right now he needed space. Time alone to think things out. Grabbing his boots and a clean shirt out of the nearest drawer, Carson fled the room, dressing on his way to the front door. He pulled on his boots, swept his coat off the hook by the door and was gone.

The sound of China calling his name made him pause outside the closed front door but only for a moment. Shaking his head, he tossed all those schoolgirl ideas of a lasting relationship back into the closet along with China. There was no future here. Not with someone who would deceive him like this.

How could he have been so wrong about the man?

§ § § §

"Carson?"

The bedroom was warm and silent. It smelled of sex and coffee. It was probably his imagination but China thought he detected the faint scent of cranberry he associated with the taste of Carson's kisses.

Towel partially over his head to dry off his hair, China walked blindly into the room, stopping when he felt the bed covers brush his naked leg.

"Carson?" He dropped the towel and peered out the open bedroom door. "If you're getting coffee, grab me a cup, too. Black." Dragging the towel down his chest he turned to locate his pants.

It was then he saw it. The photo his sergeant and friend had pressed into his hands during his last few minutes on earth, along with a request China couldn't refuse. Didn't want to refuse.

But Carson wouldn't have known. He'd have recognized the

photo and known who it had belonged to, known China hadn't been completely truthful to him. He should have explained from the start and now…now it was too late. The first time he'd ever met a guy that made him think there could be a meaningful life outside the Army and he'd fucked it up.

The photo was worn a little rough in spots, places where his thumb had rubbed over the corners. He folded it and shoved it into his pants pocket, making sure it was safely deep in the bottom. He dressed in a rapid tug and pull of pants, T-shirt, sweater, socks and boots, grabbing his jacket and cap on the way out the door, pausing only to make sure the coffee pot was off.

The snow had fallen most of the night and now, in the very early morning, the sidewalks were thick carpets of white, undisturbed by the start of the day's usual traffic. It was easy for China to track the tread of Carson's chukka boots all the way to the church. He found the younger man in a small chapel off the main hall. He guessed it was used as a place for private grieving and meditation.

He sat down on the plain wooden pew beside Carson, slightly encouraged that Carson didn't move away or make a move to punch him. He would have stopped him from moving but not from throwing a punch. No one deserved to be socked more than he did.

He leaned forward, elbows on his knees, and looked up, trying to catch a glimpse of Carson's face; desperate to see some sign that he could fix this. Carson's skin was paler than usual, his head bent, his blond curls blown around his face like a halo. China wanted to look into those green eyes and read Carson's thoughts but the other man kept them lowered, half-veiled with long eyelashes.

"Do I get a chance to tell you the truth?"

Then those eyes he wanted to see so badly were looking at him. Harsh. Accusing. Hurt. His chest actually ached when Carson demanded, "Why start now?"

§ § § §

"You lied." It was hard, accusing and cut straight through China's carefully constructed neutrality. The amount of hurt in Carson's burning glare made him feel like a heel and gave him hope at the same time. Carson wouldn't be this passionate about hating him if he didn't have strong feelings for him.

"No, I didn't." China sat up straight and slid his hand into his pocket. Despite the cold his hands were sweating. The edges of the photograph wedged in the crease of his palm, sticking. He let it stay there, needing an anchor to the reason all this happened. "I just didn't tell you everything. Yet."

"Yet? Kind of late isn't it?" Carson spun to face him, braced for a fight, a white-knuckled grip on the pews in front of and behind them.

"There's time if you give it to me. And it *will* take time. The situation is...complex." His gaze never left Carson's face—studying, searching, looking for that one shred of hope this could work out. That at least Jim's brother wouldn't hate him when the truth was out.

So far all he knew was that Carson could go white as snow and still be alive and angry as hell.

"Looks simple from here." Carson's voice broke, but he took a deep breath that let him finish fairly steadily. "You somehow got my brother's picture of me, tracked me down, stalked me, and then made me think we had *something* between us. That's sick."

China suddenly understood Carson wasn't bracing for a fight. He was holding on to the pews to literally stop himself from shaking. For a little guy, he had a big temper. He turned on the pew and faced him head on.

"Okay. I understand you're angry."

"*Angry*? Try betrayed, used, fucked—"

"Stop!" China moved closer, grabbing Carson's wrist on the front pew just to connect better. Carson liked actions more than words. Tremors ran through the arm under his grip, but he suspected hurt fueled them more than hate. "You have a right to be angry, but most of that other stuff isn't true. I didn't betray you or use you."

He touched the side of Carson's face, his chest aching at the unhealthy coolness of the porcelain-like skin. He lowered his voice, longing slipping out along with the truth. "And it was more than fucking for me." His thumb brushed lightly over Carson's lips. "Not that it could work out between us, but—"

Carson jerked his head to the side, brushing off China's caress. "Just tell me where you got the photo."

This was the hard part. Reliving it in order to tell it. He took a deep breath, trying to sweep away the memories, at least the hardest ones. He reminded himself that what he felt was nothing compared to what Carson would go through. "Jim gave it to me."

"What?" Anger drained away in an instant. Carson was left looking frightened and lost. "When?"

A hesitant knock on the door frame heralded the arrival of a young woman to the chapel doorway. She glanced in, anxious eyes studying their faces before she gave them a nod and a small smile. China pegged her for a curious church worker timidly investigating raised voices. Apparently, they were non-threatening enough to satisfy her. She left even more quietly than she had arrived.

"Just before we got hit the hardest with a ton of enemy firepower."

"You were with him when he died?" China was sure the young man would keel over if he got any paler. "Is that how you were injured?" Shaking hands ransacked his clothing, touching his chest and arms, remembering where all the deepest wounds lay. "All the ragged scars?"

Carson jumped to his feet, still holding on to China. Both his hands were fisted around large folds of jacket, hanging on for dear life. "How did it happen? Tell me!"

"Sit down and I will." China grabbed hold of Carson's forearms and forced him to sit. He kept his grip firm to ward off his own crazy thought that if he didn't Carson would disappear like wisps of smoke. "But you have to listen. I can't give you all of the details. They're classified, and they don't really matter anyway." Carson made to rise up, but China pulled him back down beside him. "But you have to sit!"

It took a moment, but Carson finally relaxed back into the pew, trepidation shrouding his expression. "So talk."

China was shocked to realize he'd give anything to take away the mistrust in Carson's eyes. The trip really hadn't turned out the way he had planned. Not by a long shot. Christ-on-a-pogo-stick, he wanted this over with.

"I joined the fire unit at the end of March. Fifth man in. I replaced a guy who went stateside. Your brother was sergeant, along with three other guys. Wilson, Vincent and Bradley. All good guys. Fair. We fit, like a team is supposed to."

China looked off toward the candles burning on the center table. Memories, good and bad, came to life in the flickering light. The faint sound of a choir singing drifted through the open chapel door, a sweet counterpoint to the nightmare playing in his head. "It can be hard when you're the new guy, but the Sarge and I clicked from the start. We got to be good friends pretty quick."

He tore his gaze away to meet Carson's expectant stare. "Facing death together everyday can do that."

Carson didn't comment. "Your brother was like that. Easy going. Quick to take to most people. Friendly, accepting, perceptive. Too perceptive, in my case."

"How?"

"Jim could figure a person out and tell him things nobody else knew just by observing him for a while. Once all five of us were getting drunk and stupid. The guys are partying and chatting up the working girls. Blowing off steam and hoping for a blowjob. At one point Jim and I both wander off to get rid of the cheap beer we're drinking. There's one light bulb in the shit hole of a latrine and the noise from the bar was so loud the door might as well have been open. It looks deserted except for us. To make a long story short, Jim says it must be hard, wanting some ass and not enjoying what was being offered by the working girls. I keep my personal life to myself but Jim had me figured out. Before I can answer him, some jerk from another unit stumbles out of the shadows and gets in my face. Calling me a faggot and threatening to make a report. Asshole is high as a kite."

"What happened?"

"Jim told him if he said a word, he'd be peeing into a cup and on his way to Leavenworth before any other dishonorable discharge papers were signed. 'Don't ask, don't tell' may be official policy, but it doesn't keep you safe from assholes with guns in the field."

"It's a stupid policy."

"I'm not arguing with you there."

"Finish. Please."

"After the first month, Jim started talking about his younger brother, Carson. Sharing stories from your letters, childhood pranks and stuff. I got to know you pretty well. Jim says how proud he is, how smart and successful you are, and good-looking, too. Eventually, he says he'd like it if Carson found someone special. Someone solid, hardworking, to share his life with. Then he hands me your picture and asks, 'Think you could do right by him? You're Carson's type.'"

"That's where you learned to pronounce my name the way he did."

"It's the only way I ever heard it said. Seemed only right."

Carson tugged and China let go of his arms, pleased when the young man didn't move away once he was free.

"He knew you were gay?"

China nodded. "I almost choked. I wanted to say he had it all wrong, but I guess having a gay brother tuned him into the subtle things. Anyway, he knew. I didn't argue with him. Just told him you were a looker." China remembered that day, remembered the first time he'd seen those amazing, green marbled eyes.

"Jim laughed and said he'd introduce me the next time we had leave stateside. Fix us up on a blind date if I wanted." This time

China laughed, a sad, tired chuckle. "Like I needed convincing after seeing your face. Hell, I was thinking the whole time that if you were half the person Jim was you'd have guys all over you. There'd be no room for me."

The wariness had faded away but now Carson's mouth was pulled tight in a thin line, his eyes rimmed with moisture. China could see fine tremors shake Carson's shoulders. It was taking everything the young man had to hold it together.

"Jim was a good man, Carson. We only knew each other a few months but your brother was the best friend I ever had. Good man, good soldier, good friend with a good heart." He rubbed his palm over the edge of the pew in front of him, the wood smooth and warm, smelling of soap and polish. "My life is less with him gone. I miss him every day. I can't begin to imagine how you feel."

"No, you can't imagine. Without Jim, I'm alone. *Totally* alone. He was my entire family!" Carson hugged his arms to his chest, face ashen. "Last night—Christ, China! I was vulnerable, raw, my emotions were exposed and you knew it. I needed to be with another human being last night. Needed to find some comfort. With someone who cared."

China couldn't take the hurt in Carson's eyes anymore. He reached out to wrap his arms around the shaking man. Carson pushed him away with both hands. China rocked back, dropping his arms to his sides. Carson's faltering words cut him to the bone.

"How could you? How could you lie and then make love to me?"

§ § § §

Grief, pain and guilt were written all over China. His face was drawn, the lines around his eyes deeper. For the first time since he'd met the big man, his shoulders were rounded, his height seemingly smaller at this moment.

Carson wanted to hate him—shout at him, lash out—anything that would release the pain waiting to explode from his chest. But he couldn't do it. China was in as much pain as he was from the look of the man. He wasn't sure if the pain was grief over the memory of losing his brother or fear he was losing the chance at a relationship that had seemed so right for him.

Or both.

Or neither.

Maybe this was what a broken heart was like.

"I couldn't tell you. I came here to check on you. Like I promised Jim. You didn't need to know the rest. It wouldn't change what happened to Jim. But last night changed things. I didn't expect to be so attracted to you. Not just a one night stand attraction but a real one. Like in a lasting relationship. But if that has a chance, you'll need to know the whole truth. I couldn't tell you before. Not sure I can now, but I need to try. Will you listen to me?"

Suddenly, he wanted to hear China explain, wanted a reason not to hate this man, this man he had been sure he was falling in love with just a few hours ago. "What's worse than deceiving me?"

"I'm…I…" China stopped to gulp a lung full of air then tried again. It took three tries before he managed to make a few words string together. "I'm the reason your brother is dead."

The only thing keeping Carson from throwing a punch was the tortured, haunted stare balefully burning him. It spoke volumes of unshared pain and the heavy burden of guilt. It showed how deeply China had cared for Jim as a friend. How deeply he cared for Carson now.

The silence was heavy, pushing down on Carson until he was sure his ears needed to pop. The muffled sounds of the choir practice faded to nothing while the hiss of the burning candles took on epic proportions.

Hands and lips numb with an unnatural chill, his heart hammered against his rib cage so hard he was sure it would be bruised. Carson shook his head. His jaw moved but words wouldn't come.

"Our unit was sent out on a mission. Details don't matter. It was an easy designated target. Quick in, quick out. We'd done it a hundred times. Jim and Vincent would team up while Wilson hooked with Bradley. One team would create a distraction. The other would cover my ass while I slipped in and did my thing."

"What's your 'thing'?" He hated pieces missing from puzzles. As much as he didn't want to know, he needed to know.

Hands spread wide, China studied them for several long seconds. He flexed them once and lowered them to his lap. "Let's just say I'm good with my hands."

"This would be a skill that translates well to the personal security sector."

"Yeah. Among others." China slipped his hands into his jacket pockets. "At the last moment, word came in that changed things. Two guys would have to go in. Jim picked himself to go with me. Bradley would take our six. Wilson and Vincent would create a diversion. There was a second unit as back up if things got heavy."

"Which they did."

"Yeah. But not right away. We did what we came in for but it took too long. There was more activity than we expected and we got pinned down. There was unfriendly activity all around us. We knew the guys were coming in for us, but we were outnumbered. Jim took a bullet in the chest. I got the ragged one in the shoulder first. We held out as long as we could but it didn't look good. That's when he gave me your photo and asked me to check on you if he didn't make it. He made me promise. I had to talk to you. He didn't care what I said; I just had to promise. And I did. Just before the lights went out. Last thing I saw was Jim's smart-ass grin."

"When I woke up I was already stateside. We all were. Bradley came to visit. Tried to apologize but Wilson had already told me what really happened."

"Don't tell me it was friendly fire?"

"No, not exactly. It wasn't Bradley's fault. His back up decided to take their sweet time coming in. Seems one of their men turned out to be the drugged-out asshole from the latrine. He knew I was usually first man to go in on this kind of mission."

China hunched forward, elbows on his knees, his big, capable hands, one fist tucked inside the other like a catcher's mitt, restrained violence in every line of the man's powerful body. "So he moved slow, letting the *faggot* get caught in the crossfire. Suddenly, I'm a designated target."

He shook his head; his voice sounding so raw Carson wished he'd stop talking. But China trudged on, pain pushed aside. Carson reminded himself this man was a Ranger, part of his brother's team. Jim always had the best men.

"He didn't know Jim had gone along at the last minute. I don't even know if that would have made a difference to him. I hope it would. But any way you look at it, I'm responsible. If it hadn't been me out there it wouldn't have happened. Jim would still be alive."

It took some time to take it all in. The horror, the pain, imagining what Jim must have been feeling when he knew he wasn't coming back.

How much did getting shot hurt? A lot he'd bet. From the look of the man's scars, China knew all too well. Maybe he'd ask. One day, not now.

Slowly Carson weeded through the dozens of thoughts flashing through his mind like a hyperactive slide show until only one seemed important to him. "Jim wanted you to meet me?"

"Made me swear to God I'd come here. I think he was trying to make sure you had someone to lean on if he was gone. I think he was hoping we'd fit."

There was something in China's dark eyes that pulled Carson closer, some element of strength and hope that called to him. It wrapped around his insides, comforting and strong, like a hug from a friendly bear.

"At least become friends. Someone you could call when you needed it. He was sorry he hadn't talked to you for so long."

Three months. That's how long it had been since Carson had actually talked with Jim. But he was often out of contact for long periods. Carson didn't think anything about it. Now he couldn't remember what they had talked about the last time they spoke. Ordinary things he guessed.

And during that time, Jim had made a good friend, a best friend. Bonds made in the service were sometimes stronger than family ties. China wasn't responsible for this. Maybe not even the other guy. These men led dangerous lives. Jim had taught him that survival needed trust. Jim had died doing something he believed in for his country. The fact that China had survived meant that Jim hadn't died alone. He'd had a friend beside him.

The same friend that was beside Carson right now. Jim had trusted this man. Maybe it was time Carson trusted him, too.

China stood up. Carson automatically rose beside him. Taking the photo from his pocket, China held it out toward Carson, offering it back, but obviously reluctant. "I'd like to keep the photo. It'll be a nice way to remember both of you."

"You don't need it." Carson took it, holding it carefully, aware this was the last thing Jim had touched of his before he died.

"Oh." China dropped his hand to his side, fingers curled and empty. "I understand."

Disappointment flashed across his rugged face then was gone, replaced by a neutral mask that barely hinted at the pain in his eyes. Carson couldn't stand it.

"I don't think you do." He slipped his fingers into China's empty hand and held on tightly. "You don't need it. You'll have plenty of time to take more. Ones with you in them, hopefully. I'm cold. Take me home."

§ § § §

The shower was precisely what he needed. What both of them needed. Neither was in the mood for more than getting warm and tentatively feeling their way back to each other. Trust had to be rebuilt a little at a time.

Carson luxuriated in the opportunity to explore China's body without the distraction of sex. Soaping up his palms, he traced the planes of hard flesh and hills of muscles that defined the big man's towering frame. His fingertips gently outlined the vivid wounds.

There were tactile differences to them. The surgical sutures were smooth and neat, like the seams of his jeans. The bullet wounds felt like irregular lumps, raised, twisted, as if the horrors that caused them were too much to be contained solely within the man.

With a tug and a murmured word, Carson drew China under the spray, rinsing away the rivers of suds until his hands caressed only firm, wet skin. He pressed up close, his chest to China's back, his arms slipped around his lover's waist, his forehead resting on the curve of China's ramrod straight spine.

China turned in his arms and swept Carson into a tight embrace, cradling Carson's head to his broad chest, his breath sweet puffs against Carson's cheek. Carson chuckled, the sound lost in the splash of water. Even in the shower, the big man was all soldier—defender and guardian. Carson impulsively rose up on tiptoe and kissed China, a caring but chaste caress of mouths. China accepted it, asking for nothing more, seeming content to let Carson make the first moves.

The water sputtered to lukewarm and they retreated to the bedroom where several comforters and an electric blanket waited for them. Wrapped in flannel sheets and layers of down-filled linen, they lay in each other's arms.

Against China's chest, Carson raised his head so he could see China's face, read his reactions to what Carson was pretty sure would be an unwelcome idea. "Do you have to go back?"

"What?"

It was hard to take China by surprise but Carson could see he had done just that. But there was no turning back now. He had to ask.

"Go back. To active duty. Do you have to? Can't you still ask for a medical discharge?"

China stared, a frown giving Carson his answer. He was feeling too vulnerable to care. He'd been handed a shot at happiness and he wasn't going to let it go easily. He knew China took his obligations to the Army seriously, just like Jim had, but he wanted the man to consider things from Carson's point of view, too. "I don't want you to get hurt again. Or worse."

China pulled Carson up to lay more fully on his chest with an ease that startled and thrilled him. They were near eye-to-eye and he saw every weathered line on China's face, saw the slight beginning of that dimple on his cheek, and got caught in the intensity of China's understanding but determined stare.

"I can't do that, Carson."

It was the answer he had expected but he felt compelled to fight it. "Why not? You said you only have a few months to go. What's a few months?"

"The difference between being where I'm needed, where other's lives depend on me, and not. I couldn't leave the rest of my unit hanging. They lost enough."

"What about—"

"But I do promise this. I won't re-up at the end of my tour."

"Anything could happen in five months."

"Carson, I'm not the kind of guy that quits. I'm an Army Ranger. A Ranger doesn't run from danger, he looks it square in the eye. I have an obligation to Will, Brad and Vincent to see them through until my time's up. It's what I do, Carson. Who I am." China ran a hand through Carson's tangled hair, dark eyes intense and determined. "But I plan on you being a part of my life from now on. That won't change."

"What if someone finds out and tells? Can't you just leave now?" Carson couldn't help it, the fear of further exposure and official retaliation against China all too real in his mind.

"'Don't ask, don't tell' is their policy but mine is 'don't run, either'."

He could see there was no point in resisting. "It'll be the longest five months of my life," Carson pressed harder against China's comforting hand, returning the same intense and determined stare, "but I'm not running either."

ROUGH RIDE

The world swirled, spinning out of control. James' vision was filled with a dizzying, white blur dotted with occasional glimpses of Bram's laughing face and the dark outline of trees that ringed the hilltop.

The early winter sun was just rising and its dim efforts put a warm, golden glow on the surrounding snow-covered woods and hillside. Barely sunrise on a Sunday morning, they were the only two people braving the cold and ice.

The glow spun and looped as James Justin was carried down a steep, hard-packed slope at what he swore were speeds higher than his car ever achieved on the road. Seated on one side of a double inner tube, he bounced and slid, spinning and flopping along, leather-gloved hands clinging to what felt like too flimsy rubber handles on either side of the giant tube.

The other side of the tube was amazingly steady, its high lip and deep hole filled to overflowing and weighed down with his lover's massive bulk. Bram Lord was a tall, broad, beefy man. He wore a dazzling grin. His pale blue eyes matched the blue threads in the Norwegian-print wool sweater that stretched over his broad, barrel chest. The ends of a red fleece scarf loosely wrapped around his neck whipped in the wind like cheerful flags celebrating the high speed ride.

Bram's cheeks were a rosy red from the cold and his honey blond hair was tousled over his forehead, creating the perfect canvas to highlight James' favorite feature on his lover, Bram's charming and oh-so-seductive lopsided smile. James caught a titillating glimpse of that smile as he rose a foot into the air.

Soaring over a particularly big hump in the long, slick trail, James bounced hard and lost his grip on the tube. Airborne, James yelped and scrambled for a new hold, but his groping hands met empty space for several long seconds before a pair of strong, restraining arms plucked him out of free fall.

"Holy shit!"

He landed with a thunk and a thud, sprawled across Bram's

lap and chest, breath slammed out of him. James grunted and concentrated on not smacking noses with Bram.

The tube twisted, jetted off another small ramp of snow and hit down hard. Suddenly unbalanced, both James and Bram were thrown off the rubber ring. They rolled and slid a dozen feet down the ice-crusted run, James tightly clasped to Bram's chest. They came to a stop in a mound of snow, the empty twin tube skittering past them, a blur of twirling black.

Relieved, James rested on top of Bram's heaving chest, then unexpectedly found himself buried in the mound of snow as Bram rolled them over, pinning James comfortably under him.

Snow clung to Bram's hair and eyelashes, his breath a frosty mint puff of warmth only inches from James' panting mouth. His pale blue eyes crinkled at the corner with laughter. His handsome, broad face was an enticing combination of light morning stubble and soft, tempting lips.

"Jesus! That was crazy. You did that as a kid?" James smacked one gloved hand into Bram's shoulder then hung on tightly to the sweater under his fist. "What were you, suicidal?"

"Nah, just *tough*, baby." Bram shook his head and snow flew in all directions, most of it into James' face.

"Asshole." James sputtered, chuckling. He shook his head to shake off the flakes, but only made more fall down from the surrounding snow.

Bram's laughter was soft and carefree, the deep, joyous sound echoing off the surrounding woods and vibrating through James' body. Pressed chest to chest, each wiggle of Bram's large, heavy body on top of his pushed James deeper into the chilly snow bank.

The unexpected touch of icy cold hit James' skin and he yelped and squirmed, rubbing their lower abdomens together in his startled frenzy.

"Shit! Get up. Snow's going down the back of my pants!" He wiggled some more to try to slip out from under his lover.

"Lucky snow." Pinning a struggling James in place, Bram slid one muscular thigh between James' legs and did a little wiggling of his own.

James' cock responded despite the cold, but as he started to protest, Bram's hovering lips sealed over his own. The kiss was slow and thorough, a languid exploration of his mouth that left him much more breathless than the ride.

The snow that had worked its way down his jeans began to melt and a slow stream of freezing wetness divided its efforts between soaking into his pants and trickling down the crack of his ass. The sensation was uncomfortable, but oddly exotic and arousing.

His cock strained against the confines of his boxers, hard as the icicles hanging from the nearby branches. A thick shaft that gave the nearby tree limbs some competition for size rubbed between his legs and over his cock.

Locking his gaze on Bram's, James felt his heart slide up into his throat. God he loved this huge mountain of a man. Surrounded by the soft morning light, the sound of the birds and the hushed fall of new snow, James felt a sense of peace and security descend around him. He knew he'd never been loved by anyone else the way Bram loved him, cared for him and understood him. This was what finding true love was really like. Looking into Bram's love-filled face, James felt his heart lock onto Bram's. They were bound forever, souls united in this single, shushed moment on this isolated park hillside. It was awe-inspiring and exhilarating. And sexy as hell.

"Want to do it again, Jamie?"

James had to swallow past the lump of emotion in his throat before he could push down his arousal to answer.

"I don't know. That was a hell of a rough ride down." James stroked his gloved palms over Bram's shoulders, hungry to touch the man any way he could. He chuckled, arching his back to shift the snow still packed under his butt, bringing their groins into closer contact. "I'm not sure it's worth the bruises."

Bram smirked, kissed the tip of James' chin and the corner of his mouth, a light, seductive caress. "Okay." He let his words tumble into James' parted, waiting mouth. "Then how about I take you home and give you a different kind of rough ride?" Bram quickly kissed him then tugged at James' lower lip with his teeth. He released it, his stare heated. "I promise any bruises you get as a result will be worth that particular ride."

James hesitated, voice momentarily lost while he imagined Bram deep inside him, their bodies clenched together in different slippery ride that was just as dangerous and breath-taking as the one they just completed. His breath hitched when Bram's voice rumbled through his chest again.

"You won't even have to close your eyes if we go too fast." Bram tossed his scarf over James' head but, instead of draping it around his lover's neck, he used it to blindfold James. "And I'll make this ride last a lot longer than the one we just took. What do you say, Tiger?"

The outside world disappeared behind a blanket of soft warmth, isolating James, making Bram's voice and lingering scent his only tangible connections to it. He instinctively leaned into Bram's body. James' pulse rocketed and his cock jerked. He panted, feeling the wisps of warm air from his mouth grow cold, their moisture condensing and clinging to his face, captured in the scarf ends that lay on his cheek.

Slowly and deliberately, he tugged the fabric loose until it fell free to his shoulders. The expression on Bram's face was hot enough to melt the entire hillside. James' cock chaffed against the confines of his jeans. There was a tightness in his chest. A flush of warmth shot though his limbs as need flowed though his veins, along with growing desire. It still surprised him that it only took a look from Bram to get him hard. He had no doubt he was in love.

James laced his hands behind Bram's neck and pulled his lover down for a searing kiss. He poured as much heat into the kiss as he could, his own lips tingling, scorched with wanting. When he pulled back, Bram was panting and James could barely huff out his answer. "You're on, Caveman."

James let Bram pull him to his feet and dust him off. Against James' better judgment, they retrieved the evil snow tube for future excursions and then walked back up the hill holding hands.

§ § § §

Chest hairs crinkling under his touch, Bram ran his hands down James' chest, the unmarked skin smooth, supple, warmed by the heat of flames from their bedroom fireplace. James was stretched out beside him on the floor by the hearth, lean, lithe and deliciously naked in the flickering light. The down comforter under them trapped their body heat and separated them from the drafty floor in the old house. Under the dancing, golden hues of firelight, the beige cover looked like small mounds of snow from the sledding hill they had visited earlier.

Bram traced the line of chest hair down the center of James' rib cage, following the trail over his lover's taunt, concave belly to the dip of his navel. Gooseflesh erupted on James' abdomen and Bram watched it ripple outward to cover every inch of pale skin. Just as quickly, it melted away.

Bram used one fingertip to draw circles around the shallow dip of navel, his eyebrows rising as a tiny shudder and a breathy moan resulted. He loved how responsive and open James was in bed, how easily affected his lover was by a single touch. Even now, months into their relationship, he found it difficult to grasp just how amazingly fortunate he had been in pursuing James after the first night. Casual sex in a back alleyway with a stranger didn't often lead to long-term commitment and love. But it had for him. For them.

As emotionally shy as James was, Bram knew James would never have pursued him. If he hadn't asked James out a second time that night, he'd have lost out on the man who was rapidly becoming the center of his world. The cold, empty loneliness he'd come to accept as the way his life was going to be began to drain away after the first night James had spent with him. It changed everything forever, as far as Bram was concerned.

After his parents' deaths and his only sister's debilitating accident, Bram was certain his future held only work, friends and the occasional one-night stand. Now his life held the promise of so much more, all of it at his fingertips right now, quivering, needy and waiting for his touch.

He straddled James' slim hips, his own naked ass and thighs delighting in the warmth that radiated up off his lover. He settled over James so their cocks bumped, the majority of his weight resting on his knees and calves. His scrotum nestled up against the base of James' jutting cock.

"Christ, Bram!" It was that breathy, strained moan that always made Bram's passion burn impossibly brighter.

"Tell me what you want, baby. You know all you have to do is ask."

"Jesus!" That struggling, growly sound James made was going to be the death of him yet. The first droplets of precum oozed from the tip of his cock.

"Sorry, can't give you that. He's busy. Try again."

James groaned and writhed, unable to move more than a twitching wiggle. The scarf from earlier was again over his eyes, but this time his wrists had been captured in the long ends as well, tied behind his skull so his head rested on the soft bonds. His elbows were bent, arms high, drawing the flesh of his torso taunt and leaving him open for exploration. Bram had been doing just that for the last half an hour or so. Exploring, touching, tweaking, tasting and teasing.

Bram watched James pull in his lower lip and bite it, James' hips bucking under his ass. Bram knew his lover was struggling to ask for what he wanted, still fighting his insecurities and natural shyness.

Bram wasn't going to make it easy for him. Far from it. Time to speed up this joy ride just a little.

"I want to taste you, Jamie. But do I want this hole?" He curled over and shifted enough to lick the tip of James' cock, lapping the bead of cum off it in a slow, wet stroke of his tongue, wiggling the tip of the wet muscle into the leaking slit. "Or do I want a taste of this one?" He paused just long enough that James would be left guessing where he was going to lick next, then dropped forward and sucked the edges of James' belly button. James gasped and jerked, a strangled sound coming from the back of his throat.

Bram slid his hands up James' sides, his hand span wide enough to cover a large portion of James' ribs, holding his lover down. He loved the feeling of James moving under him, squirming with want, burning with need, vulnerable and open. He was always conscious of the size difference between them, aware he dwarfed the shorter, slender man, his own iron muscles and ripped, construction worker body shouting power and strength.

He could easily crush James, force his will on him, dominate and subdue with bruising strength. And James would let him. James' own craving for rough domination in the bedroom was intense. But Bram instinctively knew how much James needed and could handle, and he gave it willingly, lovingly. Neither of them was into whips, chains, servitude or humiliation, but James craved strength and Bram had plenty to share.

He rimmed the shallow navel, mixing sharp, quick nibbles followed by slippery strokes of his tongue, teasing its edges until James' arms jerked up and the muscles of his abdomen fluttered in protest.

James finally moaned a low, hesitant, "Suck me, please... just...God, Bram, suck me!"

"Okay, baby." Bram licked his way up James' torso to latch onto a taut, dusky nipple standing tall and swollen. "Love it when you beg like that. So hot. Needy. Love when you tell me how much you need me."

James gasped and jerked again, trying to raise his knees, but Bram's ass effectively pinned him in place.

Pulling the teat out from James' chest, Bram let it slip from between his teeth, scraping it as it popped out of his mouth with a wet, sucking sound. James tossed his scarf-encased head and groaned, rolling his hips in frustration, but said nothing. Bram grinned and worked a trail of wet kisses across to James' other teat and treated it to the same. His hands caressed the tender flesh of James' underarms and sides.

Hunched over, Bram's cock slid alongside James' shaft in an irregular dance of missed steps and fleeting touches that had James arching his back in an apparent effort to gain more contact. Bram ignored the unspoken request, waiting for James to voice his passions. Bram knew this was the hardest part of communicating in their lovemaking for James—asking for what he wanted with words.

"Bram?" Head thrashing on the comforter, James pulled his arms outward, the small gesture tightening the knot that kept his eyes blindfolded and his wrists restrained. Sweat covered his skin, making it glisten, the firelight shimmering in the beads of moisture that pooled in the curves of his upper lip and throat. Sweat trickled down his face and into his dark curls, matting them and adding a freshly fucked look to his appearance that made Bram's breath catch in his throat.

"Say it."

"You know!"

James was begging. Blindfolded, bound, flush and writhing under him. The way Bram liked his passionate, shy lover. Needy, erect and desperate for Bram was also a nice plus. But James had to ask for what he wanted.

"What? Not what you wanted sucked?" Bram mouthed the areola around the swollen nub he'd just released, teasing the dimpled tip with his tongue. His chewed the stiff peak roughly, gauging his pressure by how fast James' groin lifted to slam into his ass.

"You have to tell me so I get it right, Jamie." Still astride James' stretched-out body, he tightened his thighs and captured James' hips, stilling them. Groans of frustration filled the air and Bram noticed James' fingers were clenched in his own hair. "Tell me, baby. Let me hear you say it."

"God!" James bit his lower lip then choked out a raw, "Suck my cock! Eat me! Damn it!"

A flush rippled through Bram's chest, sending a glow of warmth all the way to his toes. Every time James let a little of his reluctance to ask for his own needs during sex fall away, Bram felt a burst of pride. James was an amazing man. The perfect man for Bram.

He ran his hands lovingly over James' body, then leaned over and kissed James' parted, panting mouth. A soft kiss that was meant to be nothing more than a simple reward, but James responded with a hunger that fanned Bram's barely contained passions. Suddenly it was an all-consuming kiss, full of stroking tongues, gasped breath and low, needy moans from both of them.

Pulling back, Bram let his lips brush over James' mouth and chin as he said, "Suck your cock. Oh, yeah. I can do that."

He uncurled from over James' body, using his hands to propel backward, sliding on his knees until he was comfortably positioned to take James' cock in his mouth. His knees gripped James' thighs tightly, forcing them closed when he knew James wanted to spread wide for him. A rush of savage power and possessiveness surged through him, the urge to take, claim and own his lover, but he tempered it. By the time the primal emotions flowed out in his touch, it was muted from savage want to a firm confidence.

He took a moment to admire the sight of James stretched under him, James' cock straining up to curve over a quivering belly, skin slick and warm, bound and vulnerable, but most importantly, trusting. A sharp pressure squeezed his chest and stole his breath. His cock ached with the need to take what was his, but his heart ruled. Pleasuring James came first. Without another word, he grabbed a small ice chip from the wine cooler by end of the bed, slipped it into his mouth and sucked the head of James' cock in after it. He was rewarded with a bellow of surprise and three more inches of cock shoved down his throat.

God, he loved his man.

§ § § §

Surprised his back could arch that far off the floor with his legs trapped by Bram's weight, James unlocked his spine and melted down onto the comforter. Bram's mouth followed him, lips retreating to the head of his cock then swallowing it to its base. Icy cold slid along his cock's length, the extreme temperature difference searing the moment into his fevered brain.

"Ahh! Jesus!"

The wet heat slid down his shaft in one fluid motion as the chill melted away. James gasped and arched, but Bram backed off, controlling the action, teasing, prolonging the pleasure, driving James wild. Bram always seemed to know just what James needed, how much he could take, and when it was time to let him explode with passion. And Bram did make James explode, time and time again like it was the first time, every time.

Bram knew what turned him on and what made him vulnerable, helpless and crazy with desire.

Like the blindfold that took away the persuasive power of his pleading stares.

Or the tied wrists that stopped his hands from taking what he wanted or touching himself.

Or Bram making him ask for what he wanted using words, making the illusion he was an unwilling participant drop away. Making him surrender to Bram's will. Making him admit he liked having sex and making love with the massive, loving man. And God knew he loved it, and Bram. There was no one like his caveman. Rough, raw, demanding and primal, Bram was made for him.

James' heartbeat pulsed so hard he could feel it hammering through the sides of his swollen shaft, the ribbons of surface veins vibrating to the thundering rhythm in his chest and head. The flat of Bram's tongue pressed against the vessels as if his lover was counting the beats. The wet, pliant muscle then turned stiff, the tip traced over Bram's favorite spot, the one that made James gasp and groan like he was doing now.

His tongue lavished attention on that spot until James heard his own voice crack and mumble out an incoherent plea for more, less, anything to end the delicious torture. And Bram moved on, tongue jabbing into the weeping slit on top, curling under the rim of the flared head while his lips caressed the sides of James' cock, sucking and massaging every centimeter of dusky flesh.

Saliva, warm and slick, swathed his cock in a layer of heat, then swirled and rushed hard, forced into a whirlpool effect by Bram's swish and suck. It was a trick that never failed to startle and delight James, the sensations never the same twice. The mental vision of what Bram looked like, bent over him, lips wrapped around his dick, face bobbing up and down the glistening shaft, eyes half-lidded in a sultry gaze was enough to make James want to rip the blindfold to see if reality matched his fantasy.

He had to see. Had to see the lust and want in his lover's eyes that matched his own rising emotions. His arms moved, but were drawn up short, the ends captured in an unyielding hold. James tossed his head in protest.

"No." It was simple, one small word, a denial of James' desire to see, but it sent jolts of pleasure from the pit of his lower abdomen straight up his cock. James felt it pulse harder.

His body burned. His skin felt raw. He could tell his teats were standing up. The bitten, worried flesh overly hot, bared in the cooler air of the bedroom, swollen in parody of his jutting cock. They begged to be kissed again, suckled, pinched, teased. He arched, thrusting out his chest to let them plead their own case, as words failed him again. He felt a quick swipe of a wet thumb bathe them in moisture, intensifying their heat, but the touch disappeared too quickly to be satisfying, serving only to notch up his frustration.

His asshole spasmed, clenching and unclenching, empty and unhappy. He needed more, wanted to be filled, filled with his lover. He wanted the man inside him, any part of him.

"Fingers!" James gulped for air, suddenly glad *and* disappointed he couldn't see the pleased reaction he knew would be on Bram's face. "I-I want…your fingers…up my ass."

The lips caressing his cock moved up his length until they held only the head in Bram's mouth. Rustling sounds of movements alerted James that Bram was shifting position only seconds before his legs were spread wide. A press of warm flesh and the tickle of hair on his inner thigh signaled Bram's desire to move from outside his legs to inside of them.

Free to move, James bent his knees up, letting his legs fall open, exposing his ass. A blunt pressure nudged his opening. Bearing down, James tried to capture it and suck it into his body, but pressure breached his opening and plunged deep into his channel in one slick stroke. Just as he adjusted to the sudden, delicious intrusion, a new sensation exploded in his ass. A sliver of icy cold skated around his clenched hole, then it wormed its way into his ass beside the thick finger wiggling and stroking the hot lining of his gut. The burn was unbelievable, startling, exotic and unexpected. In his mind he saw the half-moon sliver the icemaker downstairs produced and envisioned its smooth, slender, curved shape sliding into his ass.

"Fuck! Holy fucking shit!" His cock lost a little of its hardness but was pulled back to instant iron glory by a few deep plunges and twists of Bram's finger in his ass and a bit of wet, firm lip pressure under the crown of his dick.

The buzz of orgasm burst to life in the pit of his abdomen. Tendrils of heat sizzled along his nerves and zapped every cell in their path to life. James rode Bram's finger like it was his lover's cock, squeezing it, milking it with his muscles, clenching his cheeks so tight he could feel the knuckles of Bram's hand buried between them. The ice had melted, but a chill trickle of water oozed from his opening when a second finger was inserted. It dripped down his crack like spilt cum.

Suddenly he felt a thickness alongside his cock, Bram's mouth stretching to accommodate more than just James' shaft. It was warm, satiny and throbbing, and James couldn't help but envision Bram's cock head stuffed into his lover's mouth beside his own. His orgasm raced up from the depth of his gut and exploded into Bram's mouth, scalding over his cock and his lover's tongue.

And whatever else was there. He bucked up hard to jam as much as he could down Bram's willing throat. He didn't need to thrust back and forth to divide the stimulation between his cock and ass. Bram's hand followed his movement, the man's fingers packed hard into James' ass, grazing his hidden gland, stroking his grasping channel. Bram's meaty fist spreading the tight ring at his opening until it burnt as if on fire.

The instant his orgasm began to fade, his body relaxed and sagged. The warm wetness encasing his cock abruptly disappeared and the fullness in his fluttering ass went with it. His muscles screamed and tried to recapture the hand, but it escaped. Before he could protest, a new, bigger pressure shoved into the void as Bram's cock slammed up his ass so far his lover's balls settled into the spread crack of his butt cheeks. It was like being impaled on a telephone pole.

"Jesus! Oh yeah, fuck me, fuck me hard!"

It felt so damn good James' still half-hard cock nearly shot a second time.

"Christ! Bram! God, I love you!"

§ § § §

There was nothing like the feeling he got when James let loose and called his name. It made Bram feel like the king of the world with superhero powers. It was exhilarating unlike anything else. Possessiveness surged through his veins and took lust and passion to a new height. His cock was as hard as steel, thick and needy, encased in James' heat, burrowing its way to the core of his lover's body and soul. There was nothing like making love with Jamie. It was nirvana. Pure ecstasy packed into one hundred forty-five pounds of wiry man.

Words almost escaped him at this point but a guttural growl rolled up from deep in his chest. "Fuck, what you do to me, baby!"

Sliding in all the way to his cock's base, Bram slammed into James' ass, burying himself in his lover's clinging heat. The groan that rolled off his lips was again more growl than sigh, a deep, primal sound that vibrated down his spine. Even his hips shook. He thrust harder, roughly taking everything James could give him, enjoying the exquisite pleasure of James' ass gripping his shaft, stretched to its limits, while James bucked up for more.

The comforter was thick and warm under his knees, but the touch of James' ass on his thighs was scalding. Bram grabbed hold of his lover's hips, dragging James closer, plunging his cock in deeper. Once he was as deep as he could get, he ground his hips in a circular motion as he thrust. Every so often James would grunt and jerk, telling Bram he'd managed to hit the spot that made James thrash with need. Like now.

"That's it, baby, tremble for me. I never get tired of feeling you under me, shaking, rocking my world like this." The need to see into James' eyes, to meet his lusty gaze, to see the raw emotion James let loose during their lovemaking was too powerful and urgent to ignore anymore. Bram bent down and kissed James hard and long. Then one hand twisted in the bit of scarf over James' eyes and pulled the scarf down behind James' head, leaving his wrists tied. Bram's cock surged and he almost shot at the dazed, sultry expression on his lover's face.

There was nothing like seeing that vulnerable, wanton, needy stare and the turmoil that swirled in those sapphire eyes. He kissed him again, hard, thrusting in long strokes, grinding his hips on the final shove and striking James' hidden nub of prostate on the slide in. He was reduced to grunts and gasps. He felt a sizzling jolt of pleasure race down his spine as James licked his dry lips and gazed up at him through half-lidded, sex-glazed eyes.

"Fuck me, Bram. I want to come!"

His chest ached and his balls tightened, the sound of James' raw, choked voice pushing him toward the edge. Pulling the ends of the scarf over James' head, Bram pulled his lover's captured hands down and wrapped them around James' own cock, a layer of the soft fleecy fabric between cock and palm.

"Look at us, baby. Watch me slid inside you, feel my dick up your ass, hammering your hole, rocking us both to ecstasy." He grabbed James' hips and yanked him hard, rolling his hips and grinding his groin against James' spread cheeks, stretching his opening until he felt it spasm and clamp down around his rod. "Look at your hands, your cock. Tied together, hot and happy." He kissed James, quick and hard, then leaned up. "Just like us."

"Fuck, fuck, fuck, *fuck*! Bastard, fuck me! " James thrashed and whimpered, legs bent back and tied hands milking his cock at a fierce pace. "Do it, oh yeah, do me, *Bram*!" His gaze locked on Bram's. The vulnerable, desperate need to be loved was so plain to see Bram felt tears burn the back of his eyes.

"Love you." Bram came, shooting long splashes of cum deep into James' hot, clinging channel, letting its clenching muscles wring every drop out of him. "God, baby, oh, yeah, take it from me!" Christ, he would never get enough of this man!

Hot strands of milky white hit his chest. He ran one hand through the spurting trail dotting James' torso, using the slippery pools to wet and stroke James' swollen teats. He loved the choked sounds the man made at the back of his throat as he worked his fingers over the hot nubs.

James shuddered and bucked, his hand groping for Bram, his mouth working but nothing more than strangled grunts and harsh breaths escaped, accompanied by the rhythmic slap of sweaty flesh on flesh. It was all music to Bram's ears, the symphony of a well-loved lover.

§ § § §

"You going to untie me any time soon?" James wiggled his fingers where they rested on his bare torso, wrists wrapped in knots of bright fleece spotted with drying smears of creamy wetness.

"Not sure yet." Bram ran one of his massive hands over James' wrists and up his arm, the palm rough, his flesh hot, leaving a scorching trail behind. He followed the path back down again, coming to rest with his palm on the curve of James' naked hip. "I kind of like that look on you—well-fucked, exhausted and helpless under me—can't go wrong there in my book, baby."

He lay on his back with the big man at his side. Head

propped up on one arm, Bram leaned over him, their bodies pressed together, stretched out on the wrinkled and bunched down comforter, the firelight making early winter shadows dance around the room.

The air was thick with the scent of cum, sweat and firewood, a heady, delicious, comforting smell that soothed James' raw senses. Making love with Bram fried all his nerves on a regular basis, but when they went at it rough and unbridled, when Bram fucked him harder and deeper than James thought he could stand it, the big man totally in control of all of James' responses, James was drained senseless. He was sore, achy and gloriously sated.

"You really are a caveman." James snorted and twisted his wrists. He wasn't really in any hurry. He enjoyed the pressure on his flesh, the drying stains reminding him of his climax. The ache in his ass was almost as thrilling now as it had been when Bram stretched and filled him, massaging his insides with his satin-steel cock until he burned as bright as the flames beside them. His ass clenched at the memory.

"But I'm your caveman." It was a smug growl of triumphant, sexy, deep-throated teasing. It vibrated right through Bram's chest and into James. No one thrilled him, understood him or cared for him the way Bram did. Not even his own family. His chest was suddenly too small to hold his heart.

"There's no way I'll ever forget that." His chest tightened and his eyes burned. He didn't know how much happiness could hurt until he met Bram. "Or regret that."

"No regrets? Not one?" Bram cupped James face. The firelight caught in the man's eyes and James could literally see the joy and satisfaction he heard in Bram's voice shining there.

"It's been a hell of ride since day one, lover." James could barely rasp out the words, his throat was so tight with emotion.

"A little rough-going some days?" Bram soothed a thumb over James swollen lower lip, a spark of renewed passion in his husky, raw voice.

"Yeah, a little." James raised his bound hands and pulled the thumb from his lip, holding it so he could lick it between words. "But remember, with you—I like it rough."

"*Rough & Ready.* That's our new family motto." Bram ran his hand through James' hair gently tilting his lover's head until their eyes meet full on. "I'll see if I can get it in needlepoint to hang on the wall in the kitchen. It'll be one of your Christmas gifts."

James smiled at the mirth in Bram's face, suddenly moved and comforted by the silly suggestion.

"You're the best gift I've ever gotten." Silly or not, it was a very 'couples' things to say. They were actually becoming a family of sorts. "I love you, Caveman. Merry Christmas."

SLIPPERY WHEN WET

The first bead of sweat that broke loose ran from the man's temple to the sharp angle of his tight, square jaw. It hung on for an anxious moment, during which Parker realized he had been holding his breath, waiting to see where the bead would land on the solid expanse of bulging hard muscle that formed the casually spread, naked thighs beneath it.

Eyes hungry, Parker hoped it would splash high on the man's leg, giving him a reason to follow its descent. He didn't actually need a reason, it was a public sauna. An on site, twenty-four hour, fully outfitted gym, pool and sauna, a perk of working for a huge corporation that promoted employee health and fitness.

But Parker still insisted on playing this game with himself. Seeing how much restraint he could muster, how long he could hold back his physical desires without the other guy suspecting. What it would take to make him finally get up and leave, towel artfully wrapped around his hips while his hands covered his growing erection. Then a warm shower to cover the quick hand job before he toweled off, dressed and made his way alone back to his peaceful but empty apartment.

Working sixteen hours days was great for his work and reputation as a dedicated researcher for the company. Not so great for his personal life. If he thought about it, his current lifestyle of nothing but work and sleep was pretty pathetic for twenty-nine year old, moderately successful forensic scientist. So he didn't spend much time thinking about it.

And there was no time to look for dating material outside his immediate circle. All of his close associates were either female or straight men. There wasn't anyone he was interested in anyway. Or there hadn't been until three weeks ago when Sir Brawny & Buff started showing up in the gym every night. Parker had nearly dropped a free weight on his foot the first time B&B had strode into the gym and began his warm up. By the time the other man had ended his routine almost two hours later, Parker had hit the head twice to jack off. Which was the only reason he'd managed to stay in the sauna with the guy for six whole minutes before leaving weak kneed and dizzy, still half hard and aching.

It didn't help any that they were always alone, the last hardcore exercise junkies in the place. Or the only people that worked long hours into the evening and still had energy to burn. Parker worked out so his body would be exhausted enough that his mind would have to shut off to sleep. He was toned and wiry, but his short, slender frame would never compete with this guy. B&B was all muscle. Muscle, muscle everywhere.

But there might as well have been a big neon 'do not disturb' sign tattooed on the guy's chest. They had been alone together working out in the gym five and six nights a week for two hours and the guy had yet to do more than stare Parker in the eye for ten seconds and nod a wordless hello. Talk about your strong silent type!

Of course, Parker hadn't offered any attempts at conversation either. He'd been content to ogle covertly and fantasize. No one else in the gym meant privacy, but it also meant no witnesses to murder if the guy took offense to Parker's… appreciative interest. But then the guy would actually have to notice before he could be offended and Parker made sure that wasn't going to happen. No way. He wanted to see his next few birthdays.

Licking his lips, Parker tasted the sharp tang of his own sweat. He closed his eyes and let his muscles relax, feeling the knots in his neck and shoulders from hunching over microscopes and keyboards all day start to unwind. This was always the perfect ending to his day, the way he unwound, the only activity truly draining enough to shut down his mind and body. Besides sex. And sex was nowhere on the immediate horizon. One handed sex didn't count. It was rewarding but not exhausting.

The sauna was big enough for ten people, all wooden slant flooring and two tiered benches. In the center of the room was a small sculptured pedestal filled with steaming hot rocks. A tiny basin that filled with water automatically was artfully designed into one side and a ladle hung from a part of the sculpture.

The sudden hiss of water hitting hot stones filled the air. Startled, Parker looked up under half-closed eyelids to watch

B&B replace the ladle, towel slung low around solid, molded-from-rock hips and ass. So low and loosely wrapped that when B&B stepped away the towel slipped. B&B casually grabbed one end of it and instead of re-wrapping it, threw the towel over his broad and brawny shoulder.

Full frontal exposure. No steroid user here! It was just like Christmas. And man, would Parker like to play with that toy! Christ, this guy was one complete package. Too bad he didn't have a personality to go with the body.

Parker's breath caught in his throat. He prayed the grunt of appreciation that escaped couldn't be heard over the hiss of the steam.

The guy radiated power, even an element of danger. Parker found that thrilling, different. He'd never been attracted to guys like this before, but then he'd never socialized in circles outside of academia and scientific research. He found it amazing a guy like this was in the same workplace as he was. He knew the guy worked there, he'd seen one of the female techs trying to chat him up in the hallway yesterday. Parker had panicked at the thought of having a conversation with the guy outside the isolated exercise wing. He'd walked right by, avoiding eye contact, blood rushing in his ears too loudly for him to catch any of the conversation between the other two.

What did Broad & Brawny do here? Security? Not likely. He was too controlled, too deliberate. This guy's whole demeanor screamed intelligence and stealth with a good dash of lethal force thrown in for good measure, at least in Parker's lively imagination. A bodyguard for one of the head honchos maybe?

Parker shook his head. He was spending too much time looking at the world at a microscopic level. But man, he would like to get a closer look at this guy, a much closer look.

Every muscle group on the man's body was developed to perfection, and not from just working out in any gym. Parker could see scars on his barrel chest, back, and his beefy left arm. They didn't look like they came from any surgeon's scalpel. A long, jagged, barely healed scar decorated his now bare right hip.

Hips that were leaner than his wide, swaying shoulders with gluts rippling with constrained power as the man walked.

Parker knew this because, instead of returning to his old seat on the bench across the room, B&B was walking toward Parker. Slow and deliberate. Was that a little swagger in those rock formations other people called hips and thighs?

The appreciative grunt turned into a strangled cough at the back of Parker's throat. The swagger was slight, but since it made the stiff, gloriously jutting erection sprouting up from the dark nest of hair bob and sway, Parker couldn't help but notice—the tiny swagger and the not so tiny hard-on. Not anywhere near tiny.

He swallowed past the sudden constriction in his throat and concentrated on dragging his gaze away from the flushed and gleaming circumcised shaft before he drooled on himself.

Self-consciously, he crunched his own towel into a concealing ball in his lap. As his gaze pulled away, he'd meant to look at the ceiling, but some alien magnetic force invaded the room and forced what he knew was a wide-eyed stared to meet the man's gray-blue gaze.

Steely gray looked less… well… steely up close. More blue, with a glint of humor and a splash of something Parker would have called interest in someone else. And was that the beginnings of a sneer or… a smile on those firm, sweat moistened lips?

Without a word, Broad & Brawny dropped to the bench beside Parker, cock at full mast, proudly on display. B&B leaned back against the wall and got comfortable. His towel became a pile of crumpled fabric on the floor. A slick hard knee bumped Parker's thigh but he was too busy trying not to stare to react to the touch.

"Hey." The voice was a little softer than expected, masculine but with a smoothing timber to it. It lessened some of Parker's trepidation. "Name's Dallas."

A large, smooth hand crossed over Parker's lap, fingers spread and grip waiting perilously close to Parker's own stiff soldier. He automatically reached out and shook hands. The heat of the guy's skin was like Parker imagined it would be picking up one of the steaming sauna rocks, slick with penetrating warmth that was almost a living entity on its own.

"Ah... hi." His voice was raspy, partly from the thick air clogging his lungs and partly from surprise.

"Come here often?" The tone was light but the laser blue stare demanded an answer.

"Huh?" Parker blinked, uncertain what he should say. He decided to play it safe. "Ah, every night, same as you."

The small smile spread into a dazzling grin. Dallas leaned his head and shoulders down closer to Parker and gently added, "It was a joke. You know, lighten the mood, break the ice. A come on line."

"Oh. Sorry. I don't... go out much." Sudden he felt like he was back in high school. "Not recently." How much of dork did that make him sound like. "Not like never... just not... recently." Oh, yeah, that was soooo much better.

"Tina says you work about 90 hours a week. Hard to work in a social life with those hours. Hell, it has to be hard to work in sleep and food with those hours."

"Tina?" Trying to ignore the sweet, staggering sight of a bead of creamy white sitting on the dusky pink crown of the thick cock only inches away, Parker fixated on the part of the conversation he didn't already know all about.

"Yeah. Says she's known you for three years? The little blond I was talking with when you breezed by me in the hallway yesterday afternoon?"

"Oh, yeah." Parker stammered and tore his gaze away, fighting the urge to lick his lips. "Sorry." The image of Dallas' cock pressed to his lips clouded his mind. He was woefully aware he sounded as if his IQ had dropped fifty points. "Tina works in testing."

Parker looked at his own lap. Fisted white knuckles wrapped in the towel stared back at him like little glassy eyed aliens. This whole conversation belonged on another planet. Surreal and bizarre.

"Testing's not my field of interest."

"So she said." In the silence that followed, Parker squirmed, trying to relax. He shot a glance at his companion to find Dallas studying his face, a thoughtful, tentative look on his rugged features and a flash of something indefinable in his eyes.

Parker felt a slight tightness in his chest. Lord, was this guy coming on to him? He hated being scrutinized, evaluated. If it involved anything other than his intellect, he always felt as if he came up short. Especially when the person doing the physical scrutinizing was bigger, broader, beefier, and better looking. Not that he was skinny or ugly; he worked out every night, but mostly cardio training, not to put on bulk or build muscles like this guy sported. Parker liked to think of himself as small but wiry.

The faint smile was back on the big man's handsome face. It tugged one corner of his mouth higher than the other, bringing a dimple to life in one cheek. Parker realized a faint white line on the upper lip was an old scar, deep through the vermilion border of Dallas' lip. What had hit him so hard his face had been split wide open? And why?

"She had a lot to say about a lot of things." There was a flash of humor in that. Unexpected, revealing a glimmer of the man Parker hadn't anticipated.

Dallas rolled his shoulders. Parker could hear his spine flex and pop. He wondered if all that power and strength came out when the guy was in bed. That proud weapon standing up saluting between his legs was like a freaking light saber, long thick and no doubt deadly. Parker had to swallow hard to keep his throat from closing up.

"But we weren't talking about work."

"No?" It was almost a whisper. He wondered where this conversation was going but at the same time, almost afraid to find out.

"I think she was trying to wheedle a date out of me."

"Oh..." Bingo. The guy wanted info on Tina. That's what this was about. Damn it. "She's... pretty."

And folks, this is why fantasies are called fantasies. They never become reality. So much for the imagined sauna blow job.

"A little over enthusiastic maybe, but... nice." He studied the folds of the towel in his lap again. Pretty soon he wouldn't need it to cover anything more shocking than a limp cock. "And... and pretty."

"Pretty is nice." Dallas didn't seem to notice Parker's discomfort and lackluster disinterest. "She talks a blue streak though."

"Yeah." He took a deep breath and wiped a trickle of sweat of his upper lip. He darted a look to his left, catching that small, slightly asymmetrical smile again. Those dark eyes really should stop staring at him with that warm, intoxicating glint. "I-I like... quieter people."

"She's not really my type either."

He chanced another glance. Yep, that warm, 'I'm looking at you' stare was still in the guy's eyes. Parker ran his tongue along his lower lip, then stopped when Dallas gaze dropped to follow the movement then returned to study Parker's face. "You like them quieter, too?"

"Um-um." Gaze pinning Parker in place, Dallas made a nondescript wave in the air that conveyed nothing.

The words tumble out before Parker could stop them. "You like them uglier?"

There was short, stunned silence than a pleasant rumble of laughter shook the bench. Dallas' upper arm rubbed against him, transmitting the vibrations so their skin touched in a thin layer of combined sweat. It felt like static electricity crackled between them, making Parker's arm tingle.

"No." Dallas shook his head once, the sweat trickling off his angular jaw to splash on his chest, disappearing in the patches of dark chest hair. "Holy Christ." It was said softly, low, disbelieving, but Parker heard it and flinched. Was he that much of a dork to this guy? "Not uglier." His gaze searched Parker's face for a moment, their arms still touching. The warmth of the room was suddenly suffocating as Parker imagined he saw more than idle curiosity burning in Dallas' intense stare. "I just like my dates to be more... male."

"Male? You?" He was surprised by how husky and low his voice sounded. Interested, maybe even... sexy. His cock was sure interested. It poked at the towel, straining the fabric, nudging Parker's hand, looking for escape. "As in men?" His gaze locked on Dallas' steady stare, wanting to look away but afraid if he did he'd misread what he was hearing.

"That's the best kind of 'male' I can think of, yeah." Both the answer and the stare held steady, an invisible thread holding Parker captive.

"You're gay?" It was still a little hard to wrap his mind around. Sure he knew there were gay men that were walking talking hunks with perfect brawny bodies and chiseled good looks, but Parker thought all of them were in porn flicks. He knew he'd never met one. Until apparently now.

Dallas nodded and that tolerant smile grew a little bigger than before. "I think I just said that."

"You date men?"

"Good lord. You need to get out of the laboratory more, Dr. Crowe. Do you talk to anyone in the world outside these walls?"

Ignoring the sarcasm, Parker shifted in the attempt to cover the stirrings of renewed interest under his own towel. "You know my name?"

"I asked Tina who you were when you walked by—without even a hello. She and I were doing something unusual. You might try it sometime. It's called social interaction. You seriously need to polish up your skills."

He leaned forward, elbows on his knees, his cock pressing straight up to touch his abdomen. But his eyes still studied Parker. The interest was still there but muted as he recited his newfound information as if he was reading a report out loud. "Dr. Parker Crowe, a certified genius with four degrees specializing in the field of chemistry and biophysics. A valued, dedicated scientist in the company's esteemed R&D laboratory. Dedicated to the point of ridiculousness. Working late into the night, every night, plus most weekends. Unlike Tina, I don't see that as a bad thing, mostly. I respect hard work." The formal, harder edge that had crept into his voice slipped away and the interest was back full force. "But you have to balance it with a life on the side." Dallas reached out and ran the back of one hand down Parker's smooth, sweat-slick chest.

"Why?" The light touch made his nipples harden and his swollen, trapped cock ache for attention, but Parker couldn't help it, curiosity always won out over… everything. It a single-mindedness that made him good at this job, but it had derailed many an intimate moment as well.

"Why what?" Now it was Dallas' turn to sound confused. "Why do I respect your dedication?"

"No, why did you ask who I was?"

"Okay. Looks like we do this the hard way." The snort spoke volumes of restrained tolerance with a large dash of exasperation. "Look, the long version is we've been working out together for three weeks without a word between us. The short version is… I'm attracted to you. Wanted some personal info on you before I made a move."

"Worried I'd be offended if you came onto me?"

"The way you've been checking me out since day one?" Dallas made that amused grunted again. "I knew you were interested."

"Uh?"

"Face it, Doc. You aren't very good at sneaking looks."

Darting his gaze away from Dallas' crotch, Parker squirmed. Dallas teasingly confided, "You'd make a lousy stalker, Doc."

"Yeah, well… you still haven't answered why?"

"Wanted to know if you were seeing anyone. Don't need a

jealous boyfriend cropping up somewhere down the line. Don't need extra drama in my life. My job gives me plenty."

"Job?" He couldn't keep his eyes off Dallas' cock. It was delicious looking, slightly curved, long in the shaft with veins that looked like ropes dangling from the circumcised crown. It thickened at the base just before disappearing into a forest of dark curls.

"Christ. Yeah, my job. That thing I do during the hours I'm not asleep or working out with you." Dallas slid off the bench and crouched by Parker's knee. His cock lay flat on his sculptured abdomen, a stark smooth pole against the tanned flesh and dark hair.

"Security?"

"Kind of, but not really."

"Then what are you?" His knees were nudged further a part, empty space replaced with broad shoulders connected to a solid mass of muscle and heat. Hands massaged his thighs, the grip firm with steady pressure that transmitted power.

"Besides a guy with a monster hard-on sitting next to the attractive guy that gave me the boner? The guy with a woody just as hard as mine?" Dallas slowly but firmly pulled Parker's towel away from his lap to let it join the other discarded towel at their feet. Parker let it slip away. "Is it important right now?"

"Ah… ah."

Warm, firm lips slipped over the tip of Parker's cock. He shuddered, gasped, and fought the urge to clamp his legs together from the sudden shock. Not that he could have closed them, not with the tree-trunk-solid torso between his knees, leaning into his body, forcing him to lie back, relax and accept. "Holy crap."

Lips traveled over the head and down one side, returning to the crown again and again, firm, moist and hungry. Ribbons of saliva mixed with sweat glistened on the dusky pink shaft.

The steam laden air filled his lungs, each gasped breath seemingly filled with less oxygen than the one before it. Mammoth hands under his ass lifted his weight, coaxing his hips to the edge of the bench. Parker blindly obeyed.

He was rewarded by having his cock engulfed in a hot sleeve of slick flesh. Dallas worked the shaft with the rough flat of his tongue. Then he applied pressure to the underside of the swollen head with the firm, pointed tip before deep-throating the newly sensitized rod.

Suction pulled Parker's cock in until he could feel the tight ring of lips pressed up against his body. Grunted puffs of hot breath emanated from Dallas' nose buried in his groin hair. The suction under his taut sac tugged on the root of his cock. The rhythm pulled and released, teasing the muscles in his perineum. His asshole clenched and spasmed, eager to become part of the action. Fingers brushed his hole then dug into his ass and pulled him closer.

"Holy—!" Parker couldn't remember the last time he'd had sex with a partner this satisfyingly aggressive. Or this sexy.

Sensation overwhelmed reason, want pushed aside his natural awkwardness, and lust granted his newfound, if temporary, lover a measure of trust he wouldn't have given easily under other circumstances. He needed to relax and enjoy it. Like, really. This didn't happen every day.

Who was he kidding? He was a scientist. His life didn't include impulsive, covert sex in the company sauna. Or anywhere else for that matter. This couldn't be happening.

Yet, here he was. Getting an outstanding blowjob from an assertive hunk who was, realistically, a complete stranger.

The heat in the room leveled off. The steam dissipated but the air hung humid and heavy, coating both their bodies in rivers of sweat.

The hands holding his hips immobile slipped. Their grip instantly repositioned. One arm slid behind his low back to drag him forward a few more inches, pushing his cock deeper into the mouth devouring it. He could feel fingertips branding their mark into his flank, the massaging pressure bruising but oddly comforting, a wordless reassurance this contact was more than about sex, their owner saying with a touch he was focused on Parker not just his cock.

Dallas' other hand slid up Parker's chest, palm flat against his skin like a surfboard skimming the rivers of sweat, riding the waves of rib and lean muscle. Quick, kneading fingers latched onto one nipple, plucking it over and over until it was hard, hot and swollen. Every twist and flick of the tiny nub sent flashes of burning pain to his cock, a fire that turned into an anxious glow of almost desperate pleasure. God, it had been too long.

The start of an orgasm clenched in his balls, his ass tightening, his cock swelling. His mind reeled at the sight of Dallas kneeling between his widespread legs, face buried at his groin, lips locked around his cock. The sucking increasing as if Dallas was determined to draw his climax out by sheer physical force. The mental picture of his cum shooting out to slide down Dallas' tight, hungry throat was all he needed to fall over the edge.

And that's when panic set in.

Reason suddenly intruded on the moment. "No! No, wait. Move! You shouldn't... you don't know if... Holy SHIT!" Parker pushed at the bobbing head but Dallas refused to relinquish his prize. And then it was too late.

A burst of bright lights and searing pleasure rocketed through his cock and invaded every one of his nerve fibers. The eruption was so intense his imagination, ever the scientist, turned his cum into liquid nitrogen and his climax into an atomic mushroom cloud.

He felt shell-shocked. Numb limbs sizzled, his muscles too weak to move. All he could do was lie like the puddle of sweat under his ass, limp and fluid, forced to enjoy the exquisite delights of being sucked dry and licked clean.

"Holy cow. Just—holyyy!" His voiced sounded as weak as his limbs.

A swift, stunning yank on his waist pulled him off the bench. Parker landed with a low grunt, a leg on either side of Dallas' firm lap, a stiff, leaking cock smashed against his own still half-hard, but fading fast dick.

Even as high as he was on Dallas' thighs, Parker still had to glance up to look directly into the man's eyes. Blue eyes stared back at him, so close he had to concentrate on not going cross-eyed while he held the gaze.

"Listen, I'm sorry. I-I tried to warn you." Parker hands instinctively moved to Dallas' wide shoulders. He used the solid wall of flesh to push his torso back a few inches, gaining mental distance more than any actual physical retreat. His back hit the bench behind him, but hands gripped tighter to his waist, preventing him from moving again. Panic surged. "I swear, you'll be okay. I'm healthy, I swear."

He eyes did cross as Dallas closed the gap between them, leaning in to nuzzle and nip at the tender skin at Parker's neck. "I know." A sudden lick and exaggerated kiss had Parker pushing into the contact. "I'm not worried."

"You know? How did—? You got access to my employee files?"

A sharp bite made him flinch. Dallas soothed the pain away with small kisses that skimmed along Parker's skin all the way up to his ear. A tingle of excitement flew along his nerves and his cock stirred. "I should be mad." He swallowed hard and turned his head to give Dallas more access. "But under the circumstances I'd be an idiot to object."

"And we both know you're a genius, so let's not worry about it."

Hot, wet lips massaged the lobe of one ear before it was sucked on briefly. Hands explored his chest and back, then both slid down his ass to fondle his cheeks, fingers kneading and spreading the small globes like bread dough.

"Listen, doc. I figure we've got about three minutes before one or both of us passes out from the heat in here. Let's finish off this last soldier."

Air felt as if it had just fully returned to his sluggish lungs, but Parker couldn't find the energy to speak. He merely nodded, wondering how he was going to return the blowjob in his present position.

Dallas's commanding hands urged him to move, but not in the direction he anticipated.

"Turn over. On your knees, chest on the bench."

He was gently flipped and maneuvered into place. Any thoughts of protest got lost in the excitement of how inappropriate their behavior was. Parker grabbed the edge of the bench and rested his cheek on the smooth wood under his chest and face. His legs were still spread, stretched wide to bracket Dallas's lower body, rising cock and loose balls swinging free in the space created below his lower belly. He was completely exposed, open to anything the other man wanted, and barely able to tolerate the wait to find out what that was.

"Yeah, just like that. Let me see that tight, little ass of yours."

Hands ran the length of his back, rubbing his skin, the touch heavy, firm, reassuring. The hair of Dallas's thighs and groin scratched against Parker's legs and ass, then the heat of flesh pressed more fully against him, weighing him down. He felt blanketed by Dallas's body, covered from neck to knee in body heat. Skin on skin. Too much skin! This was going too far. Parker had never let sexual excitement over rule reason when his health was concerned.

"No! We can't. I don't… we don't have a condom. I won't—" He pushed up, but barely managed to raise more than a few inches. His lack of success had nothing to do with the strong arm on his back and everything to do with his limp and uncooperative limbs. In fact, Dallas rolled him a little onto his side and leaned in close to reassure him, understanding in the eyes under the lusty waggle of dark eyebrows.

"Relax, professor. We aren't going to. I'm clean, but I don't expect you to take my word for it." A rough tussle of his hair ended on a slow trail of fingers down his spine. It was seductive, coaxing. He was eased back on his stomach again. "Right now—

just trust me."

"What—"

"Relax. Trust me." Lips kissed down the path the fingertips had blazed on his skin. One cheek was gripped, his opening exposed. One rough swipe of a towel dried off his skin, teasing his asshole, making it wink and clench. "I've got this one covered."

The lips moved lower, not wasting time. Dallas's tongue darted out to lavish broad, wet laps over Parker's ass, then moved rapidly into the sensitive cleft. There it wiggled and stroked until it wormed its way to the puckered entrance. Once there the broad strokes vanished, replaced by a firm penetration that darted in and out of his body in a breathtakingly fast tempo. His heart matched the beat, his cock filling with each pounding note, his lungs struggling to keep up.

Parker gasped and tried not to move. He wasn't a virgin, but this was more than any of his previous fumbling, awkward lovers had tried in the past. This felt better than anything he had ever experienced before, mind blowing, thought destroying and completely amazing.

Then things got even better.

Suddenly the tongue disappeared. An insistent pressure breached his opening, filling him with something thicker, but still slick and warm, alive. The remaining brains cells not consumed by lust recognized it as a finger, long and dexterous. It stretched the ring of muscles at his opening, making them tingle with a delicious burn. A steady downward pressure and the digit pressed deeper into his channel, rubbing, curling, reaching until it bumped his prostate. His limbs stiffened and trembled, the lancing shock of electric stimulation lighting up his nerves.

He could feel Dallas's groin rubbing against his ass while strong palms manhandled his thighs together, the man's poker hot shaft trapped between them.

"That's it. Squeeze tight." Hot, muscular flesh smacked against the outside of Parker's quivering thighs, clamping them together like a vise. "Ah, yeah, just like that." Dallas leaned over him, his weight snug to Parker's back, one arm curled around Parker's waist to grab hold of Parker's straining dick.

"I'll do all the work." The cock slid deeper then out, the smooth silky glide of sweaty flesh on slippery flesh. "You just think about my hand up you tight little hole. Fingering you. Tickling that little cherry inside you. Think about that burn in your ass." The finger inside him stroked the swollen nub. Parker jumped, grunted and then moaned into the wood bench. "Think about what it looks like to come all over my hand."

Gripping the bench to keep from banging his head, Parker did what he was told, envisioning his cum spurting out into Dallas's massive hand, the creamy white juices stark against the tanned skin. He clenched his legs, thrilled when a gasp of pleasure hissed across his back.

"Goddamn, baby! Oh, yeah, that's my man." The strained, throaty tone made Parker's passion swell higher.

The sudden clarity that this powerful man had sought him out, checked him out and then chosen to fall to his knees just to please Parker was tremendously exciting. Parker's past sexual partners had been all equally matched with Parker in physical size and limited experience. As far as Parker was concerned this interlude was a once in a lifetime experience. He intended to enjoy every fleeting, sweaty second of it.

Flexing his spine, Parker pushed back into the wall of humping muscle pressed to his ass, primarily to enjoy the solid weight. He forced his legs a millimeter apart just to feel the power in the immediate resistance as Dallas pressed them back together again with his own thighs. He returned the pressure again, and was rewarded by the arm around his waist cinching closer. The fingers at his waist curling into his flesh in a possessive hold, reminding him there was a man attached to the cock slithering along the rarely touched regions of his ass, sliding under his balls and stroking alongside the stocky root of his own swollen cock.

Inspired, he wormed a hand down under his balls and managed to grab the head of Dallas's cock as it slid forward. He pinched the spongy tip, rubbing his fingertip around the crown's edge, teasing the flesh while the head twisted into the flat of his slick hot palm.

"Fuck, that's good!" Dallas grunted his surprise even while thrusting his hips harder to accommodate Parker's limited reach.

He'd never fucked like this, never imagined it was possible for such a benign position to give so much pleasure. It was unusual and bizarre, making it exotic and unique to Parker, heightening the thrill of 'fucking' with a total stranger in a forbidden location. The mental picture of what they must look like crouched over a bench, drenched in sweat, fucking like dogs in heat was almost enough to send him out of control. Dallas's hands beat out a sensual rhythm on Parker's body—one wrapped around Parker's cock, one hand shoved deep inside exploring his ass, massaging that sweet spot again and again.

Then Dallas added that last bit of stimulation Parker needed to make the vision complete. "Ah, baby, gotta pluck that cherry right off the branch for you."

The finger in his ass poked deeper and twisted, the tip flicking the nub inside, the callused pad swirled over the hardening kernel, each bold stroke sending flashes of intense heat coursing through Parker's shuddering body.

"Gonna make that sweet cherry mine, doc." There was a harsh grunt and the plumping motion between his legs increased, friction building. "Make you come. Make you mine." Dallas went stiff, frozen in place for a brief moment, then he began a frenzied pumping that would have jarred Parker's ribs across the bench if a protective arm wasn't taking the brunt of the action.

The movement forced the finger inside Parker's channel to press down, stretching his asshole and igniting the burn as it curled, adding weight to its maddening rub.

Parker couldn't tell if it was the penetration in his ass, the luscious tug-pull-twist on his dick, or the throaty, passionate groans and claiming words mumbled against his skin, or the combination of all them, but he came, hard and fast.

"Oh, god, oh god, oh god!" Small spurts of cum pumped out

his slit in thick pulses he could feel shooting up his shaft. At the same moment wet, sticky heat bathed his legs and balls. Dallas's cum rubbed into his skin as he filled the other man's hand.

The slap of wet skin on wet skin was audible, but muffled. Breathing became difficult but Parker ignored it. He groaned and spurted once more, spent but still tingling with the afterglow of a great orgasm, the best one he'd had in a long time. His eager cock held out for more, barely shrinking to a stubborn half-mast.

The weight on his back and thighs suddenly eased off. He expected to be left lying alone to regain his breath, but the restraining arm still around his waist was joined by another arm, pulling him off the bench and back to rest against a heaving chest.

"That, my dear doctor, was a hell of a ride." A quick kiss branded his neck then he was being pulled to his feet by insistent arms. "Need a shower and some cooler air. Then maybe, maybe we'll both survive. Come on."

Parker didn't think he could talk let alone walk but Dallas wouldn't take no for an answer. He had him on his feet, stumbling out the door quicker than Parker thought was humanly possible. The man had the constitution and strength of an ox. Parker felt like a marionette with no strings attached, weak and uncoordinated.

The room spun and tilted forty-five degrees, but Parker managed to keep on his feet all the way to the deserted showers. True, the tree limb wrapped around his waist helped, but he was certain his own desire not to be found naked and dead inside the corporate headquarters private steam room motivated him just as much. Vaguely he wondered why his logical, analytical mind accepted being found naked and dead in the shower as more of a natural event, but the rush of cool air that hit him just outside the sauna stole his thoughts.

He wasn't positive, but the fact that the next thing he remembered was the spray of cool water bubbling through his hair and down his neck made him suspect he'd blacked out for a moment. He became conscious of hands briskly scrubbing his legs, his back plastered to the cool tile of the shower wall, his weight held in place by a widespread palm on his sternum. Looking down, he could see only a dark head set on broad shoulders kneeling in front of him.

"Hey." It was weak and more mumble than he had hoped, but it was the all he could think of in the situation. He couldn't remember the man's name. And damned if his cock didn't see it as an opportunity to extend itself in welcome, as well. The dark head tilted and blue gray eyes smiled up at him. Dallas. Now it was coming back to him. The perfect name for a man as big as the state of Texas. "Dallas."

"Hey, back at you, doc." The smile extended to the man's full mouth, the perfect white teeth bright against the tan skin. "You should lean back there and take a minute. I don't think you've gotten your land legs."

Dallas stood, their groins touching, his hand still planted on Parker's chest. Parker could feel his heart pounding against the restraining palm.

"I think…" dark eyes watched him, their pupils dilated, a gleam of satisfaction in them coming closer and closer as Dallas narrowed the distance between their faces, open mouth hovering just above Parker's nervously twitching lips. Water hit Dallas's back, shielding Parker from the wide spray. "I think I… lost a little time between the sauna and here."

"Just a little." That wicked smile split Dallas's face. "It was cute."

"Cute?" As weak as he was, he still thought he managed to convey all the righteous indignation the comment deserved. He was a grown, albeit slight, man, and a respected scientist, a noted professional! He was not cute!

The palm slid up around his neck and into his hair. Dallas's hefty weight held him up and pinned him to the wall. The scent of sex and soap clung to Dallas despite the shower spray. Parker could smell his own cum on Dallas's breath, warm, musky, and damn it, he wanted to taste it, to know for himself what it was to savor himself on the big man's tongue. Even now, his gaze was glued to those dusky pink lips, drinking in the sounds they made, willing them to come closer. They quirked in another of those blinding, cocky, delighted smiles.

"Oh, yeah. All kind of confused and helpless." The lips came nearer. Not because Dallas had moved, but because he'd tugged Parker's head closer by his hair. "Like I said—cute."

Dark eyes studied his face. Parker's cock hardened to full length, slipping upward to poke into Dallas's balls. A quick shift of the big man's hips and they were suddenly cock to swollen cock.

Parker gasped, his sigh swallowed up by Dallas's hovering mouth. "I do like cute, professor. And helpless has its appeal." A light kiss touched one corner of Parker's mouth then the other. "That is, if I'm the one making you helpless."

He could feel Dallas's heartbeat echoing through his chest, a slow, powerful hammering pulse easily half Parker's current thundering rate. Parker felt like his own muscles were made of putty. Reluctantly, he had a twinge of appreciation for big guy's bear-like burliness preventing him from collapsing to the shower floor. He was surrounded by heat and muscle and strength, a blanket of flesh, also like a shield.

He must be used to toting dead weights around. He has all those muscles for some reason, right?

This guy was pure stamina. Probably all brawn and not much brain. Probably. Not that it mattered right now. He had developed a certain appreciation for the man's... brawn, but he did have a reputation to salvage here.

"Helpless? I'm not helpless. Or confused!" A massive hand cupped his ass and ground his leaking cock into the solid flesh of Dallas's groin. Cocks slid shaft to shaft, the tip of Parker's dick bumping slick skin and coarse, grating hair. The contrast of sensations was enough to jerk his hips in a desperate effort of their own to increase the contact. Grinding his cock into Dallas stole some of the authority from his grunted claim. "I'm—I'm not helpless!"

"It would be more convincing if you didn't say it like it was a question. But that's cute, too."

"I don't get confused!"

A light kiss landed on his chin and Parker found himself angling his face to encourage the lips to hit a better target. If there was one thing Parker did know how to do it was kiss. It was the foreplay he enjoyed the most and the thing many of his sexual partners wanted to do the least.

"Okay then. Disoriented. Discombobulated. Fucked stupid. Pick one you like best, doc." The hand in his hair grabbed the back of his head and tilted his face up sharply. Warm breath brushed his chin, then Dallas licked the underside, slow and rough, ending with a kiss to either side of Parker's quivering jaw.

A low, raw voice whispered in his ear. "While you're deciding on that, I'm going to pick something I like best."

Parker opened his mouth to object. Warm lips sealed over his protest and a tongue slipped between his lips. It teased the tender lining of his lower lip, the electric touch firm and wet. It licked his upper lip, then slid between his still parted teeth, exploring, tasting, moving to map the roof of his mouth. He couldn't hold back a moan, the sound vibrating in his throat, encouraging the invasion. His tongue battled with Dallas's and they fell into a rhythm of stroke and rub, their hips mimicking the dance, cocks and tongues dueling, sliding, grinding against each other, neither looking for dominance, happy with an equal play of give and receive.

Parker lost himself in the kiss—the subtle exchange of power, the tender caress of lips, the gentle sucking of his tongue, the wet warmth that reminded him he was in the arms of a man who seemed to value him for something other than his brains or his corporate position. Dallas had taken the time to learn about him, not just his intimidating elevated IQ or his high security, high paying job, but about him. And miraculously, the man had looked past all of the things that usually turned off all but the most scientific minded of potential lovers. Dallas seemed amused by Parker's lack of social skills and obvious inexperience, possibly even… attracted by them. It was apparent the man was definitely attracted to Parker's body.

The kiss turned ravenous. Dallas cupped the back of Parker's head, refusing to allow him to break off the embrace. Not that Parker had any plans of doing that. It felt like Dallas was trying to suck Parker's cock off by way of his tongue.

Drawing Parker's tongue into his mouth, Dallas sucked and stroked to the same rhythm he worked their cocks with, one large firm hand wrapped around Parker's dick while his own ground against Parker's flat belly.

Water splashed and trickled between them, teasing Parker's skin, a sharp contrast to the firm tugs, tight massaging grip and hungry, heated kisses. His ass was flattened against the cold tile but his head was held in a protective grip off the hard surface. The steaming shower spray felt tepid compared to the building heat coursing though his body. Parker was lightheaded, his climax coiling behind his balls, his cock stiff and swollen. His mind linked the sensation of the warm lips ravishing his mouth directly to his groin, the bobbing sucking sensation reaching down to encompass his shaft, every swipe of Dallas's wet, rough tongue interpreted as a pre-cum slicked tug on his cock.

Suddenly Dallas groaned into the kiss, the sound low, primal and satisfied. New warmth smeared into Parker's belly, the drawn out groan vibrating through their chests. The realization their kiss had been enough to send Dallas off triggered Parker's orgasm. He shuddered, fingers digging into muscle, back arched to shove his hips and dick hard into Dallas's flesh. The hand around his cock disappeared, only to reappear a second later cupping his ass and pulling him painfully closer.

Even after the glow of climax faded the kiss continued, slowly gentling until it was barely a light touch. The pressure on his head slackened as Dallas kissed his way over Parker's face to nuzzle at the soft skin behind his ear.

His blood pressure roared in his head but Parker still heard

Dallas utter what sounded like a fervent oath.

"Christ, you're a keeper, doc."

He didn't get a chance to comment. Still holding onto Parker's head and ass, Dallas swung them around so that the shower hit them full force, stripping away the sweat and cum. Parker stuck his head under the spray, shivering a little when Dallas turned down the temperature. The cool water brought a refreshing burst of energy back to his lethargic mind and limbs. He pulled away from Dallas's now unneeded grip, nodded without looking at his partner and hurriedly left the shower stall.

The sound of the shower being turned off and muffled footsteps followed him to the lockers. He picked up a towel off the bench and dried off in record time, wrapping it around his waist before turning around to face his companion. He hoped the sudden flush making his face warm would be attributed to the heat of the water or their recent exertions, but one look at Dallas's concerned expression and that hope died.

"Hey, you don't have to run away or be embarrassed about this. Come on, doc."

The man stood three feet away, a puzzled, sympathetic frown marring his rugged face. Dallas skipped any pretence at drying off, merely securing a towel low on his hips with a casual wrap and tuck. The still healing, shiny pink scar on the man's solid hip and thigh showed between the open edges. Parker found himself hoping the whole thing would give in to gravity and fall away, allowing him one last, full view of the man.

Dallas took a step toward him and Parker held out a restraining hand. "Who are you? Where do you work here?"

"Don't freak out on me, professor. You've got nothing to worry about. Nothing to be embarrassed about."

"Who are you? You look like a bodyguard."

"What? No. Christ." Dallas planted his hands on his hips, a reluctant twist to his mouth. After studying Parker for several tense seconds, he shook his head once, wasted a little more time rubbing a hand over his face, then nodded. "Fine. I'd rather have done this over breakfast or my place or your place, but… fine. You're obviously feeling used and embarrassed about this for some reason." He raised one defiant finger in the air and pointed it at Parker, lips pulled tight in a straight line. "You have no right to feel that way, either. This wasn't a drive by."

"Drive by? I don't know what that means. And I'm not embarrassed."

"Drive by. One night stand. Don't you ever go out socially?" Dallas straightened his shoulders as if he was adjusting a suit coat, a gesture Parker found puzzling considering the man was wearing only a towel. "Listen, doc. I don't do drama and I don't do meaningless casual. I'm an ex-Army Ranger. I'm a serious guy. And yes, you are embarrassed. Your face is so red you look sunburnt."

"That doesn't tell me who you are or your function in the company. And I'm not embarrassed."

"I don't work here."

Parker stepped back a pace. A flash of trepidation washed over him, but then he remembered the cardkey with Dallas's picture on it he had seen the one evening when they had arrived at the gym entrance at the same. Parker hadn't been able to read the name on it but the picture was definitely this man. Dallas had open the keyed, locked door for him so someone had cleared him through the company's rigorous security screening and allowed him access to the building.

"Don't get all freaked out on me, doc." Dallas leaned against the lockers, his stance as casual and unthreatening as a life-sized statue of Hercules could be in a confined space. "I'm an agent with the FBI. Just transferred to the DC Bureau from New York. Yes, you are."

Ex-Army Ranger. Current FBI agent. No wonder the guy was built like a freight train. That was unexpected. Cool, but still unexpected. "What's the FBI doing here, Agent Dallas?"

"Agent Wade. Dallas is my first name."

"Agent Wade. Wade?" Parker blinked and self-consciously

stood a little taller. He had to make a grab for his towel when the slight movement sent it slithering off his narrow hips. "Like in Austin Wade? The company's CEO?"

"Yeah. Just like that. My parents are from Texas." A wicked smirk smoothed away the pursed frown and defensive glare. "Austin's my older brother."

He motioned vaguely at the scar on his hip and thigh. "I'm on medical leave, recuperating from a… work related injury. Austin suggested I work out here for a couple of weeks while I get settled into the area, instead of joining a gym. It works for me." He grabbed another clean towel and mopped off his face, running it over his short dark hair, leaving it standing tall in a rakish, spiky look. Looking back up, he caught Parker's still stunned gaze. "Worked out in a couple of good ways, if you know what I mean."

Parker could feel his eyes pop open wide. "I just…." He pointed in the direction of the sauna and then the shower. "With my boss's brother? A Federal agent? On company property?" His voice rose an octave with each question but the last came out a whisper. "Holy crap!"

A genuinely amused smile beamed across Dallas's face, a gleam of shared secrets in his eyes. "I won't tell, if you won't tell."

Still wide eyed, Parker fidgeted but managed to hold Dallas's gaze. This was the best thing that had happened to him in years. Maybe his lifetime. This guy was a freaking walking, talking statue of David. Plus he was funny, sincere, and oddly tender during sex for the he-man type. It didn't hurt any that his smile made firecrackers explode in Parker's stomach and his cock act like it had a permanent penile implant jacking it up.

Parker took a hesitant step forward, lessening the distance between them. "I'm not worried about telling."

"Yeah?"

"Yeah… ah, no." Parker shook his head, too distracted to work out the tough guy shorthand Dallas used to communicate with.

"I mean yeah. I mean, I'm not worried about that."

"No?" Dallas's expression turned cautious as Parker took another step toward him, but the gleam in his eyes said 'bring it on' when Parker let the hastily gathered edges of the falling towel slip from his fingers. "What are you worried about then?"

"Not worried. And not embarrassed." He stepped into Dallas's personal space, immediately reaching up with one hand to tug the man's grinning face down to his level. He pulled at the tucked hem of Dallas's towel until is fell to the floor at their feet.

"Just... formulating a hypothesis on how best to execute my approach. You're twice my size. It presents... logistical problems." He tugged on Dallas's shoulders until the man lowered his lips to graze over Parker's talking mouth. "Unless of course, you'd prefer to continue in the role of dominant aggressor and," he swallowed hard, his breathing growing shallow and rapid, his tongue darting out to hesitantly lick at Dallas's waiting, silent mouth, "and use your considerable strength to hold me, equalizing the differences between—"

"You were a lot quieter when you were confused." A blistering kiss prevented any response. When the embrace finally broke, slightly breathless, Dallas added, "But this is pretty cute, too."

"I'm not—" Parker hoped the flush burning his cheeks would be mistaken for embarrassment instead of the burst of excitement that rushed through him.

"Yeah. You are. Small, sexy and smarter than shit. And clueless and confused and damn cute. Learn to live with it, doc." Dallas stroked his thumb down the arch of Parker's neck, chin to sternum, a slow, tender, appreciative touch. "I plan on learning to."

SOUTH OF THE BORDER

Gabriel eased down into the large hot tub, letting his sore body adjust to the sizzling heat. He inhaled and the scented steam rose up, invading his nostrils and his mind. The heavy tropical fragrance called up recent memories of late nights on sandy beaches surrounded by exotic flowers and pounding surf. The sand wasn't the only thing getting a pounding the last three nights.

He wiggled his butt on the hard wooden seat, awakening a dull throb that resulted from those memories. Sighing at the satisfied feeling the ache gave him, Gabriel relaxed and leaned back against the tub's sides. His eyes were closed and he let his arms float just under the water's surface. Scooting his butt forward, he splayed his legs to let the soothing heat reach every submerged body part. He flexed his legs slightly, enjoying the gentle tug and pull of the swirling, fluid warmth over his open groin.

Unfazed by displaying his nude body as only the blind can be, Gabriel had shed his clothes in the adjoining bedroom. Then walked through the hotel suite, and out to the private courtyard and the waiting tub completely naked. His clothing was in the bedroom, but a handgun was never far from his reach.

The San Francisco Police Department could make him retire after his blinding, but they couldn't take away years of undercover training, a finely honed sense of self-preservation and a ton of bad habits. Years undercover had earned him a whole lot of enemies that weren't going to go away just because he couldn't see them anymore.

The bag of doctored heroin that exploded in his face during his last case left Gabriel Sandalini terribly vulnerable. It took away his sight and a lot of his independence, both for good. But it also gave him two things—a renewed sense of what he wanted from life and someone special to share it with.

The soft sound of cloth rustling captured Gabriel's attention and he smiled as the water rolled and swayed with the addition of another body, a large body by the rise in the water level and the force of the waves. He stayed perfectly still and let the new arrival come to him.

A large, warm mass of firm muscle and sinewy flesh flowed in between his legs and lodged itself tightly against his sprawled lower half. He identified the familiar scent of sweat and coconut oil milliseconds before two callused hands slid up his arms, over his shoulders and around his neck. Once there, strong fingers kneaded and rubbed the tightly knotted muscles at the base of his skull.

"Umm. God, Tony, that feels great." Gabriel sighed and melted into the greedy fingertips. "Uh, Christ, that's good." He rolled his head and let his chin length black hair fall down over his bowed face. He groaned and shifted his groin closer to Antonio's. "God, yeah, right there." Arching his neck until it cracked, he let his head loll back to rest on the edge of the tub. He pushed his hips firmly against the other man's growing erection and wiggled his ass to encourage the swell.

"You're tired" The fingertips moved to caress Gabriel's high cheekbones, then strayed down to stroke gently at his lips. The low, rich tones of Antonio's Spanish accent rolled off his cultured tongue like honey dripping off one of the sun-baked tin roofs that dotted the hillsides on the fringes of town.

Just the sound of the Spaniard's voice made Gabriel's cock swell and his spine tingle, like it had the first time he heard it two years ago.

"I'm not that tired." Gabriel wrapped his legs around Antonio's nude body and hissed at the pleasurable sensation of the hot water swirling around their touching cocks. "Don't think I've ever been *that* tired." He mumbled the word into Antonio's mouth before darting his tongue down the man's throat.

Grabbing a handful of soft dark hair, Antonio forced Gabriel's head back and down, taking control of the ardent kiss. His thickly muscled arms pulled Gabriel farther off the seat drawing the smaller man's hips forward until they barely rested on the hard surface.

Clamping Gabriel's writhing, clutching body hard against his chest without releasing his hold on Gabriel's hair, Antonio slid one hand under the water, down a firm butt cheek and along the crease that divided his lover's fine ass. His fingers unerringly found the opening to Gabriel's body and he probed and stroked the fluttering muscle, delighting in the low moans of arousal it caused in the other man. Resting the tip of one thick finger just inside Gabriel's ass, Antonio pulled Gabriel back from the kiss by his hair.

Gabriel groaned in frustration and humped his groin into Antonio's, grinding their cocks together. The heated swirling of the hot tub's scented water sent a burst of tropical aroma into the air and the added motion teased at the undersides of their swollen cocks. Gabriel panted and licked his swollen lips.

Sensing the heat of Antonio's face only inches from his, he located the man's mouth by the sound of Antonio's lightly gasped breaths. Surging forward, Gabriel licked the sweat off the man's top lip, savoring the salty/coconut flavor that was Antonio's alone.

"I want you to fuck me," Gabriel grunted and pulled at the other man's lower lip with his teeth, leaving it red and swollen.

"You are always in a hurry, querido." Antonio's talented hand kneaded the scalp under its palm soothingly, his lips laying a path of tiny kisses up Gabriel's arched neck. He interspersed the kisses with an occasional sharp nip, nuzzling his nose into the long, baby fine hair in his hand. "I may not be ready quite yet."

Moving his hands from the big man's back to grip his broad shoulders, Gabriel used the rock hard slabs of muscle and bone to pull his own slender body up and then down, forcing Antonio's cock to slide under his sac and up to his finger-stuffed opening.

"You feel ready to me, bucko." Gabriel bounced on the iron hard shaft resting against his ass, trying to force it inside along with the blunt fingertip. "Come on, man. Make me feel it for a month." He shoved down hard. "It'll help me remember you while you're gone doing that favor for Briggs."

Antonio removed his finger from Gabriel's ass and grabbed both of his lover's squirming hips, stilling them, holding the man immobile. "If you do not want me to go, I will not go, Gabriel." He pressed his lips to Gabriel's ear, his rich, soft Spanish accent rumbling into his lover's damp, hair. "You do not need to punish yourself because you can not go with me." He tightened his grip when Gabriel struggled to free himself, relenting only when the resistance stopped. He tried to keep his tone reasonable. "It is only a few days."

Refusing to talk about anything but sex, Gabriel wormed a hand down between their plastered together bodies and began jerking himself off, setting up a wave of rolling water all a round them. "Fine, be a fuckhead then, you ungrateful spick." Despite the biting words, he rested his forehead against Antonio's chin, melting into the big man's bulky frame, his long hair falling down over his sweat-streaked face. "If you won't fuck me raw for my sake," he panted, "do it for yourself. Give you something to remember me by."

Sitting back on his heels, Antonio lowered them down farther into the water. "Sometimes you are an incorrigible asshole, my love." He bit Gabriel's ear, then tipped him back against the seat and pulled the smaller man's hips against his groin, balancing Gabriel on the edge of the wooden seat.

"Fine." Gabriel grunted and squirmed, pressing hard on the tip of Antonio's stout cock. "Now get *inside* my asshole and let's do this going away party right." Quivering, Gabriel shoved his face into the crook of Antonio's neck, then whispered in a choked tremble, "I'm done talking about it."

Understanding the underlying, unspoken message of insecurity and fear, Antonio ran a soothing hand down Gabriel's sweaty back, clasped the shaking man tightly to him and whispered into the thick, dark hair under his jaw, "For now, for now."

Rising up, Antonio breached the tight ring of Gabriel's ass with one powerful thrust, gripping his lover's waist to keep him in place. He buried Gabriel's face against his chest, muffling the shout and groan of pained delight from his lover. Wiry legs wrapped around his own waist and Antonio concentrated on setting up a rhythm to match Gabriel's frantic humping.

Knowing from long experience of the younger man's need for a forceful, nearly brutal coupling when emotionally upset, Antonio let lose and gave him what he wanted.

Embracing Gabriel's entire body, Antonio slammed into him, dragging Gabriel up his cock to the tip, then slamming him back down to the root of the large shaft. He closed his eyes and focused on the blinding jolts of electric blue pleasure that shot out of his cock and up his spine. "Holy Mother, nothing compares to the feeling of being inside you, Gabriel, nothing. Even like this." Antonio increased the strength of his plunges.

"Pound me senseless, lover. You've only got four of them to beat." The bitterness was still there, but raw lust had smoothed the edges and Antonio could hear the true love and deep affection in Gabriel's voice.

Each thrust forced a sharp grunt from Gabriel, but he gripped Antonio's shoulders in a white-knuckled hold with one hand that refused to weaken as he held on for the ride.

The hot tub's bubbling surface swayed and churned, waves breaking over the sides and baptizing the nearby patio furniture and plants. The scent of tropical flowers became nearly suffocating in intensity.

Antonio opened his eyes to see Gabriel's tightly clenched eyes and arched neck. The younger man's head was thrown back and his body held rigid, meeting each brutal thrust with a grind of his hips. Antonio felt the stirring of orgasm building in the base of his cock and increased the tempo, a hand falling between them to join Gabriel's already frantically stroking palm. He added his own massive fist to the pumping action and felt Gabriel contract the muscles in his ass in response to the added stimulation.

The tight, hot sheath of Gabriel's ass milked his shaft, spasming in a never-ending stream of contractions. Feeling the need to cum racing past the point of no return, Antonio nuzzled Gabriel's head up and claimed his mouth, swallowing the protest and groans along with Gabriel's tongue. Pulsing into the burning tunnel of heat, Antonio slammed Gabriel down one last time, embedding his cock deep into Gabriel's core, pumping him full of cum at one end and devouring him from the other.

The satiny rod of flesh in his hand jerked and spurted hot milky juice that was washed away as fast as it erupted. Gabriel's erection faded and Antonio forced the fingers of Gabriel's hand to intertwine with his own as the shrinking organ slide from their fingers.

Slowly withdrawing his still half-hard cock from Gabriel's ass, Antonio rubbed over the small of Gabriel's back, soothing and gentling his moody lover. Never releasing Gabriel from the blistering kiss, Antonio rested Gabriel more comfortably on the seat. He eased out of the kiss with a series of soft pecks to Gabriel's bruised mouth, but remained leaning over his exhausted lover, their hands still entwined.

"Better?" His gravelly, soft voice reflected the depth of his understanding of Gabriel's needs. So much so, his question was answered with a whimper from his usually emotionally guarded, iron-willed partner. Taken back by the sound, Antonio smiled in relief when the expected, foulmouthed reply came a heartbeat later.

"Fuck off, asshole. You aren't that good." A small sound that could have been a sniffle made Antonio tip Gabriel's head so he could see Gabriel's expressive face.

"Isn't it time for you to leave yet?" Gabriel muttered.

Antonio smirked at the man's capacity for biting sarcasm. He wrapped his arms around Gabriel's pliant body, enjoying the way the smaller man instantly melted into him, plastering their water-drenched bodies together. He stepped from the tub, maneuvering Gabriel, guiding him where he wanted him to walk. He rubbed his jaw over the side of Gabriel's head resting on his shoulder, moving clumps of wet hair aside to find the small shell of one ear.

He tightened his grip and began walking to their bedroom,

mindless of the trail of water they left in their wake. Letting all of the love he had for this amazing, damaged man settle in his voice, Antonio growled softly into the revealed ear, tugging on the tiny lobe with his teeth.

"Not yet, Gabriel. The end of all time has not yet arrived."

JACKSON
& NICK

Storming Love: Wild Fire

The minute the automatic doors slid open and Jackson Kain stepped through them, he was transported to another world. The air smelled like alcohol, disinfectant, and a faint acidic odor most people couldn't pinpoint. Jackson knew it was the mixed aromas of stomach acid and blood. It always seemed to linger in the halls no matter what time of day it was. He had long ago mentally labeled it 'ode de emergence'. Some might be turned off by it but, to him, and every New York firefighter, it was the scent of help, healing, and hope. Lives were saved here every minute of every day.

Under the sickly, luminescent whiteness of fluorescent lighting, pale gray walls stood in stark contrast to the flashes of bright colored scrubs and white lab coats of the ER staff. They hustled between lines of stretchers parked against the walls or pushed into curtained cubicles, accessing, monitoring, and calming patients according to their degree of need.

Portable X-ray machines trolled by, lumbering ogres that had only one very slow speed. Instrument carts seemed to block Jackson's way every dozen feet or so. With practiced ease, he headed toward the center of the storm. He weaved in and out of the obstacle course, his six foot four frame and broad muscled body exhibiting a grace most people wouldn't guess at. It didn't hurt any that people naturally stepped aside to let him by, most responding to his charming smile and chiseled good looks as much as his size.

He couldn't count the number of times he'd been down these halls over the last ten years for one reason or another, most of them bad. Smoke inhalation, burns, injuries from falling debris, or just checking up on a victim or co-worker. Emergency Rooms were a fact of life for a fireman, especially in a large city. He'd come to think of them as a necessary but unhappy extension of his workplace.

Though as of late, his reasons for visiting made him look forward to the controlled chaos happening around him. The 'reason' was at the center of the chaos, he was sure. The same reason was at the center of his own personal chaos as well.

Self-conscious, he pulled at his right earlobe and ran his hand over his moderately short, black hair, letting the waves of noise roll over him with practiced ease, soaking it in, letting it fuel his determination. Handsome could only get you so far in a relationship, then substance and effort were the key to winning over a new boyfriend. For the first time in his life, Jackson wanted this budding relationship to last and grow into something permanent. And *that* was challenging as hell. Five alarm fires had nothing on the scorching power of love! He tugged at his earlobe again, but never broke his stride down the hallway.

Rhythmic, beeping machines were occasionally replaced with the anxious buzzing of insistent alarms. Multiple conversations at various levels of volume and intensity hammered at him from all sides with the intermittent groan or cry of pain. All of it was underscored by the thudding, sticky sound of gurney wheels on old linoleum. His pulse matched the rhythmic undercurrent.

Heart pounding in his chest, Jackson felt the familiar adrenaline rush building. He'd been out of the field for six weeks recuperating from a work injury and it was beginning to show. He was ready to get back into action soon. He missed his job.

Soon, but not *just* yet. He had two more weeks off and he knew what he wanted to do with them.

Jackson pushed the clamor into a subdued murmur surrounding him, just like he did with the roar and heat of a fire. *Control your response to the environment and you control the situation.* That motto had saved his life too many times to count and now he hoped it would help get his future on track.

Taking a deep breath, Jackson concentrated on slowing his adrenaline response and turned his impressive frame around the next corner, heading toward the central nurse's station. Passing the first cubicle, he was blindsided by a petite, blonde whirlwind. Christie Carlyse, ER nurse and confident to most of the unit staff. He had to grab her by the arms to keep her from falling over after she bounced off his side.

"Hey, there, crazy lady!" He gave her his best grin and winked as he set her on her feet. Christie laughed, squeezed his hand then pushed a strand of blonde hair that had escaped its ponytail back behind her ear. A purple stethoscope hung from her neck, tangled in her name tag lanyard, bright against her navy scrubs. Christie's husband, Jim, was one of Jackson's fellow firefighters and a close friend.

"I knew we would see you tonight." She arched her eyebrows suggestively. A gurney rushed by them and she darted to one side to evade the wheels. "He hasn't taken a break all shift. You are just the thing he needs to steal him away for a few minutes." Her turquoise-blue eyes grew serious. "Twenty minutes, no less. We're getting hammered tonight and he's getting the worst of it." She spun off down the hall then turned back, still speed-walking backward. "And get him to eat something! Find him some of whatever you eat, Mountain Man! He's too thin." Pausing, she leaned forward, lowering her voice just enough to still be heard over the din of the hallway, "If you two ever get to third base, he'll snap like kindling wood!" Her fingers wiggled in the air in his direction then she ducked into the cubicle to her right, disappearing behind a curtain.

Stifling a snicker, Jackson nodded a hello to a passing, eavesdropping orderly. The man's tired face lit up. Jackson was used to having that effect on people and he tried to be mindful of it. Now thirty-two, he'd been blessed with good looks and a towering, muscled body since his teenage years. Most of the time it was a positive attribute but, sometimes, like in matters of the heart, it worked against him. Some people, people who mattered, couldn't believe attractive equaled trustworthy. It was a situation he needed to gain control of and tonight was the start of his plan to do just that.

If he could weave his way through all these bodies.

He moved to one side to let two police officers lead a man in handcuffs to a bench against the far wall. The faint smell of pepper spray trailed after them. He nodded hello to both officers. They each acknowledged him with a jut of the chin or a nod. Emergency services were a small world. Cops, firemen, EMTs, hospital staff, they all inhabited the same world.

Jackson knew all of the staff working tonight. He was friendly with most and socialized with a few of them. Good people. One of the new nurses, Vicky, around twenty-one he guessed, gave him a shy wave from behind a med cart. He rewarded her with a wink that made her blush, giggle, and turn away.

He'd always thought this ER had a higher than normal percentage of pretty nurses. Some good-looking male staff, too. Still, there was only one person he made visits to the ER on his time off to see and it wasn't a nurse, an orderly, or a tech.

He needed to find himself a doctor.

A thirty-two-year-old, dark-haired, deep blue-eyed, outrageously gorgeous, brilliant, dedicated, compassionate, OCD but relationship gun-shy, doctor named Nick Kirby. Just thinking about Nick kicked Jackson's adrenaline response back into high gear. His pulse throbbed in his neck and…a few other places. What could he say? He was a man of action.

CHAPTER TWO

"The radiology computers are down, Amy." A tired sigh told the story that this was not an infrequent event. "Please see if someone can get them up. If they can't do it in the next five minutes, I need actual physical films taken on room five and brought straight to me. I believe he has a right pneumothorax which cannot wait for hours." A second sigh turned into a small yawn. "And please ask his nurse to set up for a chest tube insertion. I think it's Becka."

Dr. Nicolas Kirby turned away from the blank monitor to give the unit secretary a smile. He hoped he didn't look as exhausted as his voice had sounded. He was only part of the way through the shift and he felt like he had already worked a double. "And ask the lab to rush his results. It would be nice to have them when I see the X-rays." Amy turned toward him and he added, "Sorry, didn't mean to snap at you. Just tired of the computers always going down at the worst possible times."

"Face it. You're just tired period, Nick. It's been hell here all month." Amy White's fingers flew over the keyboard as she talked. Fifty-something, hefty in the hips and endowed with the ability to keep track of every item, report, patient, and staffer in the department, Amy was everyone's mother. "Just focus on that vacation you've got starting tomorrow."

"Yeah, maybe." Nick's comment was so soft, Amy didn't react.

Glancing up to the heavens, her eyes got a starry, school-girl look in them. "Two weeks in the wilds of sunny California with your own *highly attractive* in a Gerald-Butler-way-grizzly bear." Amy gave him a knowing glance. "If I was spending that long with a man like Jackson Kain, I wouldn't be able to walk when I got back." She sent one pencil thin eyebrow rocketing toward her graying hairline. "If you know what I mean, doctor."

She turned away before he could answer, then spun her chair back, the swivel creaking in protest at the sudden movement.

"What do you mean 'maybe'?" So she had heard him.

Nick rolled his head on his shoulders, trying to buy time, hoping someone would call his name or an alarm would sound to draw him away from Amy's unrelenting, squinted stare. When an interruption didn't come, he caught her gaze for a moment before lowering his head to flex his sore neck muscles again.

Knowing Amy wouldn't give up now that he had opened the door to the subject; he threw his answer out there. "I haven't decided if I'm going to go." There was silence for a heartbeat or two.

"You leave tomorrow. You have plane tickets." Her voice was very quiet but it cut through the constant background noise and went straight to his heart. "Jackson has planned this whole vacation just for you. He's a good man."

"I know." Nick felt color rise in his face. His cheeks burned and his throat closed a bit. A tightness gripped his chest. He felt a little lightheaded, just the way he did every time he was near open water—or Jackson Kain. Out of control, seized by an adrenaline rush. Out of fear or excitement, he never knew which.

"I know, Amy. He's a great guy. More than a great guy." It was hard to speak, his throat was so dry. "I…like him…a lot." He thought he might throw up for a minute but chalked it up to six cups of coffee on an empty stomach in the last four hours. Bad coffee. "But two whole weeks? No one else around? What if things don't work out?" He shook his head, more to clear it than anything else. "Dating is fine. A few hours here. A few hours there. But twenty-four-seven? It might ruin everything."

Amy snorted an indelicate sound. "Don't be ridiculous, Nicky. What's not to like? You're a brilliant doctor, a caring, generous person, and, if I had a daughter, I'd pray you'd turn straight and marry her so I could have outrageously gorgeous grandbabies."

It was Nick's turn to snort in disbelief. "For starters, I'm work obsessed. Most people have trouble finding room in my world. I can't just walk away from what I do. Like now." He gestured at the chaos surrounding him, the staff hustling by, the patients piling up in the hall. "I shouldn't even be leaving tomorrow. You'll be shorthanded. I shouldn't take a vacation in July. It's too busy." He caught the silent disapproval on Amy's time-worn face. "I can't help worrying." He pinched his lower lip, a nervous habit since childhood. "The list of potential relationship issues is endless." Nick ran his fingers through his dark waves, tugging at the long bits at the back of his neck. He hadn't even had time for a decent haircut. He straightened his tie, then smoothed a slight, elegant hand over the tailored contours of his dress shirt. "I like things the way they are—comfortable."

"Safe, you mean." Amy tapped a fingernail on the laminate countertop to gain his attention. "You worry too much. Stop planning everything. Sometimes you just have to jump into life. You can't keep a man like Jackson Kain at arm's length forever, Nicolas Kirby." Picking up the ringing phone, she glanced up the hallway as she turned away, adding in a more muted tone, "Grizzly approaching the campsite at two o'clock." She looked at Nick then indicated the side hallway with a tip of her head. "You need to dive in, darling. The water is *fine*." She closed her eyes, a rapt expression on her face. "So *very* fine."

Nick stood up to meet the rapidly approaching figure towering over everyone else in the hallway. He murmured to no one in particular, "Just wish I'd learned how to swim."

CHAPTER THREE

Just as he rounded the corner near the central nurse's station, Jackson caught sight of his target. Nicolas Kirby stood up from one of the wheeled desk chairs behind the short wall dividing the staff from everyone else milling around the halls. Jackson couldn't hold back the smile that pulled so hard at his face that his cheeks felt like they belonged on a cartoon chipmunk.

He was even more delighted when an answering soft, pleased expression lit up Nick's face when he met his gaze. It was a terrific smile, but it didn't erase the look of worry on the doctor's face. Since the first day they'd met, Nick's eyes seemed perpetually shadowed, almost sad. Whatever the reason for that lingering sadness, Jackson was determined to be the man that vanquished it.

They had worked out together on a few occasions, so Jackson knew Nick was athletic under his dress slacks, tailored shirt, and tie. At 5'9, Nick's slender, lightly-muscled frame was both sinuous and sensuous. His thick, wavy, dark chestnut hair framing a delicately-boned, handsome face grabbed attention on first glance, but it was the crystal clear, deep blue eyes that held it. Jackson felt like he could drown in them if he wasn't careful.

"What's up, Doc?" Jackson strode up to the edge of the half wall and leaned on it, shortening the distance between himself and Nick. He didn't let Nick answer before jumping in with, "Let's take a walk. Christie says I need to drag you out of here for a break."

He looked at Amy and gave her a flirtatious wink. He was rewarded with a beatific smile and a slight flushing of her powdered cheeks.

Amy reached out and slapped his arm resting on the countertop in front of her. "Don't ply your many persuasive charms on me, Jackson Kain." She indicated Nick with a sharp, sideways glance. "I know your heart belongs to another." She grew serious for a moment. "Though you might have to explain that to him."

Jackson squeezed her hand which she had left lying on his arm to reassure her then turned his attention back to Nick.

"What? I can't just...leave." Nick sputtered and gestured at the uncommunicative computer monitor before him and the white board full of patients' names, some written in the margins for patients in the hallways with no rooms. He turned back to his monitor as two other physicians, Dr. White and Dr. Kas, arrived, each from different ends of the station. "Not...right now."

Four nurses flashed through the sudden jumble of bodies, grabbing charts, handing off lab reports, and one pulled Dr. White back out into the hall with her. They disappeared almost within seconds.

"Maybe I can take a break later." Nick tapped relentlessly on the enter key of the keyboard in front of him, with no effect. The screen stayed blank. "If we ever get films, room five probably needs a chest tube. I haven't even seen his labs yet."

The noise level raised a few decibels with all the extra people in the small space. Dr. Kas spoke up over the dim, "Go take a break, Nick. I'm free for the moment, I can do the tube." He picked up room five's chart from the rack and began looking through it.

Nick hesitated, uncertainty written all over his tired face. "Did Becka set up for the insertion?" The question was thrown out for anyone to answer, but Nick didn't wait for one. He began to list all the unresolved obstacles in his way at the moment. "Respiratory was in there when I examined him, but X-ray needs to get me pictures. I can't do this blind." He pinched his lower lip so long Jackson thought it would be bruised in the morning. Nick sighed, "I...We can't move ahead if I—we...can't see all the potential problems."

Stepping around the short wall, Jackson latched onto Nick's arm.

"Wait. I can't just—"

He tugged and Nick moved forward with him, allowing himself to be lead down the hall and out the emergency doors, into the warm July night.

"Kas said he has it covered. Amy said to go. Christie said to go." Jackson threw his arm over Nick's shoulders, relieved when he felt the tension begin to relax out of them. "Keep walking, Doc. I need you to make it through this shift so we can catch our ten a.m. flight." Jackson pulled Nick over to a shadowed corner of the building and drew him in close, using his larger frame to block them from any prying eyes. "Two weeks of romantic romping in the beautiful California wilderness. Just you, me, and the mountain lions."

"About that—"

Jackson loved the way Nick's breath caught when he ran his hand over Nick's face, stroking his cheek and caressing his neck. Nick's neck was a sensitive spot that never failed to evoke a reaction. The way the other man's lips, flush and full, parted to let his tongue moisten them was irresistible.

The kiss was long, more sensuous than the setting usually allowed them. More direct and demanding than Nick usually allowed, especially at the hospital. Jackson could feel Nick pouring himself into it, almost like he was searching for some kind of answer in the embrace, the courage to give over more of himself. Jackson tightened his hold, pressing Nick against the cool brick wall behind them.

They had indulged in some sexual play over the last six weeks, but Jackson knew Nick was holding back a part of himself, physically and emotionally. A part Jackson was desperate for Nick to share with him.

He may have been hesitant to leave the ER but, once they were alone, Nick threw himself into the moment. He pulled Jackson's head down to gain better access to his mouth, deepening the kiss.

Jackson countered by lifting him up, aware the other man's feet were off the ground. Nick didn't seem to care. Jackson slid one hand down to grasp Nick's ass, rewarded and inspired to continue massaging the taut flesh when Nick moaned into his mouth. Jackson shifted his stance to let his stiffening cock rise, delighted by Nick's slender, growing shaft nudging his body through their clothing.

Now this was a kiss to remember.

Suddenly, Nick drew back to stare wide-eyed at him. "Mountain lions? Seriously?"

Jackson pulled him back until their lips were brushing each other's. "Don't worry, city boy. I'll protect you." Jackson locked gazes with Nick, lips brushing together, teasing, tempting as he spoke. "From anything. Anytime. Forever." He saw a tiny spark of hesitation return to Nick's eyes and he gently added, "If you want."

There wasn't any conversation by that corner of the building for some time.

CHAPTER FOUR

The drive up the mountain had been a little harrowing, the road winding, rutted and too narrow for Nick, but Jackson drove the rented Land Rover like a pro.

"You're good at this." Jackson gave him a questioning look so Nick elaborated. "Driving these roads. Anyone would think you grew up here."

"Wish I had. New York City is home but I love coming here. I've been coming up to Cousin Greg's cabin every year since I can remember. My mom's cousin, really. He travels so much now, he hardly ever uses it himself anymore. We'd hunt and fish, swim in the lake behind the cabin and ice fish in the winter. Holidays are great here if the road is passable." It was easy to hear the fondness in the big man's voice. "I think it's where I got the love of being so physical. Conquering the great outdoors!"

"So this is why you grew so big. All that fresh air and mountain climbing." Nick couldn't help taking an admiring glance down the other man's body before moving his attention back to the lush world outside his window. "I've never been out in this much... nature before." He gestured around them. Trees, hundreds of feet tall, lined the road, miles and miles of them. Their fresh woodsy scent filled the car, since the windows were open to take in the sights and sounds of the forest. Fading sunlight dappled through the branches in small, glowing patches like tiny pools of gold. "The only outside living I've ever done is a one night camp out in Connecticut."

"Connecticut?" He could see Jackson was trying hard not to laugh. "Didn't know Connecticut had any wilderness left."

"All right, tough guy." Nick blushed a bit but added, "It was a microbiology field trip for pond bacteria studies when I was eight." He gave a little chuckle and melted back in the leather seat. "Not exactly a wilderness training course."

After the hustle and bustle of the morning race to the airport and a restless six hour flight to Sacramento, Nick was starting to unwind on the long drive to their final destination.

"One whole night?" Jackson downshifted to slow their vehicle, managing to traverse a narrow section of the road where several large tree limbs had fallen onto the right side of the lane, blocking the road. He expertly maneuvered past it. "What can you learn in one night?"

Nick could see a wide strip of fallen trees through the woods on either side of the road, as if an earthquake had rippled around the mountain. The ground had heaved and shifted, disturbing the soil at the base of more than a few of the still standing, larger trees, exposing roots and tilting trunks. A few of them even looked blackened and cracked. He supposed it was some sort of blight that had weakened them. The scene gave him an anxious feeling, as if the trees were just waiting for a strong wind to push them the rest of the way down. Heavy rains might have washed away even more of the supporting ground. It still could. He was about to mention his concerns when he remembered Jackson saying it had been a very dry summer this year. They had no worries about spending their vacation trapped inside the whole time.

There he was, obsessing again. He had promised himself he wouldn't ruin this trip by nitpicking at every detail he wasn't familiar with. They were outside his element. There would be lots of things he wouldn't have control over during these two weeks, starting with his emotions and desires. He could already sense his comfort factor around Jackson increasing, it was so easy to relax beside this man, feeling his strength and confidence. It allowed him to open up a bit more than he had in a long while.

He pulled his gaze away from the eerie, fallen trees, convincing himself that nature had its own way of dealing with weakness and overcrowding. Trying to regain the intimacy level from earlier, Nick decided to give Jackson a more expansive answer than he would have normally.

"Hey, give a guy a break." Nick took a deep breath, shook his head, a tiredness edged into his voice that he knew was evident on his face. "My life's been private schools, intense advance placement courses and career-oriented programs. Pre-med and med classes, internships and work. Mother didn't approve of vacations or hobbies."

Memories of that one camping trip flooded back, the sudden rush startling Nick, making his pulse race and his skin clammy. He turned to look out the window, hoping Jackson hadn't seen the color drain from his face like he knew it had. "It was supposed to be for a week, but it got cut short." Hoping to end the conversation there, he added, "Nothing to do with me. An accident with one of the other kids."

Nick took a deep breath and hid behind a map they had picked up at a small grocery store at the bottom of the foothills, along with provisions for a week. "How much longer before we're there? It's getting dark fast and I don't see any streetlights out here."

"Don't need any. It's around the next bend." Jackson reached out and rubbed Nick's shoulder. "We managed to make it here before dark, but we'll need to drive down the mountain tomorrow and let the locals know we're here."

"Why? Who cares?" Nick stared out the window, trying to get his first glimpse of the cabin Jackson had convinced him to give a chance. He expected a rough-sawn log cabin with one room, sleeping cots, and an outhouse. Calling it 'nice', Jackson had assured him it was a bit better than that, but the fireman's idea of 'nice' was yet to be determined. They hadn't been dating long enough for Nick to second guess him.

"It's what you do when you're in the wilderness, Nick. In case of coming bad weather, lost campers, or escaped convicts." They both snorted at that. "Cell phone reception is non-existent and the radio can act up." Jackson rubbed Nick's shoulder again. "Who knows, maybe someone will need a doctor."

Nick felt the anxiety of the previous bad memory melt away under the heat of the other man's gaze. Jackson's voice was suddenly husky, powerful, and seductive. "I know I do." It was hard to keep this man at arm's length and Nick was beginning to forget why he even needed to. He kept telling himself that one bad relationship shouldn't be that hard to get over but the sting of betrayal had left a wound even his medical expertise couldn't seem to heal. He hoped time would take care of it. Time and, maybe, a good, faithful man.

The SUV rounded the bend, turned down a short winding path, and came to a stop. The outline of a structure settled inside a semi-circle of towering, ancient trees was highlighted by the last rays of the setting sun. It seemed to grow right out of the forest, as if it was a living part of it. Nick's jaw dropped a little as he watched Jackson hit a remote and several lights in and around the cabin burst to life.

It *was* a log cabin, and it *was* in the middle of nowhere. They hadn't seen another place in miles. It might even have a cot somewhere. But, it didn't look like it had an outhouse. It looked like it had everything they could possibly want a cozy cabin in the woods to have and more.

"Now that's a surprise." Getting out of the SUV, Nick moved to take his luggage out of the back. "It's amazing."

"Don't know about 'amazing'." Jackson sounded nonchalant. "I told you— nice."

Two stories high, Nick could see rustic chandeliers in the entry hall and upstairs through large glass panels at the front of the cabin. It sparkled with light inside and out, designed with a love of nature and a keen architectural eye to keep the cabin from disturbing the surrounding forest as much as possible.

A heavy wooden door swung open under the persuasion of the key in Jackson's hand. Nick walked past, giving him an appraising look. "I like your definition of 'nice'."

Jackson stopped him in the doorway and pulled him close. "Good, because I think you're pretty damn nice, too."

The kiss was blistering, lasting longer than Nick expected. It only broke when the lights flickered and died.

CHAPTER FIVE

"Okay, it looks like the power lines that come up the back of the mountain are down." Flashlight in hand, Jackson strode into the cabin to stand in front of the living room's graceful stone fireplace. A small blaze flickered in the grate, a bright, blue flame powered by the propane tank tucked up next to the east side of the cabin. At least that didn't require electricity. It was a mild July, but at the cabin's high elevation, once the sun went down the air grew chilly, even in summer.

Nick nodded. "What now?"

This situation was all new to him. He'd led a city lifestyle, where the occasional power outage meant being without lights for a few hours, maybe a few days. His solution had been to leave whatever apartment he was living in, move to a hotel where the power wasn't out or go to the hospital where emergency generators were always in use. There was always a cot or bed somewhere the staff could use. It was a small inconvenience. He had a feeling it wasn't going to be so easy to avoid the problem here.

"Backup generator won't start. The battery for the electric start is dead." Jackson put the flashlight down, then moved around the room lighting oil lanterns and candles that sat in various places all around the rustic but comfortable room.

"Is your shoulder acting up?" Nick noticed him favoring his injured side.

"Tried the generator's pull start a few times. Obviously, it isn't cooperating." He rolled his right shoulder. "I'm fine. I'll tackle it again in a bit."

Jackson's right shoulder had been separated in a fall through a weakened floor during a fire three months ago. That's how they had met. They hadn't gotten involved personally until Jackson had shifted to the care of an orthopedic surgeon. The injury was healing well but the fireman was still a few weeks away from being ready for active duty. Unless he strained it again. But Jackson didn't like being fussed over.

"This happens often, I take it." Nick gestured at the flickering candlelight.

"No, not often. But this far from everything, it pays to be prepared for things even if it is only once in a while. Usually it's a heavy rain or a bad snowstorm that takes down the lines." Jackson peered out the large glass window facing the front of the cabin.

Nick followed his gaze. It was pitch black outside. He couldn't even make out the shape of their SUV parked a few feet outside the front door. He thought he saw a flicker of light high in the sky but it could have been a reflection of candlelight off the glass window.

"I'll go back out later. I wanted to let you know what was happening. For now, we have heat and light, there's bottled water and the stove works. Let's make dinner and get settled in. It's been a long day and I know you're tired."

"I'm fine." He pinched his lower lip to keep from saying more.

Jackson came over to stand by him, so close Nick could feel the other man's body heat. "Nicky, you've been on the edge of exhaustion most of the time I've known you. That's one of the two reasons I wanted you to come on this vacation with me. Give you time to relax. Let everything go."

"It's just work." Something in Jackson's face told Nick the man wasn't satisfied with his simple answer. It wasn't like a fireman's job was easy or less stressful than his. He sighed, admitting, "Sometimes... I let it..." Nick found it hard to find the right word, "consume me."

"Especially when you're trying to forget about 'things'?" He could feel Jackson tense up, as if the other man wasn't sure it was a safe subject to bring up right now.

Nick was ready to choke down the sudden, breath-stealing ache that usually followed any mention of his two year relationship and disastrous breakup with the cheating Greg, but he was startled when no rush of emotion squeezed his chest. Instead, he felt badly that Jackson thought he needed to brace himself for some kind of backlash from Nick.

Maybe this vacation was the right medicine. Or maybe the towering, rugged man, smelling of pine and diesel, only inches away in flickering candlelight was.

He found himself leaning in, shortening up those last remaining inches between them. "Especially when I'm trying to work through 'things'." He reached up and massaged Jackson's right shoulder, noting the small flinch of discomfort that crossed Jackson's face. "Work soothes me. It's a comfortable rhythm with people I feel safe around."

Jackson gave a light snort of laughter but his gaze remained serious.

Nick closed his eyes then looked the other man in the eye. "Yes, it's total chaos in the ER, but predictable chaos. I can handle it even if it wears me out. It's my world."

Jackson eased Nick's hand down from his shoulder but held onto it. The heat from Jackson's fingers almost stung Nick's cooler skin. He left his hand resting where it was, engulfed by the strength and comfort Jackson offered, for a moment longer. Slowly, he reclaimed it.

Spell broken, Jackson nodded, empty fingers tugging at his earlobe. "Let's go unpack. Even if you're not, *I'm* tired. *And* hungry. I'll show you where everything is."

They both grabbed a suitcase and a lantern then headed upstairs.

Suddenly, Jackson pulled him up short on the staircase. Nick stood two steps up, making him almost level with the tall man, as Jackson whispered, "I want to be a part of that 'safe' world, Nicky. The one that makes you feel safe. That's my other reason for this trip. Time for us."

Nick searched Jackson's sincere expression for a long, breathless moment while he sorted through everything he was feeling. It was impossible not to be distracted with how handsome the big man was. He was strong, physically and morally, a faithful friend to a lot of people Nick knew and a damn fine fireman. Jackson was smart, fun and selfless, loving and gentle when they were together, but that had only been superficial intimacy so far. Something was telling Nick that should change. Maybe it was just Amy's voice echoing in his head. Maybe it *was* time to dive in.

"I guess it's time I learn how to swim." Leaning forward, careful of suitcase in one hand and oil lamp in the other, Nick wet his lips with his tongue then brushed them over Jackson's surprised, parted mouth. "Think you can teach me?"

"What?" Jackson's now husky voice was confused but willing.

"Just how hungry are you?"

CHAPTER SIX

After extinguishing the open flames downstairs, they barely made it to a bedroom before Jackson had stripped Nick of his jacket and shirt. The room was warm, retaining the heat of the fading summer day. Hastily placed lamps cast soft, swaying light and shadows around the room. The still air held the faint scent of spruce and linen, the furnishings rustic but luxurious in a masculine style. It was a large space dominated by a sprawling king-sized bed.

Standing at one side of the bed, Nick had kicked off his boots while Jackson slid a window part way open. It let in a light breeze and the sound of cicadas singing the praises of the rapidly falling night. Returning to his lover's side, Jackson stilled Nick's hands when he began to tug at Jackson's belt in an impatient movement.

"Why don't we slow this down, Nick?"

"Slow down? You don't want—?"

Jackson couldn't stand to see the doubt clouding the beautiful face before him. Nick didn't realize just how attractive he was. Waves of dark brown hair tumbled in all directions, framing his face but never obstructing the view. His eyes were a brilliant blue, made even more perfect by high cheek bones, dimpled chin, and precisely formed nose. His skin, though on the pale side right now, was flawless, the clean-shaven jaw line just angular enough to offset the sharpness of his cheeks. He was slender, his movements graceful, an athletic, masculine grace. Nicolas Kirby was straight out of a GQ cover shoot and didn't even know it.

"Oh, yeah." Jackson pressed a finger to Nick's lips. The warmth and softness of them against his flesh made his stirring dick jump to life faster. "I want. Believe me, I want this." He leaned down and kissed Nick, a light touch that promised more. "We've waited for this moment. It's special. You're special."

He ran his hands around Nick's slim waist then up his back, stroking over the smooth, firm planes of flesh. His skin felt like warm silk to Jackson's work roughed palms. His body responded, desire burning deep and hot in his belly. "Let's take our time, do this right." His breath caught in his throat making his voice a husky whisper. "I want to remember what every inch of you feels like." He pulled Nick closer; his hands slipping under Nick's ass to lift him up until their gazes met in a lustful stare. "What you look like, what you smell, taste, sound like." He buried his face in the angle of Nick's neck, breathing deep, tasting the salty tang of skin, reveling in the small moans of surrender coming from the arched throat under his lips.

Jackson worked his mouth up the other man's neck, feeling Nick's pulse pounding through his artery as Jackson moved slowly up to waiting, parted lips. Nick was busy tugging at both their clothing but slowed their frantic movements when Jackson slipped his fingers into Nick's hair and gently but insistently brought the other man's head back.

Pinned to Jackson's chest, neck arched and body immobilized, Nick had no choice but to focus on Jackson's voice as the man laid a trail of soft kisses and tiny stinging nips down his neck and across one shoulder. "Let me love you, Nicky. I won't let you drown. I got you."

Each tiny bite brought a shiver from the man. Jackson nipped the soft, sensitive flesh behind Nick's ear. The other man moaned and struggled against his hold, grinding their bodies together. Jackson abruptly set Nick down; his hands working free the zipper and snap of the doctor's jeans in one smooth measured movement. He could feel Nick trembling under his hands as he crouched and slid the last layers of clothing off his lover's slender form. He shoved the pile of socks, jeans, and boxers to one side.

Still kneeling at Nick's feet, Jackson ran his hands over firm, slim calves, letting the prickle of dark body hair heighten his sense of touch as he moved to the silkier flesh of taut thighs and rounded buttocks. Hands came to rest on his head, an undemanding touch. He looked up to see Nick's eyes half-closed, his body swaying slightly, tension and expectation written on his flushed face.

On one knee, Jackson continued his explorations, massaging the flat of Nick's stomach, smoothing the curve of his waist, stroking the sensitive 'v' between his thighs and torso. The fingers in his hair gripped tighter but Jackson could tell it was to keep their owner steady. Leaning forward, Jackson buried his face in the nest of tight curls at Nick's groin, breathing the other man's scent and warming the flesh beneath with every exhalation. Nick's stiff arousal brushed against Jackson's jaw.

"Jac—Jackson." Nick shuddered, whispering his name.

"Soon, lover." He knew it was a plea for more. He turned his face to meet the fully engorged shaft jutting up from the dark curls. He let it bob against his cheek, lightly rubbing the day's bristle of a beard over the satin skin. Nick jumped but Jackson held him in place, a firm grip on Nick's ass pressing the smaller man deeper into Jackson's embrace.

Jackson let his fingers slip into the crevice between the other man's cheeks, separating them, kneading the firm globes, fingertips brushing over heated flesh until they found the puckered entrance to Nick's body. He didn't try to enter it; he merely stroked it with slow circles from calloused tips, delighting in the way it spasmed and wrinkled under his touch. He felt Nick sag a bit, knees against Jackson's chest, legs going weak.

Without stilling his fingertips, Jackson licked at the base of Nick's cock, a leisurely motion that wrenched a gasp from his partner. He swiped his tongue up the length, moving to a fresh strip of skin with each long, wet stroke. A jab at the underside of the swollen cockhead produced a strangled sound from his lover. A bead of pre-cum leaked from the slit, glistening like a pearl in the shimmering light from the oil lamps. Jackson captured it on one finger then slathered Nick's puckered opening with it, this time pressing in until the muscle gave way and swallowed the tip of his finger.

Nick's hips began to jerk in a hesitant rhythm, pushing back against his hand. Jackson followed the motion, sliding in deeper but not finger fucking. He wanted to be deep inside Nick, stretching his lover, not over stimulating him. At least not yet.

Taking a cock the size of his took some relaxing and preparation. He wanted this night to be something Nick couldn't forget. Something he'd want a lifetime of.

Nick spread his legs wider as best he could in the embrace, his fingers tugging Jackson's head closer with each fresh movement of finger and mouth. His breath came in soft, harsh gasps broken by small moans of need.

"That's right, lover. Feel me touching you, inside you, outside of you." He squeezed Nick's ass cheeks together with one large hand, the finger of his other hand still deep inside of Nick's opening. Nick moaned and pushed back on the digit, eager to have it do more than tease his channel. "Relax for me, Nick."

The sounds of desire filled the bedroom, urging Jackson to step up his game. Instead, he slowed his attentions, never stopping but lingering over each bristling caress of bearded cheek or wet swipe of tongue to Nick's now-straining cock.

"Do it." Nick tried to jerk his hips forward to encourage Jackson to take him in his mouth. "More. Please. I need more, Jackson."

"Since you asked so nice." He winked at Nick then added, "And you look so damn fucking hot with your cock in my mouth."

Flexing his arms, Jackson drew Nick tightly to him, engulfing the other man's slim, leaking cock into his mouth. He took it in short strokes, lavishing his tongue around the shaft, rubbing it over the swollen knob as it moved out, never letting the circumcised head leave his tight lips.

He worked Nick's cock in a steady, building rhythm, increasing the sucking pressure until he felt small tremors in Nick's legs. Matching the movement for movement, Jackson began massaging his finger in and out of Nick's tunnel, thrusting in when he sucked the shaft down his throat and drawing out when he pulled off Nick's meat. His other hand kneaded Nick's ass, holding him close while separating the globes to give him a deeper reach.

"Christ, Jackson!"

Jackson responded by sucking harder but not faster. He could feel Nick's opening expanding and gripping tight, milking his hand, desperate for more.

Nick's hands had moved from his hair to grip his shoulders, relentless and grasping. Jackson suspected the other man needed to support himself in order to stay standing at this point. Jackson knew he wished he had removed his own jeans before dropping to the floor. His cock was straining against the confinement. It was time to up the action for both of them.

He let Nick's rod slip from his lips while he buried his face in the nest of dark curls surrounding it.

"Jesus, no! Don't stop!"

"Just getting started, baby. This is just me saying 'hello' to your delicious dick."

Barely exerting any physical effort, Jackson rose up on his knees, upper arms tight around Nick's hips as he lifted the other man off his feet.

Nick latched onto Jackson's arms. Jackson swung Nick around to drop backward onto the mattress, legs bent at the knees, ass hanging off the edge of the bed, still stuffed with Jackson's finger.

"Holy fuck!" Nick's back arched and he drew his legs up to rest his heels on the edge of the bed, giving Jackson as much access to his cock and ass as possible.

"I *am* aiming for a religious experience here." It was meant to be a lighthearted reply, but it came out a as deep, husky rasp. Jackson was stunned by the beauty of Dr. Nicolas Kirby stretched out before him, flushed with desire and need, spread open to him, panting for him. He took up the in and out rhythm of finger fucking again, thrilled by the sight of Nick's eager hole pulsing around his finger, drawing him in.

"Jesus Christ Almighty!" Nick twisted his hands in the sheets, eyes closed, mouth parted, breath coming in short, labored huffs. Jackson stared until he thought he would go blind by the sight. He dipped his head down and sucked at the scrotum packed tight against the base of Nick's cock, wetting one ball then the other, reveling in the way his lover jumped and squirmed at his every touch.

No longer supporting Nick or spreading his ass cheeks, Jackson's free hand wandered over Nick's lower belly, calloused palm and fingertips heavy in their exploration. He mapped the hollow of the slender form, tracing from belly button to defined ribcage. It was all a masterpiece in his eyes, hopefully one he would enjoy for the rest of their lives.

He rose higher on his knees, and with practiced ease, released his own cock from his jeans, sliding the offending cloth down his thighs one-handed. His dick jutted straight out, thick and long, no graceful curve or angled slope to it. Hard, hot, hefty, and huge. In his younger days, it had been compared to a battering ram by past lovers.

With experience and age, Jackson had learned to prepare his partners for both the length and girth of his manhood. Nick was aware of his size but this would be the first time they had had intercourse. It had been all foreplay and blowjobs up to now. He knew Nick's asking for this moved their relationship to a new level. It was a leap of faith, faith that had been uncertain before this trip.

Maybe it was the long mountain ride, the isolation, or maybe it was the candlelight, but whatever it was, Jackson wasn't going to lose the moment. Nick wanted him, here, now, like this, and that was all he needed to know.

"Let's bring it home, Nick."

Rubbing Nick's belly, Jackson kissed the weeping crown of the cock swaying in his face. He leaned into it, swallowing the rod to the back of his throat and then backed out halfway. Nick gasped, opening his eyes, he threw his legs over Jackson's shoulders, drawing Jackson to him.

Jackson leaned into the task, sucking on the in stroke, nibbling and tonguing the shaft on the out stroke. He massaged Nick's channel with his thick finger, jabbing in short thrusts, purposely changing the rhythm to work against the sucking action now, stimulating his lover with every touch, never letting Nick's building pleasure subside for more than a moment.

He slid his hand up the heated, quivering stomach to find a taut nub of hard flesh, rolling the captured nipple between his fingertips. He plucked at it, sharp and hard, feeling the skin burning against his hand. Passion inflamed, he let out a moan of his own, vibrating his throat around Nick's dick.

"Jesus, Jesus, Jesus!" Nick's gasps and moans were coming faster, his heels digging into Jackson's back, his hips working hard to impale his ass deep onto Jackson's relentless finger.

The cock between his lips started to spasm, Nick's scrotum rising high under Jackson's bobbing chin. Nick's orgasm began to gather in his balls, drawing his sac into a wrinkled walnut. Jackson took the rod deep into his mouth, swallowing around the shaft, registering the taste of pre-cum on his tongue, his own dick leaking a trail of slippery jism. He hooked his finger forward, rubbing over a tiny gland hidden in Nick's channel. He did it again. And again. The effect was electric.

"God!" Nick bucked and shuddered, releasing his juice, hands tearing at the linen, eyes closed tight. Nick's ass spasmed.

Jackson felt like the most powerful man in the world, connected to his lover on both ends, devouring him with his mouth while claiming him with part of his hand inside of Nick. He could sense his lover's pulse, gauge his breath, luxuriate in the vibrations of his moans. He felt like he could touch Nick's soul. Jackson was lost in the sensations of the beautiful man laid out before him.

And this was just the foreplay.

In the back of his mind, Jackson wondered if he would survive a deeper intimacy with this man, but the question was pushed away by the need to find out the answer.

CHAPTER SEVEN

Nick was sure he'd blacked out when his orgasm hit. One moment, his entire body was exploding into tiny pieces and the next, he was lying in bed with Jackson propped up on one arm, leaning over him.

The other man was leisurely drawing slow circles across his still panting chest. Each pass of calloused hand over Nick's sensitive nipples sent a shock of electricity-like pleasure straight to his now spent cock.

"Shit, that was amazing." Nick rubbed both hands down his face, trying to refocus himself in the present. He felt weak and out of breath, as if he'd run a marathon. "I think you took two years of my life."

"Sucked it right out of you, huh?" Jackson was stretched out alongside him, his warm, hairless torso plastered to Nick's. His lover rolled forward to lean over him, a suggestive, cocky look on his chiseled, smiling face. One thick arm went around Nick's waist and under his body, fingers sliding into the crease between his ass cheeks. "Only two? I'll have to try harder."

Relaxing into the renewed attentions, Nick gave his lover an innocent, wide-eyed stare. "I thought firemen were supposed to put out fires not instigate them."

"That explosion was all you, baby." Jackson kissed him, once, twice, three times. Tender, light pecks that were more seductive and thrilling to Nick than the ravenous lip lock they had shared on the stairs.

"You went off like a backdraft. Even I got scorched by the heat flash."

More of his weight lowered on Nick, but Jackson was holding himself up on his arms to keep his full weight off him. They were eye to eye as Jackson moved his legs between Nick's, urging his knees up. Happy to oblige, Nick wordlessly made room.

Nick closed his eyes as Jackson leaned down to kiss him. It was a slow, languid kiss. There was no battle of tongues or straining jaws, fighting for dominance. Nick felt a balance in their intimacy he hadn't realized was there. It had been, but he hadn't noticed it until now.

For all of Jackson's towering size and raw physical strength, he had never tried to overpower Nick, never used his alpha position in life to insist on anything in their relationship. They were equals, despite Jackson's obvious advantages to make things go his way, even if only temporarily, if he wanted.

The soft, delicate tones of a wind chime somewhere outside the cabin drifted in through the open window. It was a gentle sound but crisp and pleasing. Everything felt right here, far away from everything they both knew, in this cozy, protected haven, making love by candlelight with only the wind to add background music to the night.

His urgent need for release satiated, Nick poured himself into the passionate embrace. He wanted this, had wanted it since the first time he'd kissed Jackson Kain.

He was going to get fucked tonight by someone he thought truly loved him. He could feel it in Jackson's every touch.

And, if he was lucky, maybe he would feel it every night for the foreseeable future.

He felt his dick stir, the familiar sizzle of renewed desire tingling through his core to land in his genitals. His knees were on either side of Jackson's waist, their height difference making the larger man's cock rest teasingly under his scrotum. Spreading his thighs wider, the thick cock slipped lower to press into the cleft of his ass. Nick released a satisfied moan into Jackson's mouth, hips urging Jackson to go deeper.

The kiss broke, heavy breaths against his cheek and neck, Jackson's faint murmur in his ear. "Easy, lover. This takes time." A sharp nip to one crinkled, hard nipple made Nick flinch but moan with need. "You need to be ready."

Jackson slid down Nick's body, his large hands massaging

flesh as his lover moved until he was kneeling upright between Nick's bent legs. His lover's warmth gone, Nick gripped the linens beneath him as a cool gust of air sent gooseflesh over his suddenly exposed trunk.

"I am ready." His cock jerked to half-mast, his own hand fingering his abandoned tit. The lingering wetness from Jackson's mouth forced the sensitive flesh to contract and harden, the heat under the surface matching the sudden constriction of his asshole as his ass was clenched in powerful hands.

"Not as ready as you're going to be. Turn over." A quick wink from his lover, then Nick was lifted, flipped, and settled back down on the sheets, his knees bent. A pillow was shoved under him.

"Hey!" The sudden movement was a surprise. He couldn't help but react, but his fears dissolved when Jackson leaned down close against his back and whispered, "Trust me." Those two words, spoken in a strained, husky tone, were rich with more than just sexual need. They sounded like truth to Nick.

"I do." He twisted to look at Jackson, the other man's face flushed, his eyes clear and bright in the lamp light, full of honesty. "I really do."

When Jackson was done, Nick lay chest down on the mattress, face turned to one side, his ass raised in the air, hips on the firm, thick pillow. His cock was trapped, pointed downward over the edge of the cushion, he could feel the weight of his balls resting on it.

A light touch ran down Nick's spine, ghosting over his raised globes, teasing the crevice between them. The second pass over the same trail was heavier. He could feel Jackson's heavily muscled thighs under his own, supporting them where they hung off the pillow. Jackson's hands were moving over every inch of Nick's back and thighs, learning the slopes of his body, visiting the curve of his skin as if it was the first time they had touched.

Eyes closing, Nick's consciousness faded into the sensations. Relaxing, lulled by the warmth of the bed, the scent of the crisp night air, even the sounds of crickets and the occasional chime, it all wrapped around him like a comforting blanket. Jackson murmured above him, small acknowledgments of Nick's attributes that would have had him blushing under other circumstances. Tonight, they soothed his soul.

The first touch of Jackson's mouth to his ass pulled a gasp from him. It wasn't unexpected just more intense than he'd anticipated. It was hot and wet, an open mouthed kiss to the opening of his body. His lover wasted no time with a delicate assault. His ass was licked and kneaded, the flesh sucked on until he squirmed. Nick felt the heat of Jackson's breath on his puckered hole, his only warning before a sweet, wet jab of warm muscle poked at his entrance. He pushed back against the probing tongue, wanting more.

"Christ, Jack!"

Fire raced along his nerve endings like lit blasting powder heading for sticks of dynamite. His trapped cock engorged, coaxed to fullness with each hump against the silky pillowcase. After several heady moments of being tongue fucked, the hot wetness was replaced by a thick fingertip. He groaned into the mattress, fingers curled in the fabric of the bed.

The finger was slick with gel he hadn't realized Jackson even had near them. The familiar aroma of lubricant combined with an additive to stimulate sensitive membranes reached his senses at the same time as the first heat of it blossomed in his channel. The finger slid deeper, massaging, turning, raking his insides. Pleasure shot through him. He shuddered at the suddenness, mentally seeing the stout digit stroking his channel, feeling every millimeter of its width and length. His ass was spread, the tight muscle of his entrance stretched until a burning, luxurious and exciting sensation radiated out through his cheeks.

Jackson's rhythm was maddening, slow and steady. Just when Nick was about to beg for something more, a second digit pressed into his taut hole. The burn flashed bright then faded to a throbbing ache that pushed his desire so high he felt his own cock leaking. His balls drew up, hips rocking back and forth.

Nick desperately wanted Jackson to increase the rhythm without asking, but it didn't look like that was going to ever happen. The other man had patience and self-control at a level Nick couldn't match.

Right now, he didn't give a damn about patience or self-control. "Do it, Jackson! Please!" He surged back against the intruding digits but Jackson eased off, preventing him from getting deeper stimulation.

"Do what, Nick?" His words were soft, but the hand in the middle of Nick's back holding him still was insistent.

Nick knew he was going to have to say what he wanted, declare the fact he wanted Jackson inside of him, for them to be joined together. That final surrender changed things for Nick in a relationship and Jackson knew it. There would be no going back to the casualness they had before tonight.

Letting go of his inhibitions with a lover had always been hard for him. Nick had learned the hard way that an unguarded moment could be thrown back in your face when a relationship soured. Trust was a tough thing for him to give.

There was a brief, internal struggle before Nick took a deep breath and demanded, "Fuck me, damn it! Take that huge, goddamn, fireman's hose and DO ME!"

"I've been waiting to hear that for weeks, Dr. Kirby."

CHAPTER EIGHT

The thrill of hearing his lover demand he fuck him was so intense, Jackson thought he'd come right there. He'd been focusing on little things about Nick Kirby to keep control over his body's responses to the brilliant, sexy, panting, beautiful man in his bed. He breathed in Nick's scent; a faint mix of astringent soap, the man was forever washing his hands, and a lightly spicy aftershave that Jackson couldn't name. The feel of Nick's skin was soothing on his own rough hands, some spots tough like the soles of his feet from long hours walking up and down the halls in the ER. Some areas were as unblemished and soft as Jackson's infant nephew's skin. Every touch was exciting. Nick was like a live-wire brushing against Jackson, all sparks, sizzle and danger.

Nick wouldn't believe him if he told him, but despite how attractive the doctor was physically to Jackson, it was the man's intelligence that had drawn Jackson to him. Jackson had been hooked on the man after spending hours watching Nick work when he had been injured. He'd never seen such a sharp, knowledgeable, caring, and capable doctor. And Jackson had meet many an ER doc in his time as a NYC firefighter. Some were good, very good, but Nick beat them all, especially when you considered he was barely in his thirties.

As amazing as Jackson found Nick's brain, he knew all either of them was interested in at the moment was each other's physical attributes.

He eased his fingers out of the tight confines of his lover's opening, gaze locked on the sight of Nick's clenched opening grasping at his fingers, reluctant to release him. The wind had picked up outside, its forest scented breeze cooling the sweat sheen that covered his body, the chill helping to slow his own passionate urgency.

"Take slow deep breaths, lover." Jackson squeezed Nick's ass cheek to let him know he was taking care of him. Once he saw

Nick nod and felt the expansion of his lover's ribcage, he moved ahead.

Not wanting to lose any of the progress he had achieved with relaxing Nick's entrance, Jackson propped himself over Nick's backside and guided the tip of his now slick rod into the lubed opening with one hand. It was a snug fit, but the way his dick naturally engorged, arrow straight and iron hard, helped him breach the clenching passage.

"Huh!" Nick gasped once then resumed breathing deep. One hand reached back and gripped Jackson's arm then fell away. "More." Nick pushed his hand under himself in search of his own dick. Jackson knew he had found it when the other man grunted. His breaths came in rapid puffs from that point on.

Encouraged, Jackson inched in farther, drawing back and sliding in just a little more with each thrust. Soon he had a gentle rhythm established. It wasn't long before Nick rose up on his knees to push back, meeting each thrust, face buried in the sheets. Muffled moans escaped the doctor in a constant shuddered litany of passion and need. The overwhelming desire to turn those moans to cries of brilliant pleasure fueled Jackson's own need to a premature explosion.

Running both hands over the younger man's bucking flesh, Jackson gripped the slender hips, matching the push and pull, until he was balls deep inside Nick's ass.

"Fuck! Jackson! Seriously? You giant bastard!"

His dick was wrapped tight in the hot wetness of his lover, his long shaft buried deep in the clenching channel. He could feel the silken walls slipping over his rod, milking it like it was a throat, loving every inch of his thick meat.

"More. Harder...more, Jac—Jack!"

"Yeah, Nicky, I got you, baby. Anything you want." He pumped his hips faster, driving deeper. His cock's tip prodded hard at the end of each thrust, forcing a soft grunt from Nick's throat. The slap of flesh on flesh filled the room. The musky scent of men having sex dominated the air. Smooth linen became harsh with his knees constantly sliding over it. His own guttural groans blended with Nick's moans and gasps, drowning out the increasing but still faint wisps of the delicate wind chime from outside.

Pressing his chest to Nick's hunched back, Jackson kept one hand holding Nick's hip while the other slipped forward and under to find a rigid tit. His hips kept pumping away in a rapid, urgent rhythm, keeping the level of stimulation for the both of them building. He wanted Nick's orgasm to be the kind that lovers always remember, so rich and satisfying it becomes a memory to take to old age.

Finding the taut nub, he rolled the tiny, hard nipple between his finger and thumb, then plucked it like a guitar string. He did it again, this time pinching it just a little with his nails. Nick twisted under him, his dark head rolling from side to side on the mattress, ass pressing back with increased desire.

Jackson played the burning nub like a musical instrument, twisting, plucking, and rubbing while his strokes in and out of Nick's ass got longer, harder, and deeper. His balls slapped Nick's perineum, the lubrication they used leaking out of Nick's opening, slathering over their sacs.

Wanting Nick to come first, Jackson abandoned the hot bud of crinkled flesh to move lower. Finding Nick's hand tugging on his slender cock, Jackson wrapped his fist over Nick's and pumped the shaft harder, a calloused thumb rubbing the crown, smearing the leaking fluid he found there over the sensitive rim.

He felt his lover's orgasm burst over his hand. He tugged faster, reveling in the small cries Nick choked out in his ear. He expected Nick's eyes to be closed but when he gazed at him to remember what the other man looked like at this moment he found bright blue eyes staring back at him in wonder, searching his face, memorizing *his* expression. And then he exploded.

The orgasm was beyond description for Jackson. Nick was clenched around his shaft, the tiny, expanded rim a tight, unrelenting ring raking along him with every thrust and drag. The fine hairs on his sculptured body bristled, gooseflesh running across his flesh. The sounds and smells of sex, release and massive exertion hung in the room. His mind soared off, pleasure racking his limbs, sizzling through his nerves, making his muscles rigid then weak with satisfaction. Jackson slowly became aware his dick was slipping from his lover's shuddering body.

"Come here." Unwilling to separate from Nick just yet, Jackson gathered a still panting Nick in an embrace without getting a protest. He rolled to one side, arms and legs tangled together. Nick's head rested on his upper arm while Jackson dragged pillows into an agreeable position for them both. The sheets were a tangled heap but he managed to pull a corner over their sweaty but cooling bodies.

Several minutes passed before Nick turned in the embrace to look at him. The worry lines at the corners of his lover's eyes and mouth had eased. His face was flushed but smoother. He seemed less tired, less worried, and even younger. Jackson realized it was the first time he had seen the man genuinely relaxed since he'd met him. Nick was even more gorgeous like this—rumpled, sweaty, stinking of sex, hair in his eyes and the five o'clock shadow darkening his dimpled chin.

Nick wet his lips to speak. Jackson hoped the doctor wouldn't say anything too profound. Jackson was feeling so many things right now he didn't think he could express it all without sounding like a mad stalker. Luckily, he didn't have to worry.

"That's one damn fine hose you have there, Mr. Fireman." Their laughter echoed off the walls and shook the bed. It was long minutes before they settled into a dry, comfortable position they both could live with in the unfamiliar, shared space.

Over the top of Nick's tousled head, Jackson glimpsed flashes of lightning bursting across the blackness through the window. They were brilliant blue-white javelins cracking open the sky. The accompanying sizzles and throaty rumbles told him the storm was several miles away yet. He hoped the storm was gone by morning, but then maybe a lazy day in bed was just what the doctor ordered.

CHAPTER NINE

"Doesn't look like we got any rain to go with all that lightning we saw last night." Nick sipped his coffee, gazing out the glass door leading to the back porch and the forest beyond. The coffee was rich and strong, perked in a steel drip percolator on the gas stove. Nick had never seen it made that way and actually thought he might like it better than the coffee from his two-hundred dollar pod coffeemaker back at his apartment.

Jackson joined him, mug in hand. "There's a huge lake about a couple hundred yards through those trees."

Nick could see a footpath begin between two arched limbs then it disappeared into the thick woods.

"My first nature hike. Yeah." His obvious lack of enthusiasm was only partly in jest. "I'm kind of liking me on this side of the glass. You know, looking out at the beautiful scenery but not a part of it." He raised his cup in a salute, smiling over the rim at his lover. His face was beginning to ache from smiling this morning. "Less chance of meeting mountain lions this way."

There was an answering grin on the big man's face but it didn't seem to reach his dark eyes. "I'm going to cut you a break, greenhorn. Let's leave the nature walk for later. Right now, we're going to drive down and check in with the locals." Jackson finished his coffee in one huge swig and put the mug in the sink, all the while his gaze searched the peaceful scene beyond the door, like he was looking for something Nick couldn't see. "Should have done it last night, but I opted for getting off the road before dark over adding an extra hour to a long day."

Jackson seemed perplexed as he scanned the sky and the woods, his gaze studying the sudden bursts of wind that came and then just as suddenly disappeared, making the underbrush sway and the fallen leaves dance across the ground. "But I think we'd better get to it now."

"You've got that look on your face." Putting down his

own unfinished drink, Nick touched the other man's shoulder, massaging the healing injury, conscious that he had been responsible for giving that shoulder a bit more of a workout last night than was medically advised.

"What look?" Jackson nailed him with a steely stare that didn't manage to hide the troubled lines around his eyes.

"The one that says *'Danger, Will Robinson, Danger!'.*" Surprise shot across his lover's face. Even Nick was shocked at how well he knew the other man.

His voice softened, sincere and caring. "I saw it when you came into the ER with the three kids with smoke inhalation. We didn't even speak that night, it was so hectic. Then I saw it again the first night we met, after you came to. Before you realized you were safe in the ER." He studied the grim set of Jackson's jaw, watched him go to tug at his ear then stop himself, controlling his outward response to the situation. "Something's off. What's the matter?"

"Nothing." Jackson pulled Nick closer, hands rubbing over Nick's shoulders. "I just want to get this out of the way so we can enjoy ourselves." The embrace was both casual and intensely intimate. A sizzle of pleasure flushed through Nick's core, not a sexual buzz but pleasure at the ease of Jackson's instant reassurance. The man was not timid about showing his feelings. That was new and different for Nick. He was growing to like it.

But now there was a new edge of urgency to the fireman. Jackson kept his tone casual and steady. Too casual. "It's just a safety precaution."

Nodding nonchalantly, Nick tucked in his flannel shirt and checked his jean's pockets to be sure he had his cell phone. If they got lower down the mountain, he might find a tower signal. Just knowing they could reach the outside world suddenly seemed wise. He slid into emergency physician mode, hyper-aware and smart enough to know to follow the lead of the most knowledgeable guy in the situation. That would be Jackson. "If it's that important, let's go. I just need to grab shoes."

"Make them your hiking boots, okay?" Jackson took a ready-packed knapsack from a cupboard under the staircase. "In case we do a nature walk."

"What's that?" Nick sat on the steps, lacing up his boots. "Don't tell me you're going to relive your military boot camp days." He eyed the heavy pack, noting the small ax and large bowie knife strapped to one side. "A ten mile forced march with a fifty pound pack was not in my vacation plans."

"I think you could handle it with flying colors, Dr. Kirby." This time the flash of a smile was real. "But don't worry, this is a readiness pack. And it's just a precaution." Jackson herded him toward the front door and out into the early morning sunlight.

The sky was a slight gray and the air heavy this morning. It was still and quiet. Nick had imagined the chirping of birds and the buzzing of insects in the early morning hours of the great outdoors. A warm breeze blew his wavy brown hair into his eyes. He still needed that haircut.

"Another *precaution*." Nick pulled up short beside the car door. Jackson stopped beside Nick. He threw the pack into the backseat. They stared at each other a moment before Nick quietly said, "Tell me."

Tugging his right earlobe until Nick thought it might remain stretched an inch longer than it normally was, Jackson blew out a slow breath then stared down the road they were set to travel. "It's a feeling I have. The lightning. The power outage." He glanced at the sky and reached out a hand to let the new gust of warm air push through his outstretched fingers. "The sky." He rolled his hands into two fists before he dropped them to his sides. "The breeze is all wrong."

"Lightning? From last night? What's that got to do with anything? That was hours ago. And it didn't even storm. How can that be a problem now?" Nick got into the car, an insistent nudge from Jackson urging him along.

"Jackson?" Side by side in the car, Nick waited. "I can't make sense of things without some kind of information flow."

Sighing, Jackson started the SUV down the road at a faster pace than Nick was prepared for. He held onto the grab bar on the door and waited some more.

"I can't be sure. It's just a feeling I'm getting."

"Okay." Nick scanned the passing scenery, looking for something to give him a clue as to what Jackson was seeing. "Instincts have helped keep you alive through a tour in the service and a decade as a firefighter. You trust them. I trust you. Tell me."

"I think last night's light show was dry lightning."

"Dry lightning?" Now he really was confused. "Isn't lightning always dry?"

"Yes. And no." It didn't escape Nick's notice that the other man's fingers tapped out a little SOS code on the steering wheel as he drove. "When lightning hits the ground it can spark a fire. That's normal. Usually the rain that follows it puts out the fire and you never know about it. But, if no rain follows the lightning, if it evaporates before it hits the ground like it sometimes does at higher elevations—"

"Fires start. Wildfires."

"Yeah."

Running the whole morning through his head in fast forward, Nick latched onto a few unusual elements that now stood out to him. "The gray sky to the west isn't morning fog?"

"Don't think so."

"I don't smell smoke."

"We're up wind. Won't until it reaches us or the wind shifts." Jackson threw in the next bit just to give Nick a frame of reference, he was sure. "Lightning is about 45,000 degrees Fahrenheit when it hits."

"Toasted."

"Yep."

"Crap." He couldn't help envisioning the medical challenge

being caught in a raging forest fire would cause. Smoke inhalation, lungs damaged by superheated air, burns, getting struck by falling tree limbs…and that was if a person managed to survive.

They traveled in silence as they evaluated the facts. Nick broke the somber mood, saying out loud what the other man had probably been thinking all morning. "And we didn't check in so no one knows we're at the cabin if they had to evacuate."

"That pretty much sums it up. If I'm right. Which I might not be." It was a slim hope that was dashed as they rounded the next curve. Jackson brought the SUV to a dirt-spitting halt. Several large trees lay across the road, roots exposed, limbs scorched, the ground split and blackened for a good hundred feet on either side of the now impassable road. Bark smoldered on several of them where they came in contact with the torched earth. There were no active flames visible, but the smell of smoke was heavy in the air.

Nick jumped from the SUV, two steps behind Jackson. They both spent several minutes stamping out small, smoldering patches of undergrowth.

"Do you see a way around this, Jack?"

"Not with the SUV." He studied the thick woods, checking out the tiny specks of sky through the foliage. "It's too dangerous and too far to go down on foot. There's nothing higher up. Greg's place is the end of the road." He walked back toward the SUV, motioning for Nick to follow. "Our best bet is go back to the cabin and get the generator working. That way we can find out what we are dealing with and let people know we're here. Just in case."

The scent of smoke seemed stronger to Nick but he wasn't sure if it was real or just fueled by the sudden spike in his adrenaline that Jackson's casual tone had sparked in his gut.

He settled into his seat beside the other man, glad if he was going to be caught in a potential disaster at least it was with someone who truly cared for him. He knew Jackson had his back.

"I guess there are worse things in life than being caught in a forest fire with a real fireman."

Jackson grinned at him, a genuine smile that lifted a little of the heaviness off Nick's chest. "And I have my own trauma doctor if I fuck up. What more could we ask for?" Jackson gunned the engine, did a messy, tire-spinning turn, and headed back to the cabin at top speed for the narrow dirt road.

Hanging on tight to the grab bar again, Nick let out a slow, unsteady breath. He stared straight ahead out the windshield, watching the shadowed trees fly by them. "We're in deep shit, aren't we?"

"Probably." Jackson didn't hesitate. He had known all along what Nick was just realizing. The answer was also strong and confident. The fireman was already mentally prepared for what was coming at them. That gave Nick a sense of comfort. It kicked his own confidence and professional training into gear. They were going to have to depend on each other like they were a cohesive team if this turned out to be as critical as Jackson feared.

The cabin was just ahead, its peaked roof linear and sharp against the eclectic tangle of tree limbs behind it. Jackson's fingers flexed, letting a little of the tension out of his death grip on the wheel. Nick was a bit shocked to realize he felt more relief from seeing Jackson relax a hair then he did at seeing the solid, safe, looming cabin. Not the best circumstances to find it out, but apparently, he did still know how to have faith in another man.

CHAPTER TEN

Neither of them lost any time once the SUV jostled to a stop.

"I think the generator just needs a little persuasion. It hasn't been used in a while." Jackson headed to the shed out back that housed the generator. "There should be some first aid things in the house. I know there's a small kit in the backpack. You might want to pull a few things together."

"I know…'just in case'. Go. I got it." Taking the pack out of the SUV, Nick ransacked the house, looking for medical supplies, bottles of water, and anything else that might come in handy if they had to leave the cabin. He repacked the sack, replacing ordinary hiking supplies with items they could use only in this situation. He snagged a couple of large bandanas from one of the bedroom's dresser drawers.

Nick scanned the room he was in one last time, picked up the pack and headed out to the generator shed. He had hoped to hear the sputtered roar of the gas engine come to life before this.

The shed door was ajar. A mechanical whirling sound followed by a grunt of human effort reached him as he pulled the door open the rest of the way. He was just in time to see the second disaster of the day happen.

Drenched in sweat, outer shirt already thrown off and on the floor, muscles bulging with the strain of the repeated, unsuccessful effort, Jackson unconsciously switched the pull handle to the generator to his other hand and wrenched as hard as he could.

With his dominant arm.

His still healing, vulnerable, not-to-be-wrenched-with-yet shoulder that was attached to that dominant arm.

"Jack—" Nick knew it was too late before he shouted. Then it got even worse than just the overuse of an injured shoulder.

The cord snapped under the extreme force. Jackson's arm

yanked back, all tension unexpectedly gone. His shoulder jerked and twisted. Jackson tumbled backward to slam against the shed wall. He managed to stay on his feet but his face contorted, for the briefest of moments, in pain.

Dropping the pack on the ground, Nick raced to Jackson's side. "Christ, Jack!" He helped Jackson regain his balance. He was surprised when the man accepted help to walk outside. Jackson sat on a nearby stump used for cutting wood.

"Let me look at it." Jackson cradled his right arm to his chest while Nick carefully probed and kneaded the joint and surrounding tissue.

"Can't be sure without an X-ray but, the shoulder joint feels okay. You've re-injured the muscles." He talked while he examined the area, eyes focused on his work. He made sure he caught Jackson's gaze to add, "There might even be a tear."

"I'm okay." Jackson shook his head. "I just strained it." He gave a reassuring smile but it didn't replace the pain lines around his eyes.

Nick ignored him. "Here," he ran his hands expertly over Jackson's muscled chest, "and here," he smoothed his fingers down the man's back and over his shoulder blade, "have already begun to swell. It's 'strained' all right. I can't believe you used that arm."

"It was reflex." Voice tinged with annoyance, Jackson added, "I'm supposed to be healed."

"In a couple of weeks." Nick moved away to dig a chemical ice pack and a bandage roll from the backpack lying on the ground beside the shed door. "No nice, tailored slings from the hospital supply cart handy, but this Ace wrap will work to help keep some of the weight off your shoulder."

Despite his objections, Jackson let Nick create a makeshift sling for his arm and affix an ice pack to his shoulder. "We've got bigger things to figure out, Nick. The generator is useless now."

"Every move you make is going to aggravate this. Just humor me and leave it on for now, okay?"

The wind shifted. The smell of smoke drifted in. Jackson stood up and stilled Nick's busy hands. "We need to leave. Now."

"To where?" Nick retrieved the knapsack, gaze scanning the surrounding woods for any signs of fire.

Jackson grabbed his forearm and led Nick off toward the arched opening in the woods.

"The lake. Greg doesn't like boating but there's a swimming float about a hundred yards out. We can use that if we have to." Jackson didn't wait for Nick to respond, pulling him along at a rapid pace. The scent of smoke grew heavier and the air hotter, instilling a new urgency in both of them.

Glancing back, Nick watched the woods to the west flutter like a desert mirage. The faint sounds like the roar of ocean waves reached him. He moved faster, coughing, the cloying taste of burning wood in his throat.

It took a few tense minutes to break through the dense woods, then the ground sloped down. The undergrowth tapered off, dirt giving way to sandy grit that in turn flowed into a finer sand scattered with pebbles, bits of water-polished twigs, and clumps of marooned water plants. The air was clearer, cooler, the odor of smoke combining with typical scents of fish and open water. Nick coughed, choking on the fine particles of ash in the air. The wind swirled around him, hot, dirty and faster than before.

Jackson rubbed Nick's back with his free hand, a gesture Nick knew was meant more to soothe than to actually help his breathing. "We're going to need something to filter the air or smoke inhalation will get us before anything else."

"I got something. Hang on." He took a bottle of water from the pack then searched for the confiscated bandanas. He doused the material with water and handed one off to his partner. Both of them tied the saturated squares over their noses and mouths. The chill of the water felt good against Nick's too warm skin, but he shivered despite the relief. All the while, he couldn't keep from staring at the water.

The lake was huge. Nick could see the line of shore far across the water to the left. To the right, the lake spilled out in an endless expanse of calm, dark water, no land in sight. It was so wide and deep it could swallow a person, leaving no trace behind except a tiny ripple on its murky, mirrored surface.

And there, hundreds of feet away, was a small, blue square bobbing above the water's surface. An uncontrollable chill ran down his spine hard enough to jerk his head.

"You've got to be kidding me." It was barely a whisper but Jackson turned to give him a questioning look. Nick felt like he was eight years old again—ill-prepared and ashamed of it.

The swimming platform was their goal. Way out in the water.

Way, way out.

CHAPTER ELEVEN

A sharp crack split the smoke-laden air, so sudden it made both of them jump. A wave of heat hit them, the air filled with the sound of blazing flames and the cracking of twisted, falling tree limbs. Nick could see the bright hues of orange and white through the surrounding woods as the fire ate its way toward them at a pace so fast he could scarcely believe it.

Jackson grabbed his arm and urged him to the water's edge, crouching low as they ran. He swept his arm toward both areas to the northwest and the southwest, shouting above the noise. "Both flanks of the fire are moving faster than the head in this area. I think the cabin is keeping it busy." He stripped off his boots, tied the laces together and hung them from his neck, indicating Nick should do the same. "We're going to swim to the platform. If the wind shifts again, that might be enough."

"And if it doesn't?"

"There's a landing area and dock across the lake to the left. There's usually at least one or two boats moored there during the summer." He pointed in the direction of the strip of land Nick had noticed earlier.

"What good is that going to do us?" Nick had the sinking feeling he knew the answer. The land was viewable, but still very far away where he was concerned.

Jackson looked like he thought Nick had suddenly dropped his IQ. "We can swim to it. It's only a mile."

"Your shoulder! You can't swim that far." As desperate as he was for another answer to their problem, he was concerned for the other man's safety. What if he got out in deep water and couldn't function? How would Nick help him? It would be a repeat of that disastrous summer when he was eight.

"It's not that far." Jackson yanked the make-shift sling off his arm, letting it hang from his neck. He carefully flexed his arm to demonstrate as he waded into the water. He gestured for Nick to join him. "We'll take the boat out to the middle of the lake and try to raise someone on the radio. There's always someone monitoring the radio waves." He sloshed in a few more feet, stopping only when he realized Nick hadn't entered the water. "Come on, Doc. Let's go."

Heat raged down from the now shimmering trees behind him, forcing sweat to pop out all over his body. It was inconsistent with the chill Nick felt gripping his insides. He knew that gut-wrenching ice ball wasn't because of what was behind him. He could face the fire, Jackson would help him get through that if it was at all possible to survive. His real fear was right in front of him, his toes soaked with the cool, terrifying wetness of it.

And this was the point where his relationship would tank. His life depended on a skill everyone in the world knew except the brilliant, talented Dr. Nicolas Kirby.

"I can't swim." He knew he sounded helpless and small and lacking. That was the way he felt. And now Jackson would know it and feel it, too. He'd be little more than a weak, useless anchor around Jackson's thick, powerful neck from this point on. How had he ever believed he had a future with an outdoors, accomplished man like this brawny fireman? He'd been kidding himself. This had all been a mistake.

Nick could hardly bring himself to look at Jackson but he was forced to when the other man appeared in front of him.

"Why didn't you say so?" Snorting in disbelief, Jackson grabbed Nick's arm, pulling him into the water until they were waist deep. It only took a few steps, but it was getting harder and harder to see more than a few feet away in the smoke-filled air. "Half the population of NYC can't swim. I'll tow you. It's easy."

"You can't tow me all the way to the dock. It's a *mile*." Wait, wasn't Jackson supposed to be leaving him behind? Nick panicked as the water rose up his chest. His feet slipped on the slimy rocks at the bottom but Jackson kept him upright.

"Don't plan on it." Jackson took the sling off from around his neck, gripping it with his injured arm. He placed the other end of the loop in Nick's hands, wrapped it once around a wrist forcing Nick to grasp it. "Hold on to this. No matter what, this never leaves your hands, got it?"

"You're sure?" Nick examined the slim piece of fabric. It was sturdy but there wasn't much of it.

"It's a professional rescue maneuver." Jackson flashed a killer grin. "Just in reverse. I'm taking you deeper into the water, not out of it." He pulled Nick closer by the neck, yanked both of their masks down, and kissed him, quick and hard. "Trust me, Nicolas Kirby. I won't let anything happen to you."

Floundering for a moment, caught off balance by the sudden embrace, Nick gasped then choked as both smoke and water hit his throat. Jackson helped him position his bandana, then adjusted his own. The backpack was abandoned on the shore.

"I do trust you." The moment was broken by the explosion of a small tree as it burst into flame a hundred feet away. Both of them moved deeper into the water.

"Let your body float. Close your eyes if you need to. I'm leading this dance."

Swimming one handed, Jackson put distance between them, drawing the Ace tight enough Nick had to extend his arms to hang on. He let the water take his weight, panicked but handling it as he dropped further under the surface.

"If we can't make the boat, where are we going?" Eyes tightly closed, his voice sounded muffled, hoarse and strangely calm considering the way his heart was hammering in his chest.

"*I'm* still going after the boat." Jackson swam out, steadily dragging them toward the floating oasis. "Right after I drop *you* off at the platform."

"What?" Eyes springing open, Nick kicked awkwardly at the water. "You're leaving me?"

"I'll come back for you with the boat." Jackson had to shout to be heard over the roar of the approaching forest fire at the shore. "And stop doing whatever you're trying to do." Nick ceased flailing his legs. "Just let me do the work. It's easier."

He hadn't added 'on my shoulder', but Nick knew the big man's injuries, old and new, were taking the majority of the physical exertion. "Okay." Closing his eyes again, he concentrated on keeping his head above water and keeping terror from eating his insides up. He was convinced he would disappear beneath its inky surface and never be found.

He'd give anything to be able to trade this unscheduled swimming lesson for the comfortable chaos and overwork of his simple, safe ER. There he knew how to approach every situation and how to solve almost every problem. Nothing there terrified him. No open bodies of water, no strong, wonderful men he wanted to attract and impress. In the ER, he wouldn't fail miserably at it.

Though he had to admit, he'd been blindsided by Jackson's off-handed, immediate acceptance of his inability to know how to swim. He had taken it in stride as if Nick had confessed to not knowing how to cook instead of throwing a stumbling block to survival at him. Nick was sure the athletic fireman would be shocked and appalled, maybe even amused by his failing. Others had been.

His last serious boyfriend, Greg, had seen any shortcoming he thought Nick had as a personal insult, as if Nick's lack of skill or knowledge in some area reflected on Greg himself. The only thing the other man had contributed to their three-year relationship was to instill a deep sense of mistrust in any future partner Nick would have in the following years. Until now.

Injured, sore, exhausted and looking at a one mile swim, Jackson Kain was literally saving Nick's life. And doing it at no small cost to his own chances of survival. Jackson didn't have to tow him to the platform. He could have headed straight for the docks with a promise to come back to shore to get Nick. He could have saved his strength and the use of his bad shoulder to ensure his own safety. But then Jackson Kain wouldn't have been the badass, decorated, respected fireman he was if he had.

Something solid bumped his shoulder. Nick opened his eyes and found himself face to face with the badass in question. The solid object was one of the floats supporting the swimming platform.

"Already?" Jesus, even hurt the man was strong.

Still holding on to Nick's tether, Jackson climbed the short ladder onto the platform.

"Climb up." He pulled Nick to the heavy steps and helped him out of the water. Both of them lay on the now bobbing surface, panting through the saturated bandanas. The air was a little clearer here but it was turning thicker fast. Nick lay on his back and stared up at the sky. Though still morning, the sky was dark, overcast, without a hint of sunshine.

Jackson hauled Nick upright. "I want you to stay on the raft until I come back for you."

Nick snorted a derisive retort. "*That* will not be a problem."

They were eye to eye again. Jackson's stare was more intense than Nick could remember ever seeing before. "Well…it might be."

"What?" The dread had eased since they'd climbed on the float but it surged again in an instant. Nick choked and coughed on his own word. The air was getting foul. Even Jackson was more hoarse and coughed more frequently than when they had entered the water.

"We're not the only things running from the fire, Nick." He touched Nick's face, fingers stroking down the angle of his jaw, as if memorizing his features. It was touching and terrifying at the same time. "Every wild animal in the forest will instinctively come to the water to escape."

"And?" Nick was sure Jackson was leaving something out, waiting for him to see it. But he was too damn tired to puzzle it out. He was a city boy for Christ's sake. Who knew what wild animals did?

"Some of them will know how to swim."

"Crap." Understanding dawned for Nick but acceptance was a little slower.

Jackson jerked a long pole with a hook at the end of it off the side of the raft. "This is a pike pole. It's used to retrieve things in the water—life float, boats, whatever." He slid it closer to Nick. "You use it to keep things from climbing out of the water."

"What kind of 'things'?" Eying the wicked-looking, but blunt, metal hook, Nick picked up the pole. It was heavy, a sturdy weapon if needed.

"Raccoons, bears, Bigfoot. Anything you don't want to share your lifeboat with." Jackson was already slipping back into the water.

Nick moved to him and hung over the edge. His glance darted over Jackson's face, mapping the lines, the color of his eyes, the way water beaded in the cleft of his chin and the corners of his full lips. "I suppose this is where I profess my undying love and faith in you and beg you to sacrifice me for your own safety." He locked eyes with the big man, floored to see love shining back at him in that dark brown gaze. His voice cracked but he managed to croak out, "But fuck that. I expect you back here to save my skinny ass before I'm barbequed or some crazed raccoon gnaws my leg off."

He leaned in and kissed Jackson, a deep, passionate kiss that explained everything he couldn't say right now. Just as abruptly, he backed away. "Now go. I'm desperate to find out if small boats make me as seasick as large ones do."

Jackson's answer was a devilish wink. "I'm pretty fond of that skinny ass." Then he was gone, only the sound of water rippling marked his progress. Nick hung on to it for as long as he could until the noise of spreading fire took it from him.

CHAPTER TWELVE

He'd made this journey a dozen times every year since he was sixteen. At first it had started out as a challenge. The young man keeping up with his favorite uncle, forcing himself to go the distance, straining every ounce of his fit body into the task. It had been difficult the first summer, pacing himself, getting the most out of each stroke of his long arms, every scissor of his legs, but soon the mile swim from the cabin to the dock was a leisurely one. Sometimes, he had done it twice a day just for the exhilaration of the exercise. Jackson kept telling himself today wasn't any different.

Except he had to rely on instinct and his ability to swim in a straight line since he couldn't see more than a few yards ahead. Breathing was hard. He'd had to let the bandana fall around his neck. It had become so waterlogged it was impossible to get air through since his face was underwater eighty percent of the journey. His injured shoulder had been painful when he'd started out, more painful than he wanted Nick to know. It didn't take long for the strained muscles and ligaments to object to further abuse. The burn started in his upper arm, spread to his shoulder then across his back. By the time he was halfway to where he thought the boats should be, his entire upper body on the injured side was screaming for relief. Nick wouldn't be happy about this.

Nick. What was happening to the man right now? The heat and the smoke was nearly unbearable back at the platform. Jackson knew the other man could handle that. He was a smart, resourceful man. But was he safe? Had any burning trees fallen into the lake and managed to float near the platform? Anything still smoldering could ignite the float. Had anything else looked for escape from the fire in the safety of the lake? Had he left Nick behind to fall victim to some unforeseen new danger? As if smoke inhalation, drowning or being consumed by a raging fire wasn't enough.

His rhythm faltered just for a stroke or two. Jackson shoved what might be happening out of his mind. He couldn't allow anything to shake his concentration. He worked through the pain, the one in his body and his heart. Controlling his emotions was the key. *Control your response to the environment and you control the situation.*

Control, control, control. The chant rolled through his head every time his arm cut through the water. He didn't know when the chant changed to: *Nick. Nick. Nick.*

§ § § §

When it came, it wasn't a crazed raccoon, a bear, or Bigfoot.

Stationing himself in the center of the raft, focusing on where he thought Jackson might climb out onto land, Nick had managed to avoid eye contact with the murky water. It was getting harder and harder to see more than a few feet in any direction. The sky was dark. The air was heavy and hot, suffocating. Sweat bathed his skin, drenched his clothes and plastered his hair to his head and face. He doused the bandana with water from the lake at increasing intervals, eventually laying the fabric over his entire face. His eyes burned, bloodshot from ash and sweat dripping into them. His throat was raw, his breathing labored as his lungs tried to pull oxygen out of the gritty, depleted air. He was exhausted just lying there.

What did Jackson feel like, battling his way to the shore over a mile away, swimming a marathon through a veil of smoke, one shoulder probably useless by now, not knowing if there would even be a boat at the dock when he reached it?

Lost in these unhappy thoughts, Nick didn't hear the splash of water or the labored panting until his attention was pulled back to the here and now by the sound of something sharp scrapping against the wooden surface of the platform close to his head. He rolled over and came face to face with a pair of squinting, yellow eyes staring at him between two massive, clawed paws.

"Seriously?" He couldn't help voicing his anger. How many times had the other man teased him about this? He thought it was all just a joke to scare the city boy. "There really *are* mountain lions here?" The other man had never let on it was a real possibility. "Jackson Kain, you *bastard*. If I live through this, I'm going to kick your awesome, tight ass."

A mountain lion's head was much larger than he'd imagined it would be. Their eyes were rounder than he'd expected, too. And their claws were much, much longer and sharper than he'd thought possible. The ones piercing the platform a foot away from his face were as thick as his little finger and just as long. The fur on this particular large feline head was matted with soot, patches scorched, with one ear in bloody tatters. He vaguely remembered hearing something about not making eye contact with wild animals that could kill you, but he couldn't help it. Those yellow eyes locked on his and he couldn't drag his gaze away. Or maybe it was the hypnotic nature of the throaty rattle of warning vibrating constantly from around the beast's bared teeth.

Once the shock faded, terror set in.

"Nice kitty." Nick began a slow, full body, slip-sliding motion, easing himself across the platform surface toward the other side of the float. The pike pole was in his grasp the entire time, but he couldn't bring himself to use it, not yet. Without the benefit of the ladder, it was a difficult climb over the flotation blocks and the added depth of the thick beams of the platform. He comforted himself with the idea that the exhausted animal couldn't drag itself up onto the raft.

Like so many other things on this trip, the big cat proved him wrong.

Scratching and clawing with its powerful front legs, the cat gained purchase on the raft inch by hard-won inch until Nick realized it had managed to dig its hind feet and claws into the portion of the raft underwater. Before he could do more than scramble to the far corner of the float and bring the pole into a defensive position, the cat was standing on all fours, ten feet away.

"Nice kitty."

The animal's once tawny coat was singed in multiple areas, bare spots of black encrusted, bloody skin marking its back. As Nick watched, the cat limped a few paces toward him, panting, eyes crazed with fear, crouched low, a deep rumble still resonating from its throat. It was as long as Nick was tall, broad shouldered with muscles that rippled and tensed all over its thick, sinewy body with each low hiss and threatening growl. Nick could tell it was injured but he doubted that lessened the threat it posed.

"Now I know where they get the 'lion' part of your name. You're freaking huge, my friend." Nick stole a glance at the surrounding water to be sure his new companion was alone. If there was anything else out there in the few foggy yards he could see into, he couldn't find it. The roar of the fire along the shore was deafening. The heat waves blistering.

He moved closer to the edge. Any dread he held for the dark, murky water or the raging fire paled next to the alternative in front of him. Tightening his grip on the pike pole, he cautiously pushed himself up to his knees. He needed more room to swing the pole if the cat advanced on him.

For several long, agonizing seconds, they stared at each other, then without retreating the big cat lowered himself to the floor, its gaze never leaving Nick. It lay panting, sides heaving, teeth bared and eyes narrowed against the smoke drenched air. The noise from its throat ceased only when it gave way to a startling, strangled cough. Nick shifted farther away, the pole scraping against the wooden planking. The metal hook managed to give out a raspy screech.

Without warning, the cat sprang forward, claws extended, jaws open to expose curved fangs and rows of sharp teeth leading to a cavernous throat. Nick swung the pole, lashing out at the beast with the hooked end. The cat batted the pole aside time after time, angered by the solid jabs to the chest but unharmed. Nick realized a blunt stick and his meager human strength were no match for the frightened animal. One of them would have to leave the raft. Nick desperately didn't want it to be him.

Pushing the cougar off the platform was the only attack Nick could think of standing a chance of accomplishing. Drained as the cat was, Nick was still no match for full grown wild cat.

It gave him a vague sense of unease to think about forcing the animal back into the water. Nonetheless, he got into a position braced against a short post he imagined was used for tying up floats or small boats to the platform. Hoping to take advantage of a surprise offensive, he lunged at the animal, trying to force the cat off the edge with a sideways sweep of the pole.

Before Nick could process what had happened, the cat sprung around on its hind legs, grabbing the wooden handle of the pole with its forepaw's claws and swept the stick back at Nick. Both the pole and Nick flew backward. The pike pole thudded to the floor then rolled off into the water. And so did Nick.

He hit the surface flat on his back, arms spread wide, the boots still dangling from his neck flying up to smack him in the face. He touched down with a huge splash that was gobbled up by the constant din surrounding him. The impact dazed him, forcing the air from his lungs. He shut his mouth and eyes out of reflex, more to block out the sight of the charging cougar than to go underwater.

As awkward as it was, landing spread-eagle helped keep him from going too far below the surface. Sputtering and coughing, Nick flailed his arms and legs, trying to keep his head above the water. He seized the edge of the platform. The sudden appearance of a fanged muzzle and powerful claws made him falter in his hold on to the structure.

"Son of a bitch." Panicked, he sunk below the waterline.

Kicking and pawing his way back to the surface, he tried to inch farther down the side where the ladder might provide a handhold out of the cat's reach. It was luck that placed the handle of the pike pole in his struggling path. The metal hook had caught on the metal brace of the ladder steps. Nick latched on, willing his trembling body to relax enough to stop struggling and just float. The pole put him roughly six feet away from the pacing wild cat. Still close enough the cat could reach him if it wanted to but not easily. But then, wounded animals were known to do desperate things.

For now they seemed at an impasse. The cougar strode along the edge of the float while Nick figured out how to tread water without swallowing half the lake. His whole body ached from coughing. The water was cold just under the surface despite the superheated air above it, fed by mountain streams brimming with melting snow packs. Shivers racked his entire frame, making his teeth chatter and his outstretched, tired arms go numb.

Nick became aware something was different. The cat had stopped patrolling the edge. Stopped growling deep in its chest. But it was still staring. Crouched on the very edge, not six feet from Nick's face, the cat's head swayed in time with the rippling water as Nick floated at the end of the pole. It was coiled like a spring, muscles bunched at its shoulders and hips, eyes wide, staring, like yellow-gold orbs of glistening glass. Nick couldn't see anything in those eyes. No fear, no interest, not even pain anymore. They had the cold, blank look of a predator sizing up its prey. Nick knew it could smell the fear radiating off of him, making the animal more brazen and aggressive.

Just as the creature tensed to make its move, the sound of a boat motor cut through the backdrop of the fire. Seconds later, a small cruiser emerged out of the smoke-laden air, so close Nick floundered to stay clear of being crushed against the float.

"Jackson?" Seizing the rope mooring tied along the edge of the boat, Nick huddled against the craft. Nearer to Jackson meant being one step closer to being out of this mess.

"Nick?" Unbelievably hoarse, the other man croaked out, "What the hell?"

The motor cut off, the tail end of the boat almost touching the platform, placing Nick in a protective triangle between the swim raft and the side of the craft, away from the motor blades. A familiar silhouette appeared topside. Nick could barely make out Jackson's features in the ash-filled air.

"You are freaking *Superman!*" Relief rushed through Nick like a high speed train only to be replaced seconds later by renewed terror. His voice squeaked, raw from disuse. Something in the cat changed in that instant. Nick could see it gather up its energy, coiling like a snake about to strike.

If he could barely see Jackson, Jackson probably couldn't see the crouching beast a few feet away. "Christ, Jack—"

The warning came too late, but the attack wasn't aimed at the new interloper. The cat decided he had enough from the talking head in the water. It cleared the short distance between them, silent and deadly. Nick was sure it would come down on top of him. He clung to the boat's slippery side, the dry rope cutting into his palms. The sight of the huge cat pouncing through the air at him was so surreal he couldn't take his gaze off it.

And it was just as well he hadn't or he'd have missed the even more surreal sight of his boyfriend punching a mountain lion out of the air.

The cougar leaped off the raft in an impressive arc that sent it sailing right past the boat's occupant on its way to Nick. In midair, the feline shuddered. The full force of a massive fist connected with the side of its broad skull. The animal twisted, paws flailing wildly, finding nothing but empty air. Right up until it splashed down in the lake. It went under once but came up paddling, now intent on regaining the solid ground it had just left. All thoughts of annoying humans apparently gone.

By the time Nick realized he was in the water with the beast, he was hauled on board the small cruiser. His feet had just hit the deck when a soft, light blanket magically wrapped around his shoulders and he was deposited on a bench.

"Sit." Nick was happy to slump back against the seat, the vibrations of the engine soothing with the sweet promise of safety.

The engine roared to life under Jackson's expert handling. Dazed, Nick watched as the swimming platform disappeared from sight. Only the hazy, fiery glow of the shoreline marked the distance they were putting between disaster and salvation. It shimmered and danced with the heat, hypnotic, almost beautiful in its fierceness. The farther they went into the darkness, the cooler the air became. Eventually, not every breath made him cough and the burning in his eyes receded to the point where he could blink without feeling like his eyelids were lined with sandpaper.

He didn't remember when the boat stopped moving or even when Jackson had come to sit beside him. It was the sudden warmth of the arm wrapped around him, the one that drew him close and held him there that brought him back to himself. He slipped one hand out of the blanket, found a calloused, slightly trembling fist and held onto it. He noticed Jackson's other arm lay useless and still at his side. They sat for a long time like that, silent, thankful.

Eventually, Nick stirred. "Why is the boat stopped? Are we at the other side of the lake?"

"Nope. Out of gas." Jackson tucked Nick's head under his chin, pulling him closer. "I raised the forestry service on the radio. They're sending help. It'll be a while." He grunted a little as he shifted to a more comfort position on the bench. "I told them we were fine."

Nick snorted in disbelief, but it came out sounding like a muffled cough. "Liar. Your shoulder is probably in worse shape than it was when you fell through that burning floor."

"It aches a bit." Jackson flexed his injured arm, unable to hide the small grunt of pain it caused. "But I'll live. *We'll* live."

"I didn't think we would for most of the day, but yes, we will." Nick ran his free hand over his face, ending the gesture by pinching his lower lip.

Jackson gently pushed Nick away until they were facing each other. "Can I ask you something?"

"Okay." It was still difficult to see but Jackson's dark eyes were studying him intently.

"Earlier. On the shore. You were more than scared to get in the water, you were terrified. Life and death terrified. It was more than just not knowing how to swim." Genuine concern pushed the tiredness out of the other man's voice. "What was up with that?"

Nick sighed, deciding to face the issue full on. Jackson deserved the truth. "It's not just swimming. It's boating, fishing, skipping rocks. You probably haven't noticed, but I even avoid puddles on sidewalks."

"I have noticed that." Jackson gave him a quirky grin. "I thought you just didn't want to get those expensive shoes wet." Nick was known for being something of a clothes horse.

Nick sighed again, deeper this time. Tugging the blanket closer around himself, he started with his story. "Remember when I said I went on a field trip when I was eight?" Jackson nodded, encouraging Nick to continue. "It was so long ago, but I remember every detail." He looked out into the night, staring at the faint lights appearing on the far shore.

"There were twelve of us, all overachievers from private schools. We were attending a camp for future scientists." He gave Jackson a halfhearted smile. "My darling mother had her heart set on me being a research scientist for her father's firm. I was eight." He shrugged, acknowledging a simpler time in his life. "It sounded like an adventure. I've always been into science so it seemed like a great idea." He drew in a deep breath and let it out slow. It was a moment before he continued.

"It was the second morning there. After breakfast, the counselors trooped us all down to a small pond near the camp. We took our specimen jars and little fishing nets, excited about gathering pond scum and plant life to examine under microscopes later." He chuckled, remembering how thrilled he'd been about being allowed to actually get dirty.

"One of the other boys was an odd little guy, one of those quiet kids no one takes the time to notice. His name was Angus, Angus McCarthy. He was exceedingly smart. He would have been a terrific scientist." Nick glanced at Jackson as the other man gripped his hand tighter. "Sometimes I wonder what he would have become."

"What happened to him?"

"Nothing good. We were all up to our knees in the pond. I don't think it was more than three feet deep at any point. We had scattered along the edge, three counselors moving from kid to kid, checking on our progress, encouraging us." He blinked, squinting his eyes as if that would help bring the memory into better focus. "Angus was next to me, fifteen feet away, reciting details about plant names and bacteria strains." He shook his head. "I wasn't really listening. There were tadpoles in the water and I was trying to net one. Then I heard Angus yell, like he was surprised. When I looked up, there Angus was, flailing around in the water. I thought he had slipped on the muddy bottom. It was only about twelve inches deep where we were standing. I can remember smiling, waiting for him to sit up so I could laugh with him about it. One of the counselors called to him. I think she was waiting for him to sit up, too. After a few seconds, he stopped splashing. It was so silent then. The counselor tried to run to him as fast as she could but," he shrugged again, "the mud, the water—when she got to him—it was too late."

"He drowned?"

"I thought so. Everyone thought so at the time. But later I overheard one of my teachers telling someone Angus had died from anaphylactic shock. No one, not even his parents knew he was allergic to bees." He gave Jackson a mirthless, little smile. "We don't see a lot of bees in New York penthouses. That was probably why he yelled. He got stung. And then he died." He briefly closed his eyes to clear his blurred vision. "My parents never discussed it. Not once."

"That's a shame. Might have helped you cope with it."

Nick just nodded. "I still remember trying to help the woman lift him out of the water. How cold his skin was." He made a loose fist, rubbing his fingers over his palm, remembering the touch of lifeless flesh of the other boy. "Then watching while the adults tried to revive him, thinking I should be able to do something to help. *Something* to make a difference."

He stared off into the distance for a moment. "Sometimes

I wonder what great things we haven't discovered yet because Angus McCarthy didn't get a chance to grow up." He ground the heel of one hand into his tired, burning eyes. "I never wanted to feel that helpless again. So…" This time the smile he gave Jackson was real. "I decided to become a doctor that day."

They were both silent, lost in their own thoughts. Nick pinched his lower lip until Jackson reached out and hauled his hand away from his abused mouth to say, "For what it's worth, I think the universe was trying to make things right again." Nick gave him a puzzled look but waited for him to finish his thought. "If one person leaving this world before their time convinces another to dedicate his life to helping save thousands of others, some good does come out of the tragedy."

"That's one way to look at it, I guess." His hand was still cradled in Jackson's. Nick decided it was fine where it was.

"Life is messy sometimes." Jackson indicated the entire surrounding area with a sardonic, eye-rolling glance. "Doesn't always work out the way we want."

"On that subject." Nick sat back, putting a little distance between them. The other man had proved himself to be an extraordinary person in the last twenty-four hours. Nick couldn't lead him on anymore. "I have a confession to make and it should be sooner than later." Jackson deserved the truth from him if their relationship was to continue. "After last night, I thought I was in love with you." He saw the stillness settle into his lover's handsome features, frozen, clearly bracing himself. "But I have to tell you, that was just lust."

He wasn't prepared for the total lack of any movement from the other man. Jackson didn't blink, didn't seem to breathe, didn't flinch or shift his weight. Only his eyes seemed to change, their expression moving from confused to haunted to steely determination in the span of a few seconds.

"You should know I've been in love with you since the first time I saw you." Jackson's tone was strong, unrelenting, determined not to surrender. "I practically became a *stalker* trying to find the right way to meet you without looking like some macho jerk trying to get inside your pants." His gaze softened along with his voice. "Luckily for me, I fell through a floor when you were on duty."

"Jackson. Let me finish—" Thick, sooty fingers closed his lips.

"What I feel for you is much more than lust, Nick." Jackson took away his hand only to drop it to touch Nick's heart. "I love you. Don't cheapen what I know in my heart because you don't feel—"

"Let me finish." Nick hadn't meant to yell but that's how it came out. Jackson fell silent again but Nick could see the frustration in his face. "I *know* that was lust because after *all this*, after seeing what you did for me, how much you sacrificed, the genuine physical torture you endured during that swim to come back for me…" He faltered, needing a deep breath to choke back the turmoil of emotions. "I just can't describe it any other way than…I love you. I *love* the man that did all those things *for me*."

He couldn't help it, he laughed. A nervous, wavering laugh of relief and disbelief. "Christ, Jackson, you literally fought a *lion* for me!" He threw his arms around Jackson's neck and yanked him into an embrace. He didn't want to let go of him. Ever.

After a moment, Jackson relaxed into the embrace. He patted aside a tousled mess of Nick's dark hair to counter with a comment full of suppressed mirth. "A mountain lion. There's a difference."

"Like hell there is." Nick pulled back, then settled again under Jackson's arm, side by side, waiting for rescue. "Didn't you see him? He was *huge*."

"He was still just a mountain lion. A cougar."

"It was dark. You were blinded by the smoke. He was gigantic. I'm naming him Simba."

"Was it a male?"

Nick thought about it for half a second. "Surprisingly, I didn't take the time to check. But," he rolled his head so he could see

Jackson's face, "considering how demanding and unreasonable it was, it may have been female." He nodded to no one in particular. "I'll call it Marion instead."

"Marion?"

"My mother's name."

"Ah." Jackson drew him back into the crook of his arm.

"After this, she'll want to meet you."

"Okay."

"You say that now. After you do, you'll know firsthand what I went through spending time on the platform with a crazed wild cat."

"I look forward to the challenge."

"You say that now."

Trademarks Acknowledgment

The author acknowledges the trademark status and trademark owners of the following wordmarks mentioned in this work of fiction:

Land Rover: Jaguar Land Rover North America, LLC

Ace: 3M

GQ: Advance Magazine Publishers Inc.

Superman: DC Comics

About the Author

LAURA BAUMBACH is the award-winning author of numerous short stories, novellas, novels and screenplays. Her favorite genre to work in is manlove or m/m erotic romances. Manlove is not traditional gay fiction, but erotic romances written specifically for the romantic-minded reader, male or female. Married to the same man for almost 30 years, she currently lives with her husband and two sons in the blustery Northeast of the United States but is looking for a warmer location to spend the second half of her professional and family life.

Laura is the owner of ManLoveRomance Press, founded in January of 2007. You can find Laura on the internet at:

http://www.laurabaumbach.com/

http://groups.yahoo.com/group/laurabaumbachfiction

http://www.mlrpress.com/

http://groups.yahoo.com/group/mlrpress/